WHEN KRISHNA CALLS

AN ANITA RAY MYSTERY

WHEN KRISHNA CALLS

SUSAN OLEKSIW

FIVE STAR
A part of Gale, Cengage Learning

GALE
CENGAGE Learning·

Farmington Hills, Mich • San Francisco • New York • Waterville, Maine
Meriden, Conn • Mason, Ohio • Chicago

GALE
CENGAGE Learning®

LIBRARY OF CONGRESS CATALOGING-IN-PUBLICATION DATA

Names: Oleksiw, Susan, author.
Title: When Krishna calls : an Anita Ray mystery / Susan Oleksiw.
Description: First edition. | Waterville, Maine : Five Star, a part of Cengage Learning, Inc. 2016.
Identifiers: LCCN 2016001570| ISBN 9781432832254 (hardback) | ISBN 1432832255 (hardcover)
Subjects: LCSH: East Indian American women—Fiction. | Americans—India—Fiction. | Murder—Investigation—Fiction. | India, South—Fiction. | BISAC: FICTION / Mystery & Detective / General. | GSAFD: Mystery fiction.
Classification: LCC PS3565.L42 W48 2016 | DDC 813/.54—dc23
LC record available at http://lccn.loc.gov/2016001570

First Edition. First Printing: August 2016
Find us on Facebook– https://www.facebook.com/FiveStarCengage
Visit our website– http://www.gale.cengage.com/fivestar/
Contact Five Star™ Publishing at FiveStar@cengage.com

Printed in the United States of America
1 2 3 4 5 6 7 20 19 18 17 16

For Roger and Juliet

ACKNOWLEDGMENTS

Once again I am indebted to several individuals for helping me with this book. Usha Ramachandran explained several technical aspects of life in contemporary India. Dr. Charlene Allison caught my mistakes on life in traditional India, as well as many other missteps. Elenita Lodge offered valuable insights and suggestions on early drafts.

My publisher has been generous with attention and support, especially Alice Duncan, Deni Dietz, and Tiffany Schofield. Deirdre Wait has designed beautiful covers perfectly matched for the stories in the Anita Ray series.

CHAPTER 1

The little girl tugged on the tether hooked onto the goat's collar. The bell tinkled and the goat backed away. Determined, the little girl pulled the goat closer and wrapped her small arm around its neck, pressing its snout onto her pink dress. The goat began to snuffle and nuzzle until it found a spot it liked especially. As the animal nibbled at the child's dress, the girl pushed it away, but now the animal was the one who wanted to be entangled. The two wrestled until the goat collapsed onto its knees and the girl fell on top of it. The goat dropped its head on the ground, and the little girl rested hers on its belly. A wave crashed on the shore beyond the compound wall. The goat bleated, but no one at Hotel Delite was awake to hear.

It was well after midnight. From her hiding spot behind the bushes on the slope, Nisha watched her daughter fall asleep inside the compound, where she would be safe until morning. She felt a wave of relief flood her limbs, bringing warmth against the chilly night air. She released the branches and let the window through the shrubbery close as she knelt on the ground and decided what to do next. She had brought the child to safety, but she couldn't stay here. She had to move on, to get as far away as possible. Her husband's village lay to the north, but she couldn't go there. She would go north, and then east. She knew the jungle, the paths, the old homesteads and back roads. But she had to hurry.

After one last look at the child asleep on the other side of the wall, Nisha pushed up hill, avoiding driveways and hotel guards snoring on verandas, the occasional dog rummaging in the gutter for food. She crossed this road and another, and then another until she was running along a dirt path into a sparsely settled area, still thick with trees and shrubbery and vines. She ran on.

She didn't know how long she ran. She lost feeling in her feet, and her legs felt like they were moving through air. Her nurse's aide training told her to stop, see to the cuts on the soles of her feet, the gashes on her arms from thorns. But she couldn't stop. She didn't dare. She hurried on until dirt paths turned into badly paved lanes, small huts turned into two-story houses, and little shops turned into office buildings.

The farther she ran from the shore and the compound that enclosed her beloved daughter, the harder it was to tamp down her panic. She could not deny it now. She felt like she was running for her life. She tried to tell herself she was exaggerating, that her mind was playing tricks on her, but then she remembered Panju and her child, and the terror and confusion of the night swept back. She felt a burst of energy and ran faster.

In the distance a car engine turned over. She skidded on pebbles and pressed herself against a wall. The old narrow concrete water channel that ran beside the road was dry. She lowered herself into it, covering her body with leaves and debris as she worked her way under the concrete slab that served as a footbridge to a private gate. The driver revved his little engine and the scooter made the corner and sped up again. She waited. When she heard only her own breathing, she climbed out. Her uniform sari—green cotton with a white and gold border—was soiled beyond recognition. No one who saw her climb out of the old gutter would know she was a member of a respected profession.

The night confused her. Shadows leapt where the sun burned

clear in the day, darkness hovered where crows pecked at trash scattered by feral dogs and cats, flecks of stone in seemingly dead rocks flickered under the caress of moonlight.

Nisha paused at a corner, listening. Silence. The humid air grew heavier, pressing the earth down, seeking out every corner, wrapping itself around every breathing creature, as if to squeeze out what little life might remain. The northeast rains, *thulavarsham,* hadn't come yet, but the land ached for them. The southwest monsoon had been light, and the land suffered now. The ground was hard, the red dirt dry and cracked.

Along the quiet lanes few lights broke up the dark, but on the main roads tube lights burned, turning night into day. A shadow came toward her—a man out walking, going nowhere special, perhaps to a tea stall to visit with a friend. The shadow rippled forward, then was spliced by a compound wall and disappeared. She leaned against a wooden gate, trying to catch her breath. She raised her hands to her chest and flexed her fingers. She felt the crust of dried blood crack and pull on her skin.

Once again the sound of a motor vehicle reminded her of her precarious situation. She couldn't stop here. She had to keep moving while she had the safety of the night. This was the dead zone, the time of night when little moved—no trains, no buses— just two hours of resting before it all started up again. She had been on the move for almost five hours.

At first she'd thought about hiding in the convent at least for a few days, but that was too dangerous—too near what she had to flee—and she passed it by, heading toward the museum and the zoo. She moved stealthily through the university campus, clambering over walls, slipping through gates too narrow for most adults.

Up ahead she saw the Palayam Junction underpass. But no. It would be too easy to be trapped in there. When she saw a man sauntering down the middle of the street as though he had nothing better to do in the world, she retied her sari, pulled off her petticoat and twisted it into a head load–carrying base. She fitted it onto her head, and stepped into the street behind the man, just another laborer on her way home from a long day, an extra job that kept her late but promised more badly needed money. The man looked back at her quizzically, but once on the other side of the road, she ran for the trees. She dodged handcarts covered with plastic tarps for the night, ran past old men sleeping on the pavement, and past a woman at a brazier boiling water for tea. The squatting woman glanced up, and for a moment interest flickered in her eyes. She poked her fire and stirred it to life. As a small flame spurted, Nisha offered up a silent prayer to Agni.

Nisha clambered over a wall and fell onto the hard ground. Stunned and dizzy, she stumbled to her feet. Overhead a mass of white flew by, then settled on a nearby roof. The screech owl peered about. He ruffled his feathers, looked here, looked there. The owl gazed down at her, his sharp yellow eyes assessing her—her size, shape, value. He tipped his head to one side, then drew back, ruffled his feathers again. The moon sought him out and kissed his whiteness, as if paying homage to another who brought lightness into the dark. The bird gave a call, adjusted his wings, and flew away. Nisha watched him, her hand rising as though to call him back. With his flight, she felt abandoned, more alone than she had ever felt was possible. His white feathers and thickly framed eyes seemed to promise guardianship to those lost in the night. His incurious glance had seemed to offer an assurance of protection. But no. He ruffled his feathers, rose aloft, and flew off. She was alone without a protector.

The night had fallen near to silence. She listened. Where were the night creatures? She let herself slide down, to sit among dead leaves and broken twigs. She was tired, bone weary. She could stay here forever, she thought, let sleep overtake her; she was ready to slip from the world as though she had never been born. And why not? She had nothing to go back to now. She had given her all and it had cost her everything. Her beloved Panju was gone, husband in this and every other life, father of her child.

The moment of rest gave her time to gather herself, but her fears lodged themselves in the crevices of her thoughts, sneaking in among her unguarded feelings. She could not forget why she was fleeing, nor why she had to keep going. She pushed herself up and began to dust the crumbling stone from the wall from her hands but stopped. It was still there—all that blood. Dried, crusty, covering every finger, her entire hand—both hands—splattered all the way up her forearms. She remembered the feel of it as the blood spurted onto her hands, the sticky warm thickness of it, the way it slithered along her skin, seeking out the folds and wrinkles of her hands, running along the lines of her palm that had promised her a long and fruitful life with little hardship but much work. She folded her hands into fists and sent a silent call to Vishnu to protect her.

Over the next half hour Nisha worked her way through the brush. She could hear the sounds of the animals at the zoo, some asleep, others restless in their cages. Some seemed alarmed at the agitation of others. Nisha heard a squeal, a low grumble as one rhino heaved into another, a loud yawn from a lion prowling in a cage, a crack as one creature climbed out onto a weak tree limb. Someone had told her these were comforting sounds—they meant the animals did not fear danger approaching. They too, like birds, went silent when danger was near. Nisha peered over the stone wall bordering the museum walkway beneath the champaka trees.

Atop the hill, on the steps in front of the Napier Museum, sat a man, his head propped in his hand, elbow resting on his knee. He rose slowly. Another one with nothing to do, she thought, as she kept herself hidden. The northeast monsoon was late. The heat was intensifying. Anyone who could find a place to enjoy the cooler night air was sure to take advantage of it, and the park would be one of the coolest spots in the city. Its many trees and higher elevation and open landscape promised a respite from the heat. Despite the locked gates, the man must have found a way in.

He descended the steps slowly, stopped at a landing, and pulled a cigarette from his shirt pocket. Down he came, one step at a time, rolling the cigarette in his fingers while sauntering in the night air. At the bottom of the steps he placed the cigarette between his lips. He held up a wooden match, snapped it with his fingernail, and watched the stick burst into flame. After admiring it, he drew it toward the cigarette and soon his head was wreathed in smoke.

Nisha lowered herself silently in the dark, careful to keep her sari out of the moonlight lest it find the flecks of fake gold in the border pattern and make them shimmer. She waited for the sound of his footsteps, then reached out for the pallu—her sari end was especially nice beneath the dirt and grime, with embroidered gold flowers. She wanted to hold it close to her, to keep it out of the moonlight. But someone else reached it first.

CHAPTER 2

At seven o'clock in the morning, two men perched atop the short flight of stairs leading down to the entrance to Hotel Delite. They wore the long white wraparound garment called a mundu and white shirts hanging over the folded fabric at the waist. They wore black sandals turned brown with dust, had neatly combed hair, and sported mustaches. The minute Anita saw them, she knew they weren't new arrivals just off an incoming flight and looking for a room. The men glanced at each other, and the shorter one straightened the black briefcase under his left arm; they began their descent looking uncertain and confused.

"Police in mufti," Anita whispered to Auntie Meena behind her at the registration desk. "I wonder what they want."

"Welcome, welcome, Sar." Auntie Meena stepped forward and rested her hands, palms down, on the counter. Even at this early hour, she looked prepared for all comers—her black hair in a neat bun, her sari clean and pressed, her earrings reminding the world that she had once had a husband of means. She smiled and lifted her chin. "You are so welcome. You are wanting a room? Yes, rooms are available." She offered her best hotelier smile and glanced behind them for the bearer with suitcases she knew wasn't there. Anita settled on a stool to watch the policemen's discomfort when they realized they'd have to admit who they were to Auntie Meena.

"Good rooms we have heard," the first one said. He pressed

his arm against the briefcase, holding it tight against his chest, and grasped it with his hand, for good measure.

"And who is it who has said such kind things?" Auntie Meena looked pointedly at the floor, her eyebrows raised, noting the lack of suitcases.

"Yes, water view?" The second one started to walk toward the windows looking out over the terrace and ocean.

"Ah, it is for guests only." Auntie Meena came out from behind the counter and stepped toward the hall, keeping up with the man. She offered the most reasonable of smiles but this one said clearly that nothing was to be gained by challenging her. She might dither over the accounts, cry with guests over a missed train, or be equally horrified by news of a theft. But she was no pushover where her own hotel was concerned. The parlor was off limits to outsiders. "Please. You are wanting?" She led him back to the registration desk. Perched on a stool near the window, Anita enjoyed the scene.

The two men glanced at each other and seemed to come to a decision.

"We are looking for one Nisha Eappen," the shorter one said. "She is in your employ?"

"Nisha?" Anita stood up and came forward. "Why are you looking for her?"

The taller man glanced at Anita, lifted an eyebrow, and turned back to Auntie Meena. "You know Shreemati Nisha? We are requesting to know where she is. When does she arrive for work?"

"And you're asking because?" Auntie Meena lifted an eyebrow.

After another shared glance, each man lifted a small black plastic card case from his shirt pocket and offered it to her.

"Hmm," she said.

"Again," the shorter man said, "she is arriving for work when?"

"She doesn't," Anita said, refusing to be ignored. She had been toying with her dupatta, but now she flung it over her shoulder. "She is working only as needed. She is a health aide. If a guest falls ill or has had some minor surgery and asks for nursing care, we seek out Nisha and she comes to the hotel. She is recommended by local doctors. She is highly thought of. But she has not been here to aid a guest in a number of weeks. Two weeks, I think."

"It is important that we are contacting her," the second one said. The first one shifted the black briefcase under his arm and Anita wondered what was in it. It seemed to be flat, so nothing bulky, and looked too small to hold the usual sized paper for business. It didn't look like it even had a newspaper in it.

"We will tell her you are looking for her if we see her," Anita said.

"Yes, we are doing this." Auntie Meena raised her hand to forestall any protests. "It is small kindness we shall undertake. As soon as she is appearing, we are informing."

Both men glared at the women before turning slightly to each other. Their way of communicating, it seemed to Anita, was to look at each other, guess what the other was thinking, and begin again. She waited to see if she was right.

"Let me say," the second man said, "this is a matter of some importance."

"If that is so," Anita said, "why have you come here?"

"One of Nisha's neighbors mentioned you as her employer," the second man said.

"Then that neighbor also knows where Nisha has gone to, perhaps another employer," Anita said.

"It is a matter of importance," he repeated.

"Yes, very important," the shorter one said. "This is a matter of murder."

"Murder!" Anita moved to the center of the hallway, pushing Auntie Meena aside. "What are you talking about? Has something happened to Nisha?"

"We have not heard of anything happening to Shreemati Nisha," the shorter one said. "It is only a matter of seeking information from her."

Auntie Meena pulled the pallu of her sari to her face and dabbed at her forehead and mouth. "That is a great relief, Sar. Nisha is such a lovely young lady. To imagine some injury to her would be most distressing. So very distressing. Your assurances are most appreciated." Auntie Meena began to sigh deeply and fan herself with her pallu.

"Hmm," one man said to the other.

"What information are you seeking?" Anita asked. She sensed they were withholding something important. "What is it you want of her? If you tell us, we can do our best to locate her."

"Yes," Auntie Meena said. Her back straightened, any sign of a smile gone. "Why are you wanting her? You said this was a matter of murder."

"Yes, madam. We want to question her about this matter."

"What matter?" Anita said, leaning forward.

"Her husband, Panju, was found dead this morning. Murdered."

Both women gasped.

"How did it happen? An accident, surely," Anita said.

"With a knife in his stomach?" the shorter man said.

"A knife?" Auntie Meena fell back a step.

"And you think Nisha is also injured?" Anita asked. She watched both men, trying to tease out their true intentions.

"We are thinking she knows about this event," the second man said.

"Oh!" Auntie Meena said, turning to look at Anita.

"You think she stabbed her husband?" Anita said, knowing they did.

The two policemen let their eyes close, one lifted his hand as if to say perhaps, and both nodded.

"Ayoo! Shivayashivoo! You think our little Nisha murdered her husband!" Auntie Meena opened her eyes wide and crumpled into a heap on the floor. Anita rushed over to her, and the two officers in mufti leaned over the counter to marvel at this display of emotion.

A thread of steam spun its way into the air above the table, but every time Auntie Meena reached for the handle on her delicate cup, the cup rattled in its saucer, and the sinuous line was broken. Too unsteady to pick up the cup and drink, Meena ended up jiggling it and slopping coffee into the saucer and onto the table. Anita leaned forward and grasped Meena's hand, trying to calm her. Anita was equally distressed by the news about Nisha, but the policemen's behavior warned her that much had been left unsaid.

Auntie Meena began to hiccup. "Our poor little Nisha! What has become of her? She is in danger, Anita, I am sure of it."

"We don't know that," Anita said, taking a closer look at her aunt. The older woman only got the hiccups when she was frightened.

"Who would kill her sweet Panju? Such a nice young man. So suitable in every way."

Anita wasn't surprised at the lament. Nisha's family had approached Auntie Meena for information about Panju before finalizing the marriage arrangements. Meena had helped with the family investigations and in the end had given a good opinion of the young man. The marriage had gone forward.

"Oh, Panju gone! Nisha gone. It cannot be!" Meena began to twist her sari fabric.

"I did not know you cared so much for Panju and Nisha," Anita said. "You are frightened for her."

"She is just a child, Anita. A mere child. She . . ." Whatever else Meena was going to say was lost in a clatter of hiccupping.

"We don't know what has happened, Auntie, not really. It is too soon for us to fall apart." She smiled at her aunt, who rewarded her with a pathetic look of misery. Meena looked older this morning to Anita, her jowls thicker and lower. "All we know is that Panju is dead and Nisha has disappeared. That is all."

"But murder, Anita. Murder! They think Nisha murdered her husband! It is madness!" Meena clapped her hands over her mouth as the hiccupping intensified.

"Yes, Auntie, it is madness. But we do not have to participate in this madness." Anita leaned back in her chair, growing thoughtful.

The police didn't say anything directly, but clearly they thought Nisha was involved in her husband's death. And worse, they had come to Hotel Delite. Why? Because a neighbor had told them Nisha sometimes worked here. That made no sense. Nisha worked in lots of places. She attended patients in hotels, in private homes, in small hospitals when additional staff were sought, and wherever anyone wanted a private nurse. This was Nisha's job. The two police could not be drawn about whether or not they were visiting other employers, but Anita sensed they expected to find something significant here. *But what?* Anita wondered.

It was odd, Anita realized now, that they didn't ask about Nisha's relatives. After all, her family members were the ones most likely to know where she was, or the ones she would most likely go to for help. But the police hadn't asked about other members of the family, or where Nisha might go to hide if she were frightened.

"Oh, our poor little Nisha." Auntie Meena slumped in her chair and shook her head. She was no longer trembling and had managed to get the hiccups under control, but she still looked haggard. "What will become of her?"

"We will do everything we can for her." Anita stood up. "I will see what I can find out." She smiled down at her aunt. "Do not distress yourself, Auntie. I will help her." Anita waited for the usual objections Meena raised whenever Anita involved herself in other people's troubles, particularly crimes, but Auntie Meena was eerily silent.

Anita turned the pages of the heavy ledger, running her finger down the carefully written list of names and addresses. She found Nisha's listing and wrote down the information. When she returned the book to its shelf, she saw the dhobi in the doorway, bouncing from one foot to the other. His arms for once free of laundry, he flapped his hands to get her attention.

"What is it, Brij?" Anita asked.

"I think you are coming to the compound."

"I have to go into Trivandrum right away," Anita said. "This can wait."

"No, madam. You are coming this very minute." With that oblique demand, he bobbed his head and dashed out. When Anita looked up all she saw was a flash of plaid fabric out of the corner of her eye. She sighed and got up to follow him.

In the near corner of the compound a little girl tugged on the goat's tether, and the goat pulled back. They jockeyed for position over the rough ground. When the girl fell, the goat wobbled on its legs and approached her, nuzzling the top of her head. Brij stood to one side, watching.

"So, what did you want me for?" Anita asked.

Brij waved his hand at the goat and the girl. Anita looked at them.

"Who is she?" Anita asked.

Brij shrugged. "I am arriving at my expected time, gathering and preparing to do laundry. Then I am noticing the goat is not in its usual place, so I am looking and there, over there, the goat is lying and sleeping by this little one." His face softened into a warm smile. "I am not knowing who she is. But she is refusing to leave the goat."

Anita quickly looked around the compound, but nothing else seemed out of order. The black guard dog the hotel had purchased at the end of the season, in April, was poised like the Sphinx in the elbow between the stairs and the hotel, resting in front of the kennel it would soon return to for the rest of the day. It prowled at night, a common sight now in private homes in the city but less so at tourist hotels. It didn't seem bothered by the child.

Anita walked over to the little girl and knelt down. Anita estimated the child was about eight years old. She looked vaguely familiar, but Anita abandoned that thought as she took notice of the girl's dirty clothing. The dress was pink with large peonies splashed across it and a white bib. But down the front was smeared a thick line of something. Anita took hold of the little girl's hands and examined them, as well as her forearms. She had dirt and something crusty on them, like mud or perhaps sap. Anita sniffed at the child's hands.

"Amma?" Brij stepped forward. "What are we to do with her?"

Anita looked into the little girl's eyes. "Did your Amma leave you here?"

The child stared back, wrapped her arms around the goat's neck, and snuggled closer to the animal.

"Who is she? Am I to be calling a constable?" Brij asked.

"No, we mustn't do that." Anita stood up. It was strange, she thought, that the child could find her way here, get over a compound wall some time in the night, and not alarm the dog. Nor was she calling for her amma.

Brij leaned over to peer at the child. "Her parents will be desperate to find her."

"Not right away, I am thinking." Anita studied the little girl's features, her arched eyebrows, the straight nose as though it had been sculpted.

"But who leaves their sweet little one alone in a strange place?" Brij looked around the compound.

"Someone who is very frightened, Brij." Anita turned to him. "I think something has happened to her mother and she has been left here for her own safety. I think also we are being asked to help. That is why she is here, alone, unexpectedly." She paused. When she spoke again, her voice was barely a whisper. "You must tell no one she is here. You will take her into the workers' quarters and give her a bath. She can stay here and play. For now, she is your cousin's child, for you to keep with you while your cousin is having an operation."

"What operation is that?" Brij asked, looking worried.

Anita reached for the little girl's hand. "Tell me your name."

The child shook her head. She began to look scared, no longer as confident as when Anita first saw her. Anita didn't have much time before others arrived to begin the workday, or stopped to chat over the compound wall. Whatever she decided to do, she had to do now. She knelt down again and studied the girl's features more closely, the curve of the ear, the color of the eyes. She noted the little girl did not flinch or pull away but stared right back at her.

"You have seen me before, haven't you?" Anita said.

The little girl hunched her shoulders up to her ears and looked around, as though planning her escape.

"And you know the dog too, don't you?" Anita waited while the child glanced at the dog and looked away. She shut her mouth tight, as though afraid she might blurt out answers to Anita's questions.

"I wonder if your amma left you here. Did she tell you to wait for her here and not to speak to anyone until she came for you?"

The little girl's eyes opened wide and she leaned forward, the hopefulness and eagerness painful to see. But she pressed her lips together, perhaps to keep the truth from bursting out of her. Anita smiled, relieved she was on the right track.

"Since you are here, you must have a name," Anita said. "Suppose I guess what would be a good name for you? Is that all right?" The child nodded.

"I have a name for her," Brij said.

"Thank you, Brij, but I think mine will suit." She smiled at the child. "I will call you Theti." Anita was gratified to see the child's eyes open wide and her shoulders give a little jerk. "Yes, that is a good name for you. Theti it is."

CHAPTER 3

Brij led the child into the workers' rooms, chatting away about the goat and the tether and what they would have for breakfast. They seemed to become friends at once, and Anita wondered if Nisha, for this was surely Nisha's daughter, had told the girl to stay close to Brij, knowing he would be the first to find her in the compound.

Anita climbed the stairs to the office. With each step she decided to tell Auntie Meena, then not tell her, tell her, then not tell her. By the time she reached the office, Anita had changed her mind at least half a dozen times. She ended by deciding to wait before telling Auntie Meena for a very simple reason. If Nisha had decided her situation was so dangerous she couldn't leave her daughter with a neighbor or another relative, then her situation was dire indeed. And Auntie Meena would sense that in a second. No, Nisha's daughter would have to remain Anita and Brij's secret, at least for now. The child was safe in Brij's care, and would be confined to an area Auntie Meena tended to avoid. To prevent any suspicions from taking hold about Anita's behavior, she decided to keep to her original plan for the day, at least as far as Meena was concerned.

Anita turned into the office to tell Auntie Meena she was headed into Trivandrum. At least that was the plan until she caught a glimpse of her aunt. Auntie Meena clutched a handkerchief in one hand and a crumpled letter in the other. When she heard Anita, Meena shoved the letter into the ledger and slammed the book shut.

"What is it?" Anita asked, leaning over the other woman.

"What is what? What do you mean? There is nothing, nothing. Can you not see I am working?" Meena turned away and shoved the chair back as she tried to escape through the opposite door. But Anita was too fast for her. She blocked the doorway.

"It is not nothing. Look at you! You are distraught. Am I blind?" Anita shut the door and grasped her aunt by the shoulders, gently moving her back to the chair. "You must tell me what this is all about. Am I not your most trusted relative? Tell me what is wrong and let me help."

"It is nothing. I am a foolish old woman. I fret and fret. You know what I am like."

Anita did know what she was like, and that made her all the more determined to get a real answer. "What were you reading?"

"Reading? Oh, that is nothing." Meena waved her hand, as though she could magically dismiss every problem in the world.

Anita pulled up a chair and sat directly in front of her aunt, so close their knees bumped. "You must tell me what is troubling you so. There is nothing more important."

Meena's face softened as she gazed lovingly at Anita. "For all your faults, you are a good daughter to me." Neither woman touched the unspoken coda—better than Meena's own daughter, Padma. "It is nothing. Just foolishness. I am recovered. Am I not? Do I not seem my usual self?" Meena forced a brittle smile.

Anita studied her aunt. The woman's mood certainly was changeable this morning. In an instant she had moved from misery and worry to resignation without fear. Meena was right that Anita could only press so far, but still she was reluctant to let the matter go. She hated to see her aunt unhappy. The hotel was a burden sometimes, but Meena loved it—it was her life. And now it was Anita's life as well. She wanted to share in the burdens as well as the successes and pleasures.

"I think you should trust me and confide in me, Meena Elayamma." Anita squeezed her aunt's hands.

"I will. Truly, I will. But not now. Eh?" Meena smiled and patted her niece's cheek. "Now I am satisfied knowing how much you care for me. It is a great comfort."

"And you want me to be satisfied with that?" Anita scowled affectionately at her aunt. "All right. But I won't forget. You owe me an honest explanation."

"Where are you going now?" Meena asked.

Anita decided to let her aunt have her way—for a while. If Auntie Meena's problems could be postponed even for a day, Anita would go along. The morning had already proven to be full of shocks, between the police in mufti, the questions about Nisha and about Panju's death, and the appearance of a strange child. And Anita still had her own worries, albeit minor ones in comparison. "I have a meeting with Anand at the gallery."

"Eh?"

Anita sighed.

"You are exasperated with me?" Auntie Meena said.

Surprised, Anita tipped her head to one side and smiled. "Not at all. I didn't want to dwell on my appointment, knowing how you feel about Anand." Anita—and everyone else in the family—knew how Auntie Meena felt about the man.

"I only want for your happiness," Meena said, but her assertion lacked conviction this morning.

"You sound weary, Auntie," Anita said.

"Not at all, no, no. This is about the art exhibit, yes?"

"Yes, it is. This is something that will be wonderful for me," Anita said. "Rahul Singh owns a very important gallery in

Trivandrum and he has offered me a solo exhibit."

"So you will be a famous artist?" Meena gave a heavy sigh. The change in her was unmistakable. She leaned forward and smiled, with a shadow of the look she often had when she had stumbled on an opportunity and was trying to figure out how to exploit it. But Anita noted the faltering enthusiasm despite her aunt's knee-jerk reaction.

"He is a good friend of Anand's, Auntie, and I think this is more of a favor to Anand than a testament to my great artwork. I don't think I will be famous."

"Anita! You are too modest." Meena pulled her sari tighter, and gave Anita her most imperious look.

Anita laughed. "Perhaps. But first I must collect my camera from Shiva's Emporium, and then I'm off to the gallery. Yes?"

Meena reached out and took Anita's hand and kissed it. Anita didn't try to conceal her surprise.

"Oh, dear, Auntie. You have heard from Padma, isn't it?" Anita said. Her cousin Padma lived overseas, and meant to stay there. She and Anita had been close as children, but they drifted apart as they grew older, going to different schools and finding different friends outside the family circle, choosing different paths into adulthood. Now they rarely spoke and Meena often kept news of Padma to herself.

"So exciting her life is," Meena said, but she didn't look like she meant it.

"What is it now?" Anita said. Padma had a habit of writing about her exploits in breathless prose on email, and then yawning during overseas phone calls. Anita wondered if Padma remembered what she'd written, or even if she sometimes made it all up.

"A trip to Washington, D.C. She is meeting a senator." Meena looked both proud and confused. "A delegation."

"But she's not a citizen. Why is she going?"

"She is assisting the delegation." Meena seemed to take Anita's skepticism personally, as an insult to her daughter's standing in America. "She is crucial to their endeavors."

"Oh." Anita shrugged. She had her own views of Padma.

"And you are ready for this gallery business?"

Anita laughed. "First you think it is wonderful, and then you think it is nothing."

"Is it important—to you?" Meena asked, and this time she seemed genuinely interested.

"Yes, it is. This gallery business, as you put it, Auntie, is very important to me. And a little scary. I am being taken seriously as an artist." For all Anita's attempt at nonchalance about her photography, whenever she spoke of the upcoming solo exhibit, she was a bit dismayed. She didn't like thinking of herself as an artist. It seemed pretentious. She worried that someone would come along and point out that she only photographed the kinds of things people found on postcards. It wasn't true, but at moments like this she felt uneasy and very lacking in self-confidence.

"I always take you seriously," Meena said. "Perhaps I will go there and I will meet a suitable boy for you. I will take note and we will talk. Yes?"

Anita shook her head. "You never give up hope."

"Of course not. And your mother would never expect less of me."

"My mother lives in America and she expects much less of you," Anita said. "Don't despair, Auntie. I am in no danger of marrying anyone anytime soon. I only ask that you like Anand as my friend."

Meena rested her elbow on the table, her head on her hand. "You do not need a friend. You need a husband."

"Then so does Padma."

The look on Meena's face so startled Anita that she could think of nothing to say.

The bus shuddered to a stop just before the entrance at East Fort. Women clambered down in a huddle after the men. The sun beat down. Anita pulled the dupatta over her head and let it drape over her forehead. She separated herself from the crowd and headed through the white arch.

The first item on her list for the day was a visit to Shiva's Fine Photography Emporium, to collect her camera. She had discovered a spot in a series of photos she had taken and concluded that a speck of dust had somehow found its way onto the mirror. The camera had been left for cleaning.

Shiva's Emporium, as the customers called it, had an excellent reputation for quality of service, and the owner treated the staff well. Anita knew this because Nisha's cousin Nirmala worked there in part as the result of a recommendation from Auntie Meena. Anita climbed the cement steps to the shops on the second level of the open-air gallery. She pushed open the door to Shiva's Emporium and was met with a blast of cold air.

A short man in his early forties, his blue shirt neatly tucked into his dark gray slacks, gave Anita a nearly imperceptible nod as she entered. George owned the shop, after purchasing it from its founder, and had managed its growth over the years until it became known as the most reliable camera shop in the city. He acknowledged Anita and returned to the customer facing him across the glass counter. Two other counter assistants, one male and the other female, tended to other customers, and another two customers, middle-aged men, hovered at the end of the counter waiting their turn. Only they weren't really customers. Anita knew the minute she caught sight of them out of the corner of her eye that here were two more police in mufti, their civilian "disguises" looking almost like a different kind of uniform.

So, they know where Nisha's relatives are, she thought. Anita took a seat against the glass wall and waited. The female assistant completed the sale of a flash attachment and turned to the two men next. The policemen dithered and otherwise tried to give the impression of being ordinary customers who knew little about cameras. *They need acting lessons,* Anita thought.

"Yes, she gave us advice." The first man shook his head and lifted his eyebrows in a sign of confusion. "Yes, she worked here. What was her name?" He turned to his partner, who looked equally at sea. "We are friends taking up this new hobby."

"We are the only ones working here," the assistant said. George approached the men at the counter.

"If I may, sars, what day are you coming in?" George asked.

The two men dithered some more but couldn't be certain.

"And how did the young assistant appear?"

Again the men dithered. George sighed and turned to his assistant. "Bring out Nirmala." The young woman pulled open a panel covered with bright posters for luxurious vacation sites, and slipped into the back. A moment later she reappeared with a young woman barely in her twenties. Nirmala was short and slight, her oiled black hair hanging down her back, over her bright red khurta, falling almost to her jeans.

"Sar?" Nirmala looked at George with huge worried eyes.

"Did you assist these gentlemen?" he asked.

Nirmala gazed at the two men. "No, Sar. I don't remember them. I am not working on the counter."

"Thank you, Nirmala." He nodded to her and she walked backward to the door. She noticed Anita and stopped to offer a smile of surprise and delight.

"I'm here to pick up my camera," Anita explained.

"I shall get it for you, yes?" Nirmala scooted behind the panel, and Anita turned her attention to George and the two men.

"There is a young man in the back," George said.

"No, no," one man said as he clucked. "It was a young woman."

"She is reliable, this one Nirmala?" the other man asked.

"Very." George was growing annoyed with the same question asked in different ways, and didn't conceal it. After another few rounds, the two men gave up and stepped back near the wall, where they could argue in private.

"They go about their work in peculiar ways," George said *sotto voce* to Anita when he returned to his place at the counter. He dutifully inquired about Auntie Meena and the hotel, and then after Anita and her gallery. "You have come for your camera. It is ready. I left it sitting in the lock box last night."

"I think Nirmala went to fetch it."

George raised an eyebrow and turned to the panel door. Nirmala appeared a moment later, deposited the camera on the counter, and disappeared back into the workroom.

"That's it." Anita felt like she had lost an old friend and now it had come back to her. She reached out for it.

"Please be looking to be certain you are satisfied." George rested his palms on the counter and lifted his chin. He was shorter than Anita and probably most of his other customers, so he had a habit of stretching his neck and lifting his head, to gain height. It made him look both myopic and snobbish, and he was neither.

Anita held the camera up to her eye and sighted it on the wall, the counter, the two men by the glass wall, and the row of chairs. She pronounced herself satisfied. "Excellent work, as always, George."

"Most pleased, madam. Most pleased." George smiled. "Is there any other matter?"

This was George's usual comment as he began to fill out the

charge slip, but Anita surprised him by saying yes, there was. She was interested in using a certain filter but worried it might produce effects she didn't want. What was his advice? George looked at her as though she were speaking a strange language whose swear words alone were recognizable, but he rested his pen on the counter and turned to the glass case behind him. Anita rested her elbow on the glass top and leaned forward, as though she were in Tiffany's to select a crystal pattern.

George slid open the glass case and drew out a box of filters. "These may be of use to you, madam." He placed the box on the counter and opened it, each movement taken with care and, Anita realized, some doubt this was really happening. She tried to get involved in his explanations, but she kept the two men in mufti in her peripheral vision until they pushed open the glass doors and walked down the steps. Abandoning their roles at the bottom, they marched off to the Fort entrance, swinging their arms and chatting. Anita was the only customer left in the store.

"The police are looking for Nirmala's cousin Nisha. It seems her husband, Panju, was found dead and Nisha has disappeared," Anita told George.

"They did not question her," George said. "As you saw. Nirmala!"

Nirmala appeared in the doorway, her eyes even wider, if that were possible. She glanced at George and Anita, and stepped into the store. "Sar?"

"I have just learned about your cousin Nisha," George said. Nirmala's eyes filled and she began to sniffle. George offered gentle condolences, as did Anita.

"How did you find out?" Anita asked.

Nirmala stepped back and seemed to compose herself. "A neighbor. Someone heard something. It is terrible. I only know Panju is dead and Nisha is gone."

"Do you know the police were just here?" George asked.

"I wondered if those two men were police. A man in uniform came to the house early this morning after a neighbor told us something had happened." Nirmala paused and gulped. "I don't know these two men." She nodded to the counter area where they had stood. "They didn't say they were police."

"I suppose they are trying to keep a low profile, to give themselves more room to maneuver. I am so sorry, Nirmala. If I can help, please call me," Anita said. Nirmala thanked her and, with a nod to George, returned to the workroom.

Anita reached for her camera. "I don't know how they knew about her though. They have already been to Hotel Delite and did not ask us any questions about Nisha's relatives. I found that odd."

"She has a daughter," George said. "Nirmala talks about her all the time. What has happened to her?"

Anita pulled the camera to her chest and examined the covered lens. "Well, that is another problem the police will have to figure out, isn't it?" She slipped the strap over her neck.

"Of course." George offered a smile but his eyes were more curious than kind.

CHAPTER 4

Anita stepped out into the sunshine and stared toward the East Fort entrance, the direction the police had taken. There was nothing unusual in the police having come to Hotel Delite in search of a missing person who was known to work there. But the police came in mufti, didn't identify themselves, and did not ask the expected questions. And the police continued to go about their investigation as though it were a secret. Why would they pretend to be customers at Shiva's Emporium, when all they had to do was ask if Nisha's cousin Nirmala was there? What was the need for subterfuge? Did they suspect Nirmala of having some involvement in Panju's death? The idea was laughable. But the whole business gave Anita a greater sense of urgency. She headed to the Fort entrance and hailed an auto-rickshaw.

The little taxi set off, and in less than twenty minutes the auto crept over a bridge and slowed to avoid deep ruts left by the southwest monsoon just a few months earlier. The auto followed a lane running parallel with the canal until it came to a turning, and continued on. Halfway down the lane, a young constable rose from a white plastic chair, where he had been sprawled reading a newspaper, and waved the auto to a stop.

"Is it the road?" Anita asked.

"No, madam. The road is passable but it is being closed."

"The police came to Hotel Delite this morning asking about my employee who lives here. I know something has happened. I

35

came to help the family if I can."

"Name?"

"Her name is Nisha Eappen." Anita paused, waiting. She realized more was expected of her, and gave her own name.

The man looked uncertain, but after a moment he turned away and pulled a walkie-talkie from his waist. He chattered into it. When he turned back, his face was still blank, but he motioned her to park along the side of the road. "You can walk to the house, just there. Ten houses down on the right." He nodded farther down the lane. The driver parked and Anita began walking the short distance to Nisha's house.

The houses were tidy and attractive, the neighborhood quiet. Ahead a guard stood outside a pink-painted one. The grounds showed signs of neglect—no one had swept the yard in a number of days, a few rags lay scattered about, a dying shrub had snagged a plastic bag. No potted plants decorated the front stoop. Brown weeds dying in the heat straggled over the path to the front door. Anita felt uneasy at the air of neglect and implied poverty. This wasn't how she had seen Nisha at all.

A second constable watched her approach, and spoke into his walkie-talkie. Another policeman emerged from the house and sauntered down the path. He gave the impression of barely noticing her, but she knew he was sizing her up. She tried to get a good look at his badge, to determine his rank, but all she could see before he turned away was a red ribbon along the edge. So, above a constable but below a superintendent. He held his walkie-talkie against his chest, resting it against his shirt, concealing his nametag and badge.

"She is an employee," Anita explained. "The police came to Hotel Delite this morning but they left very quickly after finding she is not there. I came to see if I could be of assistance. I want to offer my help to the family." It was thin, but it would have to do.

"A good employee?"

"A very good employee. Can you tell me what has happened?"

"She has worked for you how long?"

Anita told him.

"You have papers?"

Anita pulled out an ID card.

"Hmm." He held the card in his hand, reading it slowly, turning it over in his fingers as though he had never seen one before and he wanted to get a good look at it before he had to give it up. After he handed it back, he did her the courtesy of studying her as well, perhaps trying to decide what he could learn just by looking. He harrumphed once more and said, "Her husband is dead and she is missing."

"Panju's dead? Yes, that's what the police said."

"You know this already?"

"But they didn't know what happened to Nisha. I am very concerned. What has happened to her? Do you know anything?"

"Missing. Am I not saying?" His upper lip twitched. "Neighbors are reporting an argument in the night, previous nights many times. Many nights running they are arguing. Then nothing."

Think fast, Anita told herself. "Her family. What about her family?"

"There is a child, at least one, perhaps two, we are told. But now no one is here."

"And other relatives? Have you learned about them?"

"Neighbors are providing—aunt, cousin, others."

Others, Anita thought. But the policeman clamped his mouth shut.

"Does she have a mobile?" he asked.

"I think so." Anita gave him the mobile number Nisha had originally given her, and he punched it into his own phone. She heard a ring inside the house. Both turned to look. A constable came to the doorway holding the phone, the two men nodded to each other, and the man in the house flipped open the mobile and cancelled the call. *The first dead end,* she thought.

The little three-room house was one story with a flat roof reached by a narrow outside staircase. The little portico filled out the shape of the footprint, making a square. It was the perfect spot for someone like Nisha to sit of an evening, chatting with her neighbors while she rested after the day's work. Staring at the adobe and plaster wasn't going to get her anywhere, but Anita couldn't force herself to turn around and walk away. She needed information, something to tell her which direction to take, some hint about Nisha and what had gone wrong.

Anita could sense the policeman watching her out of the corner of his eye. She had a better view of his badge and now saw he was an assistant sub inspector. He was just beginning to make serious progress in his career, and his belly protruding over the black belt testified to that. He had the look of incipient prosperity and self-satisfaction, but he was still at that level where he had to be careful to be certain about whom he was talking to. He seemed to size up Anita as someone he could be generous to if he felt like it but could dismiss if he wanted to. This usually worked to her advantage, so she was glad to let people make their own assumptions.

"Do you know what happened?" she asked.

"We are examining evidence and all individuals will be questioned."

"Yes, of course." This wasn't any better than no answer at all. "How did he die?"

"Stabbing."

"Stabbing!" Even though the police at Hotel Delite had

confided that Panju had a knife in his stomach, in the back of her mind Anita had assumed there was more to the story, that Panju had been hit on the head, pushed off the roof, poisoned—ways of death that were hard to attribute to a particular person on the face of it. She had assumed the knife was ancillary to the real cause of death. But stabbing! "Oh, my. That seems very violent, quite extreme," she added. "I suppose there was a lot of blood."

"Very violent. A thrust to the stomach. Very much blood. Everywhere."

If the man was stabbed in the stomach, Anita had no doubt there was "very much blood everywhere." There would have been blood gushing all over the place, all over the victim and all over his attacker. "Has anyone looked for Nisha in this area? Perhaps she was also injured and she ran off into the, the . . ." Anita looked around her for the kind of place where someone might run off to if they'd been stabbed in their own home. A few trees shielded the house from those on the next street over, but there was no jungle anyone could get lost in.

"We are looking," the man said, giving her a tired smile.

Anita turned her attention to the house. The place must be a mess, a sticky gag-inducing horror, she thought. "May I look in the doorway? Just from here."

With more uncertainty than not, he waggled his head yes and led her closer to the door. She craned her neck to peer in, shifting from one foot to the other, trying to see around corners, into other rooms, down a short hallway to the back door. She noted the portico was mostly clean and the few stains dotting the cement could be anything. She studied the dirt path leading around to the back, but that revealed nothing either. She suspected that whatever might have been there to discover had been trampled by the police when they first arrived.

"How did you know there was a matter of concern here?" she asked him.

"A neighbor is worrying that no one in the household has been seen in the early morning. So she is knocking on the door and peering inside the open window and seeing the ghastly scene. It is creating much distress in the neighbor lady."

"This side?" Anita leaned toward the house on the right, and when the assistant sub inspector didn't contradict her but avoided giving a complete nod she hoped she had guessed right. "A good neighbor indeed. She must have heard something, yes?"

"She heard nothing, no."

"Oh. Too bad." Anita began to inch her way into the yard.

The ASI turned around to look at the house, looked at Anita, and puffed up his lips in thought. He had progressed from cradling his walkie-talkie at his chest, to holding his hands rigidly at his sides, to letting one hand slip into his pocket and the other hold the machine while resting it on his shoulder as though it were heavy instead of a small plastic device not much bigger than a cell phone. If he saw her as a harmless nosy woman who couldn't get him into any trouble with his superiors, he might toss a few tidbits to her and let her peck at them like a crow; but if she seemed a serious presence in the world, he would clam up and watch her for his own safety.

"Knife is found there. Coconut knife," the constable said.

"That would make quite a gash in the body." Anita had a healthy respect for the broad sharp knife coconut harvesters used.

"Very big gash." His nose quivered in disgust.

"And he is in the police morgue?"

"Where else?" The question seemed to try his patience.

From farther up the lane came the sound of a car approaching. Anita looked in that direction and saw an official car emerge from the shade of a tree, where it had been parked. The ASI turned to the constable and muttered an order that implied the crime scene would soon be returned to the owner's care. Abruptly, the ASI turned to Anita. "Tell me again why you are here. It is really morbid curiosity?"

"She is my employee, Sar, and I was concerned."

"Have the police not come to Hotel Delite this very morning?"

Anita nodded yes. "But I was hoping to offer my help to the family. I had no idea so much had happened."

He studied her while she spoke, as though he was weighing her words and how believable they were. After a while he said, "Ugly and violent. One dead, one missing."

"Will your people do more work here?" she asked.

He shook his head no. "We are finished. Now we only wait till the owner comes. The constable will remain as a matter of course in case anyone of interest appears." He paused and gave her a stern look. "And to keep away hooligans."

Anita tried not to look annoyed. She was either a person of interest or a hooligan, it seemed. Of course, if the police knew about Theti, she might actually end up in one of those categories. She smiled at the ASI.

"Then I could approach and look inside, at least through the windows?"

"Why?"

What sort of reason could she have? "I feel responsible for my employees and I want to understand what has happened. May I approach?"

Once again she felt herself being evaluated, or maybe he was thinking of the errands his wife wanted him to do on his way home from work, some few little things his driver could collect from one or another of the new shopping venues that made life so much easier and more gracious for the middle-class families of the city.

"No photographs," he said, nodding to the camera hanging around her neck.

She readily agreed. She walked gingerly up the path to the edge of the portico. The ASI gave a curt order to the constable, climbed into his car, and was gone.

In her years helping Auntie Meena run her modest tourist hotel, Anita had faced numerous crises among the guests. She had taken in hand a retired civil servant who had inexplicably gone mad and dashed himself against a wall time and time again. She had discovered a man who had rented an outlying cottage off season and there committed suicide; he not been found for over a week when a laborer, who lived barely within sight, came calling out of curiosity, hoping for a job. She rescued a cousin who was deemed possessed and locked in a windowless room for three weeks. But she wasn't ready for what she saw through the open door of the little pink house—the blood smearing the walls, sinuous lines widening into puddles whose fluidity had gelled like a surrealist painting.

Anita felt her stomach seize and twist; she turned away lest she begin vomiting. She shifted to the other side of the portico to peer into a side bedroom, where sheets were tossed across the end of a thin mattress and towels lay crumpled on the floor. The armoire door stood open and the neatly stacked saris stared out in proud defiance of the chaos before them.

With another step, waiting to hear an order to desist rumble behind her, Anita perched on the doorsill, scanning the floor for blood spatters, but the trail led back, into the kitchen area, not forward to the front door. The furniture—only one settee for two people and one straight-backed wooden chair caned in bright blue and white plastic, both shoved against a wall—was stained with browning blood. The man must have bled to death in this room, she thought, and Panju's body seemed to materialize before her. It would have been a terrible death. Unconsciously she clenched her fists and crossed her arms over her stomach.

Anita moved around the house counter clockwise. The back stoop was sticky with blood. A tiny print of a sandal was the only evidence someone had left this way—a child had come out this door and the little shoe had left its mark. Anita peered in the open kitchen window and saw splashes and smears of blood along the floor. Had he fallen and crawled here? Had he stumbled around the sitting room, panicked and flailing his arms, sinking into shock as he coughed and choked on blood? Would he even be able to? Had he struggled to reach his assailant and defend himself? And what about the assailant? Where were those footsteps? Was it Nisha who fled this house in terror? Alone? With another?

Anita walked along the back wall, peering into another room. Again the shutter was open and through the barred window Anita saw a small pallet on the floor. Three books were tossed in a corner and a towel lay draped over a low stool. Odd, she thought. Most families kept their children with them when they slept. Children didn't get their own rooms until they were much older. Only very modern families now gave their children their own rooms. *I didn't know Nisha was so modern,* Anita thought. Then she remembered the ASI's words about a second child, and guessed this must be that one's bedroom.

The last window on the remaining side opened into the parents' bedroom, the pallet on the floor with its sheets in disarray, the half-opened armoire that declared the previous orderly life of the occupants of the house, the towels lying at the doorway to the bathroom, waiting for Nisha to collect them as she set the room in order.

It was a confused place, the signs of a busy home with a child mixed with the evidence of a rage so great it all but consumed the building, drowning it in the blood of murder. Yet all around Anita was a quiet, semi-rural neighborhood punctuated by little pastel-colored houses with green palm trees leaning over them protectively, shading the pepper vines and flowers growing in pots along the borders. Anita walked around to the front of the house, avoiding the constable's eye. She moved to the open front door and gazed inside once again, adding up all she had seen.

She walked along the lane, viewing the small house from different angles, as though that would somehow tell her more, reveal something not already visible. Two school-age boys in the standard uniform of white shirts and blue shorts watched her, their gaze steady and focused.

"Dead!" the taller one said.

"Did you know about this?" Anita asked.

Both boys shook their heads.

"But you knew the family who lived there?"

The boys seemed undecided. They knew about the family, it seemed, but not much else.

"Were you friends with the child?" Anita gambled they knew the family well enough to play with Nisha's daughter as just one more child in the neighborhood.

The younger boy turned up his lip and clicked disdainfully. "No fun."

Surprised, Anita glanced back at the house. Theti had seemed a very ordinary child, playful with the goat and easy with Brij. Was it the second child they were referring to? "What was that one like?"

The two boys screwed up their faces and flicked their fingers in disgust. "He is not playing good games," the taller boy said.

So, Anita thought, an older child, a boy, Nisha never

mentioned. "What was Panju like? Did he get along with the neighbors? Did he have friends here?"

The boys shook their heads. "He is a photographer," the taller one said. "He has a camera with a big lens." The boy held up his hands, moving them wide apart. "Bigger than yours."

Anita's hand went to rest on the camera hanging around her neck. She knew Panju worked for a local newspaper, but she had understood he held only a low-level position. "You saw him with the camera?"

"Practicing," the taller one said. He wrinkled his nose.

"Not very good then," Anita said with a smile. "Did you see his photos?"

The boys shook their heads. "But I can tell," the taller one said. "Only looking here, looking there." He pointed to the surrounding trees.

Anita considered the setting. Nothing here was exotic—coconut palms, mangos, a jackfruit tree, tamarind, and in the distance a young banyan tree. Occasionally a goat wandered by, which would interest tourists but not locals. Most of the houses had pots of flowering shrubs, azaleas and bougainvillea, but nothing special that she could see. But each artist was different, and she could see this was a place where Panju could learn about composition, color, light, shapes. The odd part was that Nisha had never mentioned Panju had any interest in photography.

CHAPTER 5

The tall cast-iron gates of the *Kerala News* offices sat open just enough to let one person through at a time. Gone were the days when cars and motorcycles could zoom up the slight incline to the front door of the glass and steel building, or park along the pedestrian ramp. The guard watched every arrival with a steady eye from his bench inside the hut. He emerged from his guardhouse to open the gate only for the publisher or someone of equal importance. Anita walked past the hut and on to the main entrance.

If Nisha had fled because she was involved in her husband's murder, or had been taken and also murdered, then it was time she learned more about Panju. Anita pulled open the glass door and stepped into an air-conditioned lobby. A guard, much younger than the one at the gate, stood up behind his desk and nodded to her to approach. She asked for the head of photography. After the obligatory half-hour wait, Anita was led to the second floor and an office in the rear. A man in his thirties with short black hair met her at the door.

"So, we are making news as well as reporting it." This cynical remark was the only greeting from Dhanu, the head of the photography department of the *Kerala News,* a local language newspaper. "Yes, Panju was my assistant. Actually the office assistant. He did a little of everything to help others. He was very eager."

Anita followed Dhanu into a small room with piles of paper,

stacks of old newspapers, boxes, file cabinets, and a desk with three chairs, one in back and two in front. There was barely enough room to turn around in, but Dhanu made it to the other side of his desk. He was much shorter than Anita and his jeans were crisp and sharp beneath his striped shirt. He had a partial beard that probably would never be full. He was cocky too, and had that world-weary look of someone who has come to believe he's important.

"What kinds of things did he do?" Anita pulled out one of the white molded plastic chairs and slid into it. The other one was piled high with papers, with a leather jacket draped over everything. "I'm trying to figure out a motive behind such a terrible death. He was stabbed, as you probably know."

"Ah!" Dhanu sat down and sprawled as though he had just delivered a juicy secret. "What did he do? That's a good question. I can't imagine anyone less significant than Panju. A nice boy. But really, a village boy. He wanted to be successful in Trivandrum, but he was so unaware of how things are done." He shook his head, a sad smile spreading across his features.

"Did he cover any stories that could have been dangerous?"

"Hah!" Dhanu threw his head back and laughed. "Panju? He was a gofer! If he went out on a story with a photographer, it was to carry equipment."

"He didn't do any of the photographing himself?"

Dhanu slowly shook his head back and forth, his smile changing to one of disdain. "He barely knew which end of the camera lens to look through. Wait, I think Randall offered to teach him a few things. Randall!" He shouted to someone in the next room. A man in jeans and a cotton shirt came to the doorway and Dhanu waved him in. "Did you teach our poor Panju how to photograph?"

Randall was a tall lanky man, perhaps in his forties, with a careful look in his eyes. Anita pegged him as Anglo-Indian with his brownish hair and light brown eyes. "A bit. I am showing him the technical aspects and letting him take a few shots at the temple festival in Karamana last week."

"How did he do?" Anita asked. Randall had been speaking directly to Dhanu, but with Anita's question, he took his hands out of his pockets and looked down at her.

"Not bad. He had a good sense of composition."

"That must have pleased him," Anita said.

"Yes, you would think."

"Did he go out on any jobs with you that might have brought him into contact with dangerous people?" Anita ignored the contemptuous laughter from Dhanu and kept her eyes on Randall, who paused to give the idea some thought.

"He is only going out with me a few times, and these were the usual. Protests in front of Secretariat, marches down MG Road, a new *mandapa* being inaugurated, a dance program at Jubilee Hall, that sort of thing." Randall frowned and pursed his lips. "But he is worried about something."

"Worried? How do you know? Did he tell you this?" Anita turned in her chair to get a better look at Randall. Dhanu had grown quiet and was now sitting up, listening.

"I didn't notice anything," Dhanu said.

"Panju wouldn't want to bother you," Randall said.

"What did he tell you?" Anita said, afraid Dhanu would distract Randall from what he seemed ready to share.

"We were watching a group protesting land distribution in the hills. They wanted the land given out a certain way, and Panju said, 'Do you think they know what will happen if they win?' " Randall paused. "I thought it was a foolish thing to say. I told him, if they win they get land. But they won't win. It's such a long shot and the government has other ideas for that land."

"What do you think he meant?"

Randall shrugged and looked over at Dhanu. "He was getting moody this last week, wasn't he?"

"I don't know about moody," Dhanu said. "But I told him if he ever took out a camera again without permission, I would fire him and call the cops. That was thousands of rupees he was risking. Bloody asshole." Dhanu hunched forward, resting his arms on the desk.

"What do you mean, he took a camera?" Anita swung around to face him.

"One night he took a camera with him at the end of his shift," Dhanu said. "He told me the next day you said he could." He looked at Randall as if waiting for confirmation. "I guess I forgot to tell you that."

"How long ago was this?" Anita asked. Randall and Dhanu looked at each other, each waiting for the other to answer.

"Maybe a month ago? Maybe less?" Randall said.

"The first time maybe, yes, that long ago," Dhanu said.

"So he did this more than once?"

"Randall, what would you say? Three, four times?"

"About that."

"Did he say what he was taking pictures of?" she asked.

Both men shook their heads. "Just said he was practicing," Randall said. "Said he wanted to be able to keep track of things."

"What things?"

"Just things."

"His daughter growing up?"

"No, not like that. I think it was more business than family." Randall leaned against the door jamb, his fingers hooked on his jeans' belt loops.

"Was there anything special about the camera?" Anita asked.

Randall shook his head. "It was just a digital SLR. Standard. He had his own card."

"Did that seem unusual to you?" she asked, sensing uncertainty in his reply.

"He didn't ask to have free prints made?" Dhanu asked. Anita had forgotten he was there, listening to it all.

Randall shook his head. "Nope. And I offered."

"And he didn't want them? That seems strange," she said. "Did he give you a reason?"

"He only said not yet. He didn't have all that he wanted." Randall pushed away from the door jamb and stood up. "It's too bad. He seemed nice. Sorry about him dying that way."

"They think his wife did it," Anita said.

"Nisha?" Randall stared at her. "Never. I met her a couple of times when she came by to meet him after work. Sweet woman. She'd never do something like that. Maybe someone from his village."

"Why do you say that?" Anita asked.

"No reason really," Randall said with a shrug. "He just seemed angry about how things were changing out there. He supported the land protesters because he said they were like villagers everywhere—losing their land to people who didn't care what happened to hardworking farmers as long as they made their own money along the way. The farmers would grow the country's food but die of starvation and poverty."

"Panju said that?"

Randall nodded.

"Damned little revolutionary," Dhanu said. "Hid it well too."

Randall hung a camera over his shoulder and headed out the door. Like many tall people, he loped rather than walked along smartly. Anita thanked Dhanu and hurried after the photographer. When she reached the front entrance a step or so behind him, she called out. He waited for her on the ramp.

"Do you mind another question?" she said when she reached him. The heat was intense, and made even worse after sitting in the air-conditioning for so long.

"Go ahead." Randall led the way to a small portico, shading them from the sun. "Panju was a nice sort. Don't mind Dhanu. He thinks he has to be cynical and tough-sounding to fit the role of supervisor. He wants to move up fast." Randall laughed.

"Back there, when you were talking about Panju, you sounded like you worked well with him." She paused. "He was a good sort, from the little I knew of him. Nisha worked for my aunt at Hotel Delite, and we all liked her."

"She was sweet the few times I met her," Randall said, "but I can't say I knew her."

"You said you complimented Panju on his photographs but he didn't seem to care, or something like that. What did you mean?"

"I saw one of his photos—some unusual flowers—and I told him the focus was good, sharp, and the color too. That's what people respond to," Randall added. "He seemed, not quite embarrassed, but awkward, almost testy, as though he didn't want my opinion."

"What did he say?"

"He said that wasn't the point of the photos, getting people to like them."

Anita considered this. "I'm still surprised Nisha didn't mention this interest in photography. I wonder if she even knew about it."

Randall shrugged and shook his head. "Can't help you with that."

"Was that the last time the question of his photography came up?" Anita asked.

Randall shifted the weight of the camera hanging off his left shoulder. "I came into the office a couple of weeks ago. It was late and everyone else had left. I came back to leave equipment and pick up some personal stuff." Randall waited while a motorcycle revved and roared away. "I didn't expect to see anyone else but he was there, returning the borrowed camera, only no one knew he had borrowed it."

"Did he say what he wanted it for?"

Randall shook his head. A horn honked and tires squealed, and his head jerked up; he was ready to head for it, already considering the best angle for a shot. "Sorry," he said when he saw her watching him. "Professional liability. You know that, don't you?"

She nodded, grimaced. "I once nearly knocked over a *pandal* and stepped on the priest at a wedding in my rush to get a shot," Anita said. *We're colleagues now,* she thought, hoping this would prompt him to share more information. "Did he show you what he shot the last time?"

"No. I picked up the camera and started going through the shots. It upset him and he grabbed the camera out of my hands." Randall laughed. He had a friendly guffaw as he recalled the incident.

"That seems extreme." Anita frowned as she considered this. "What were the pictures of?"

"Nothing special that I could see. Mostly people in front of houses. It looked like he was photographing gardens. I told him he needed to get closer to the subject, get people in motion. But some of his compositions were okay."

"Anything you remember in particular?"

"They were all men. I remember that because to get real color in a shot you need women in saris. Otherwise, it's gray and brown and black and white."

"All men," Anita repeated. Not much to go on there as far as she could tell.

"And one elderly gentleman who looked quite stately. He looked familiar, but so do most elderly stately men because they all look alike at that point in their lives." Again he laughed.

"An elderly gentleman." Anita sighed. None of this seemed to be of much help. "Well, if you think of anything, I hope you'll let me know."

"I wondered if he had another job, or was getting one." Randall stepped out into the sun. "It makes sense if you think about it. If any employee gets caught doing something wrong, wouldn't you expect him to be apologetic and obsequious? Panju was none of that. He was almost defiant. But I think he was troubled. I think he was up to something that was more important to him than his job. And in this economy, that must have been important indeed."

"You liked him, didn't you?" Anita said as they walked to the street.

"He was young and eager," Randall said. "I did like him. But he changed. I'm sorry about what happened to him, but I think he got himself in serious trouble."

"Why do you think that?"

"He showed no interest in photography when he started," Randall said, resting his hand on the seat of a motorcycle in a line of them. "He was more interested in the business side of things. I knew his wife sometimes worked at hotels along the beach, including yours, and I've seen your gallery out there, so when he came one day and asked to borrow a camera, I jok-ingly asked him if he got the photography bug from you."

Anita smiled. "What did he say?"

"It isn't what he said. It's the way he looked. He looked sick. Then he said, this has nothing to do with them."

"Them?"

"Them. That's what he said." Randall slung the camera strap so the camera shifted to his back and climbed onto the motorcycle. "Need a lift?"

"Are you going by the Bourne Studio?"

Chapter 6

Nisha leaned back against the dirt wall and pressed her fingertips against her eyelids. Inside the room all was dirt—floor, walls—except the ceiling and door. She kept her eyes shut and within this black world watched swales of color form and reform, like water bubbling up in hot springs or clouds forming on the distant horizon and scudding across the sky. The colors grew from creamy white to red and orange tinged with gold. When the colors faded and the black seeped through, she pressed her fingertips to her closed lids again. Streaks of gold and pink shot through the black. It was the only light she had.

When she grew tired of this and her eyes and mind ached, Nisha lay down on the mat and stared into the darkness. She didn't know how long she'd been here, but it had taken some time at the outset before she had the courage to search the small room with her hands.

When the man grabbed her from behind in the bushes, tying her pallu around her throat and dragging her along the ground, she had thought this was her end. She thought he meant to kill her. But he shoved her down a path and knocked her into a car, and there a man with a cigarette watched her fall. He didn't speak to her, he didn't ask her anything at first; he just watched her tumble over the ground. The other man kicked her when she tried to get up and she fell again, clutching her side. She slid to the ground and curled into a little ball.

Only when the man with the cigarette spoke to her did she

understand. Panju, her husband, had described the voice—like raw silk, it felt smooth but it snagged. This was Dipak, the moneylender from Panju's ancestral village. She dug her nails into the palms of her hands to control her panic.

"You know what I want."

It wasn't a question. She opened her eyes and stared at the tire and undercarriage. Both were spattered with dirt, dry dirt. The monsoon hadn't come yet. But when it did, everything would be spattered with mud, and then washed clean by the rain.

"I don't know."

"Where is your husband?"

She drew her arms in tighter, anticipating blows. They didn't know. Of course not. How could they? "He's dead."

The man who held the end of her pallu, as though she were an animal on a leash, yanked it hard. "Don't lie to us! Let me—"

"Shut up. How do you know?" Dipak asked her. He paused in carrying the cigarette to his mouth, then lowered his hand. "Tell me."

"I saw him lying on the floor, bleeding. He is surely dead."

"Who did this?" When she didn't answer, he repeated the question.

She held her breath, waiting, but all she heard was a cricket in the underbrush nearby. Where was the kick? Where was the pain? If she opened her eyes to look at him, would he rip them out of their sockets? Would he cut out her tongue if she spoke without telling him what he wanted to know? She felt herself getting smaller and smaller, with no way to defend herself against these men. Panju had told her about Dipak, as though this moneylender were one to challenge the gods.

Dipak gave an order to the other man, who bent over and yanked her away from the car. He ran his large soiled hands over her body, touching every part, even pulling apart her bra.

Her protests earned her a slap and another kick.

"Nothing," he told Dipak.

"She may have thrown it away somewhere." He pulled out his mobile and spoke rapidly into it in a dialect she did not understand.

"Where is the child?"

"I don't know." Another kick.

"Not here," Dipak said. He looked up at the sky as though expecting to see something there despite the darkness. "We need the truth from her, not something likely to put me off. Into the boot. I need to think." The man let go of the pallu and pulled out a rope. Before Nisha could get to her feet, she was trussed and gagged and tossed into the trunk of an old dark car. The lid slammed shut.

Nisha chanted a prayer to hold terror at bay. She told herself she was ready for this, strong enough to face whatever came. Her child was safe, and she could do whatever was necessary to keep her safe. She braced herself against the motion of the car, trying to memorize the route as the car went down a hill, turned onto a paved road or a dirt lane, sped up, or slowed for another turn. At each jostling her head banged against the wheel well, a can of kerosene sloshed, the vapors almost suffocating her. She buried her face in her shoulder and the edge of her pallu. But the fumes overwhelmed her and she must have slept because she awoke to fresh air and the night sky. Once again, she was roughly handled. She was blindfolded, pulled from the trunk, and shoved into a dirt room.

Nisha tumbled into the cave with only a few seconds of light to introduce her to her prison, but in those seconds she had seen the signs that her situation was meant to last. She saw a hole in the ground—a toilet of the most primitive sort. A bucket stood nearby with so little water, it turned out, that she would surely die of disease if she didn't go mad from thirst. A pallet on the ground told her it would be a long stay. One tin plate and a tin cup told her they meant to keep her alive, but for how long? And why?

In those first hours, Nisha had felt along the hard-packed dirt floor to the pallet and crawled onto it, terrified that a rat or snake would protest her usurpation of its home, but she met no other creature. She pulled her knees up to her chest, wrapped her arms around her legs, and made herself into the smallest possible body, a little nothing that perhaps the universe would forget about and let escape into another life, too insignificant to be caught up in any thrust of violence. Or perhaps the universe would take pity on this tiny form at the mercy of so much evil. But the universe did nothing. It ignored her pleas, did not sense her anguish, and was silent at her desperation.

After a few hours a harsh voice ordered her to the wooden door, and to take the rag off the hook and cover her eyes. She crawled toward the sound of the voice, patted the wooden planks sealed with mud and tar like the boats that plied the inland waterways carrying coir and sand. Her hand found the rag and she tied it around her eyes, letting the fold cover her nose and mouth. When the voice came again, she answered yes, she was covered. She heard the door open, then close. She didn't have to take off the rag to know what had happened. She pulled the cloth away from her eyes, letting it fall around her neck. With or without it, she sat in blackness.

She could smell the rice and dhal, thin and watery as it turned out. The fragrances told her it was yellow with ginger and turmeric, dotted with green curry leaves, just a hint of coconut milk and cardamom. She placed her hand carefully on the ground and moved it across the dirt, slowly so as not to upset the bowls she knew had to be there. But it wasn't a bowl. It was a plastic bag. The watery dhal and rice were in the bag. She picked it up and held it to her, then felt along the floor for the tin plate. She poured water over her hand to clean it, then poured the rice and dhal into the plate. Watery, yes, but the plate with its raised rim held the poor meal safely within its cold embrace. She listened for the feared creatures but nothing came, no sound of feet stealthily crossing the dirt floor, slithering down the walls, drawn by the aromas that sent little waves of comfort through her.

Since this could be her only meal of the day, she lifted the bowl like an offering to the gods. Here, my holy one, see this meal, how simple, how modest, yet how rich in the great goodness of the earth—the rice, the dhal, the spices, the clean water for cooking. Be pleased to notice each fragrance, then notice each one again with its companions, how they are richer together than alone, like mridangam and violin and ghatam supporting the singer who only wants to praise your virtues to the world. Like Radha to her Krishna.

She held the plate, soothing herself with promises that she would survive with care and tenacity. Into the silence came a buzzing, perhaps from a machine somewhere beyond the walls. But to Nisha it sounded like a bumblebee in a garden. She shut her eyes and listened long after the sound had faded.

Oh, Krishnaaya namah, I am here, your devotee. I hear the bumblebee and I know you will hear of my devotion. She lost herself in prayer until the silence came to her again.

Nisha lowered the plate to her lap. This meal was a treasure, too valuable to waste, too precious to devour without thought. She could barely stand to think it would soon be gone, but it had to be. If she did not eat she would die. She could not say for certain how long she had been captive, but her hunger pangs had dulled. She knew she could lose a sense of orientation in less than a day. She thanked Krishna for his care and turned her thoughts to her meal.

Nisha felt along the edge of the plate to make sure no rice or dhal had spilled to the edges or over the side. She touched the pile of food in the center of the plate, to make sure it was what she believed it to be—did the smells and texture match? She mixed a little pile of rice and dhal, held it in her fingers, then popped it into her mouth. Was the taste correct? Was there any taste that shouldn't be there? She chewed, letting her tongue flick little bits of dhal and rice from her teeth, tasting each morsel as though it were the finest vegetable covered with a sheet of silver, perhaps topped with a tiny dollop of strawberry jam.

She was careful to keep the balls of rice and dhal small so that no grains rose to the second digit of her fingers, where they could dry and fall to the ground. If she had known how many grains were in the meal, she would have counted each one, tracked each one, tasted and savored each one.

Once in a while she felt a brush against her hand, but she knew that feeling—just a spider looking for a likely spot to begin work—so she twisted her hand and the creature fled. An ant bit her but its comrades did not appear. Nisha kept the bowl well away from her pallet—a single grain of rice could bring a line of red ants desperate for food—and when she was done, she held the bowl over the hole in the ground and poured water over the bowl to clean it. Not a speck of food remained to draw bloodthirsty creatures.

All of this excessive care was not merely to ward off the fear, to occupy her time, to feed her starving soul and body. No. Nisha understood that carelessness in her self-care in this hole would kill her.

The darkness of her hours in the hole forced her in on herself and she filled the space fear carved out with images of her loved ones, facts about her captivity and her travel, her recollection of everything Panju had ever told her about Dipak, any sounds that seeped through the thick walls. She racked her brain for ways to escape, or to manage her captors. She would not die here, she promised herself. She would not. She had resources Dipak knew nothing about.

CHAPTER 7

The Bourne Studio occupied the first floor of a new building in the Vanchiyoor area, well away from the old courthouse, along the newly widened road. This had been a neighborhood of small shops similar to those that once defined MG Road, open-front stalls that had climbed the hills from Chalai Bazaar and East Fort up to Secretariat and beyond. With the new money flooding in from Indians working overseas, even outlying areas were turning into smart neighborhoods. Anita felt a little thrill even now at being part of this gallery. She pushed open the door and felt the air-conditioning chill the sweat on her arms.

At the opposite end of the gallery two men leaned close in conversation, a stack of papers between them. One laughed softly. They pulled apart as Anita came through the door. With her mind full of images of Nisha and Panju, Anita was slow to recognize them, Anand and his friend Rahul Singh, the owner of Bourne Studio.

"I'm late, aren't I?" she said, walking over to the men. "I hope you're not upset with me." Anita spoke lightly but she wondered if perhaps the two were upset with her. Anand had always been casual about time, and that was brought home to her when he returned from a trip last spring and waited more than a week to call her. And then came the offer of the gallery.

She was glad she hadn't stopped for a meal even though she was starving. Randall had offered, but she had put him off, too focused on catching up with Anand and Rahul. When she realized how late she was, she gave up any idea of food till night-time. She hoped at least Rahul would offer her a cup of tea with milk and sugar, anything to put in her stomach.

"It is not every day that I offer a solo exhibit to an artist and she is one hour late for a planning session." Rahul crossed the polished concrete floor with his hands outstretched and a relaxed smile. He stopped short of embracing her and instead seemed to hug the air around her. She tipped her head to one side to offer a smile and greeting to Anand as well. Hmm, no tea, she thought.

"We had such bad news this morning," Anita began. She explained what had happened to Panju. Anand's face tightened, and Rahul's smile faded into a polite nod. He took her arm and pulled her over to the desk.

"Terrible, I am certain." Rahul waved a hand in front of his face. "You will think me heartless, but you must put this terrible business from your mind. It cannot contaminate your thinking. We must focus."

"This is all I've been thinking about," Anita said, realizing too late what she was saying. Fortunately, Rahul didn't seem to hear her, but Anand did. She wished she had a moment to explain to him, to counter his barely concealed disapproval.

"This is what I am thinking," Rahul said with a lift of his left eyebrow. "Here, look here." He turned a large drawing of the studio layout to face them. "You are selling very commercial items at your gallery at Kovalam, isn't it? Well, here you will show the work you do for yourself, the ones that are important to you, the ones that tell me who you are as an artist." He turned to her with a challenging, excited look.

"Are you ready?" Anand asked. He perched on the edge of the desk, his hands clasped loosely in front of him.

"Just about," Anita said. "I have one or two more shots that are dependent on getting the moon rise at a certain time, on a clear night. That's tonight, so I have just a few things left to do."

"Good!" Rahul sounded like a businessman who'd just been told the deal was ready to close and all was in order. He was a man who liked things in order, she knew, and she had vowed to be orderly and organized herself throughout the entire project. Easier said than done, Anand had told her.

"Just those one or two shots," Anita repeated.

"Good! Then let's consider the space." He began to walk around the room talking about whether or not he would use panels, the hanging system that would be best, the lighting adjustments he would have to make. Anita followed him, looking where he pointed, up at the ceiling, across to the opposite wall, by the broad glass doors. Every now and then she glanced over at Anand, who remained at the desk, following their perambulations around the room, watching both of them with interest. He smiled. She smiled. Rahul pursed his lips and studied angles and light while his eyebrows rose and fell. For several minutes the only sounds came from the traffic outside.

"Tomorrow." He swung around to face her and spoke with such suddenness and firmness that Anita had no choice but to agree.

"Tomorrow," she repeated. "What exactly do you want tomorrow? A list of the works—"

"No, no!" Rahul cut her off. "Bring the digital cards and the contact sheets. Well, for you"—he glanced at her—"the sample prints. Small ones will do. I want to have a better sense of the images."

"They're not finished," Anita said.

"I know that, I know that!" Rahul waved away her protests. "When they are ready, bring the prints here and my man will mat and frame them. I do not trust anyone else."

"Here," Anita repeated.

Rahul marched back to his desk and flipped open a large

date book, picked up a pen, and began recording his notes. "Tomorrow the proofs. It will help me imagine the arrangement. Agreed?" He didn't bother to look up at her for agreement. "I have a reception tomorrow evening. It is Tuesday evening," he said, turning to her just in case she didn't know what day it was. "Every Tuesday evening is booked for something into December," he said, half to himself. "So you are not to come after four o'clock. Agreed?"

Once again Anita nodded and mumbled yes, but she had the feeling he wasn't even waiting for her to agree.

The moonlight was the merest lightening of the penumbra of a cloud. None of the tourists on the beach seemed to notice or care that they were walking beneath stunning natural beauty. They strolled along the beach, letting the waves wrap around their ankles for a moment before swirling away into the sea. The lights along the tiled promenade shone brighter as the darkness deepened, and the touts called out their wares. A few dogs trotted among the tourists, intent on the middens they knew would have new waste for them and barely stopping to sniff at the fish laid out on iced tables to tempt the passersby. Anita barely saw any of it anymore. The people changed year to year, with a few regulars she had come to know and enjoy, but otherwise the entire resort was a moving, amorphous mass of people that had little meaning for her. She wondered if this was a sign she was becoming jaded.

The moonlight draped itself over the water, picking out the shallow evening waves like so many steps on a ladder. Anita felt a shudder and tingle. She'd been waiting for this shot for weeks, waiting for the right time of night, the right moon, the right weather and near cloudless sky, the right path along the beach to the breaking waves. Her camera was ready. She had an extension on the camera to work the shutter. She clicked the button. Nothing.

A cloud moved across the sky. Anita glanced at it and felt a chill. She had only seconds before the shot would be lost. She'd been dreaming about this one, planning it, thinking about it, fantasizing how perfect it would be, and now it was slipping from her because of some unexpected snag. She checked the shutter extension and quickly removed it. She stood ready, waited for the cloud to clear, waited for another boat to drift across the moonlight, and clicked the shutter. Nothing.

This couldn't be happening, she thought. This was why she'd had the camera cleaned. Yes, she thought she'd seen a spot, a speck of dust, on a photograph a while back and wanted to make sure the camera lens was perfect, clean and perfect. She hadn't noticed any other problem, and over the years she had confidently relied on the technicians at Shiva's Emporium to catch any problems early. Anita pressed the menu and ran through the possibilities, glancing up at the moon every other second. She was about to blame herself for doing something wrong with the shutter when she caught it. There, at the edge of the screen, not where she'd been looking at all, was the answer. The batteries were dead. Dead?

They couldn't be. She'd changed them before she took the camera to Shiva's Emporium. Her camera required lithium batteries, and Shiva's didn't keep them on hand for testing a camera when they were finished working on it. She always handed over the camera with four new lithium batteries in it. But the symbol was clear. The batteries were drained, empty, dead. Anita shut her eyes and groaned. She looked up at the moon. As if to taunt her, it shimmered with a light she rarely saw, the water was like Kanchipuram silk, the old sailboats in perfect position. A shot in a million. Lost. Perhaps forever. She wanted to cry.

Anita packed up her camera and ignored the questions from tourists who had stopped to watch her work. She headed across the beach to Lighthouse Road. She didn't know if she should be furious at herself, Shiva's Emporium, or whoever had sold her the batteries. To work off her frustration and anger, she marched up the hill at a hard pace. The shopkeepers who usually greeted her with a friendly hello or a nod stopped short when they saw the expression on her face. She knew she must look grim but she kept on going till she reached Hotel Delite. She marched up to her private suite and almost threw her camera onto the bed.

"Really," she said, "how could I have missed that? Dead batteries." She pulled open her closet where she stored her camera equipment and materials and pulled out a package of four lithium batteries. They were hard to get here and she was careful with them, at least she thought she was. She sat down on the sofa and grabbed the camera. She opened the compartment, tipped the camera upside down, and four batteries slid out. And so did a slip of paper.

The batteries bounced on the roughly woven bed covering. They clacked against each other and came to rest in a little pile. The slip of paper floated to the end of the bed, its torn edge snagging on the cloth. It was an ordinary piece of litter, the kind that floats from the hand of a well-dressed businessman unwilling to take the time to drop the offending item into a pocket or a waste bin.

For a single brief moment Anita felt a flash of anger. How could anyone be so careless as to let a piece of paper get among batteries being installed? But the absurd thought startled her back to her senses. She was the one who had put in new batteries the day she took the camera to Shiva's Emporium. The batteries had been new—she had opened a new package. She picked up one battery and turned it over in her fingers. It was scratched and dented as well as being alkaline.

This camera could run on both lithium and alkaline, but only lithium was recommended. These batteries were nearly empty; they wouldn't have taken a single shot. They were also dirty, sort of grimy, as though someone with dirty fingers had been handling them. Anita picked up each one in turn, examining it closely. No one who worked with cameras would want to use these, or even think to install them in a good camera. Anita turned her attention to the slip of paper.

The paper was a fragment torn from the corner of a daily newspaper; at least it was the kind of paper used by the dailies. On one side someone had written something in pencil. Anita held the fading letters up to the light and tried to make sense of them. She turned it upside down and right side up. The paper read two numbers, two letters, and four numbers: 11 CH 2001.

Anita stared at the writing. She supposed it could be a house number in a remote part of the city she wasn't familiar with. It could be a date. Or it could be someone's notes that made sense to them but not to anyone else. Was it a code that only one or two people could understand, or was it simply something Anita didn't recognize but many others would? Anita turned the paper over again but nothing else about it seemed important. She folded it up and slipped it into her coin purse.

Someone had intentionally replaced her batteries and hidden this paper among them. There could be only one reason. Whoever had done this wanted her to find the paper sooner rather than later. If they had left her new batteries in the camera, she might not have found the paper for weeks or even longer. Her lithium batteries could last for months, especially if she wasn't working on a photographic project and wasn't photographing every day for a few hours. The question was, who had changed the batteries, and what was the significance of the note? And why her? Was she expected to do something with this?

A light breeze lifted the thin cotton curtain in the window overlooking the parking lot. A child's laughter floated up to her suite. Nisha's daughter was at play. If Nisha was driven to leave her daughter here, abandoning her in the middle of the night out of desperation, could she have gotten into the camera shop? Did she also somehow get into Shiva's Emporium and tamper with Anita's camera? Did Nisha leave the note with Nirmala and ask her to deliver it to Anita surreptitiously?

Anita could hear the sound of Sanj, the night guard, calling to Theti and hustling her back to the compound, shushing her before Auntie Meena heard her. Anita listened to the sounds of their voices. Sanj and the child sounded so innocent, playful in a safe world, sweet and unafraid. Brij apparently had enlisted other staff to help him manage the child.

It was naive to think Nisha could have sneaked into the camera shop without being detected. A more likely culprit was Nirmala. Anita replaced the old batteries with new ones, and closed up her camera. She would have to return to Trivandrum to question Nirmala.

Anita put away her camera. She'd had her heart set on that shot of the moon over the water, and when she saw the way the moon was rising, the light falling, the waves shaping and moving, she thought she'd get something truly special. This was going to be the one shot that mattered in her exhibit. She'd already had fantasies about how people would stop to admire it, comment on both the sharpness of the image and the detail that lifted it almost to a pure abstract of beauty. But she'd lost that. There was little or no chance the same image would appear tomorrow night. She'd have to come up with an excuse for not having the promised shot.

She had thought Rahul would be angry today when he realized she wasn't quite ready. But he seemed agreeable to working with her on a delayed schedule. Later she thought perhaps he was angry and she didn't know him well enough to recognize it. The other surprise had been Anand. He was unusually quiet, and she sensed he disapproved of her coming in late and still not being ready. She could hardly blame him. He had gone out of his way to persuade Rahul that her work was worth taking seriously, and here she was acting like she was the one who didn't take it seriously. She owed them both an apology.

CHAPTER 8

The following morning Anita commandeered the Hotel Delite car, and set off with Joseph at the wheel. She had worked out a schedule for the day that would allow her to gather more information about Nisha and her disappearance, confront Nirmala at Shiva's Emporium about the alkaline batteries in her camera, and get her materials to the Bourne Studio on time. She had stayed up a good part of the night printing out images for Rahul to examine and work with. For once she felt like she had everything under control. She wouldn't let anyone down this time.

Joseph honked the horn, turned a hard left, and drove down the hill, maneuvering the Hotel Delite tourist car through a morass of autorickshaws, motorcycles, and small cars. He veered out of the path of an oncoming bus and swerved around a gaggle of schoolchildren. The car edged into an intersection embracing eight lanes of traffic from four roads, with cars breaking from their lanes and simply heading wherever they wanted to go. Even a traffic officer would have been hard-pressed to tell which car was in the wrong spot and which in a correct one. After a few minutes Joseph emerged on the other side of the tangle and headed up the hill. He slowed as he approached the next intersection and Anita told him to pull over.

The Thempagadi intersection was a poor excuse for a crossroads, with tumble-down wooden shops facing each other across the pavement, but not a single stop sign to suggest that this intersection mattered, that it was worth slowing down here to notice street signs, of which there were none, or watch out for pedestrians, of which there were many. Joseph pulled over to the side of the road and put the car in neutral.

"Not going to Bourne Studio?" Joseph asked. He pulled himself around with his arm on the back of the seat, a worried look on his face.

"Not yet."

"Today is Tuesday, yes?"

"Yes, today is Tuesday."

"Meeting is some time before four o'clock, yes?"

"We have plenty of time," she said, ignoring his obvious worry. "This address, Joseph." She handed him the slip of paper and he looked back at her, instead of reading the paper. "Do you know it?" She had found the address for Nisha's next of kin, in case of emergency, and had decided a visit had to be her first task of the day.

Joseph sighed and squinted at the paper, and then leaned out the car window. He banged on the door to get the attention of customers standing at the tea hut nearby. When two turned out of curiosity, Joseph called out the address. The two men consulted each other, the tea wallah, and another customer. Coming to agreement, they shouted directions and waved toward the north. "Just there," Joseph reported.

Joseph put the car in gear and pulled onto the road. A jolt and a crunch shook Anita out of her seat and she landed in the well. They hadn't even gone a single car length.

Joseph jumped out of the car and pulled open the back door, wailing and calling her name. Every half second he turned around to swear at another car.

"What in the name of Shiva's Nandi!" Anita climbed out of the car, shaken.

"A fool! An imbecile! A menace! The son of a goat! The

husband of a pig! Even a crow won't lick his corpse!" Joseph pulled on Anita's arm to help her but instead knocked her off balance. She fell back onto the seat and had to crawl out of the car. She felt a headache coming on and rubbed her hand over her forehead, looking for mushrooming bumps. The jolt had startled and disoriented her, but after a silent inventory of her limbs, she seemed all right.

"Oh, madam, madam, I am so sorry, so sorry." A slim little man in a white shirt and khaki pants scurried around the bonnet of a large black car and bounced up and down in front of her, pressing his hands together in anjali as he offered a thousand apologies to the good lady and her driver and calling down a thousand curses upon his head for his stupidity. Anita couldn't get a word in edgewise.

"Oh, shut up, Mahmud."

A fragrance she couldn't identify enveloped her. She looked up as a tall man appeared behind her. He waved the short man away as he approached Anita. He nodded politely to Joseph, which Anita knew would reduce her driver to a shriveling mass of gratitude. He turned to Anita.

"This really is too annoying. I hope you will accept my apologies. My driver is an idiot."

The man who spoke was about her age, tall, with dark brown hair and light skin—Kashmiri, perhaps, or maybe Bengali, Anita guessed, though she couldn't be sure. In truth, she couldn't tell one North Indian from another; they all looked alike to her. But no one could miss the sharp planes of his face—his forehead, cheeks, chin—or the broad shoulders and delicate hands whose long thin fingers ran over the crushed steel of her car fender, its creamy luster scraped from its sides.

"Really, an idiot." He stood up and smiled, shaking his head in apparent disbelief at his driver's imbecility.

Anita had to pull her eyes away from him and force herself to look at the damage. Looking at him made her want to say, "Really, it is nothing." And then she'd smile stupidly. But really, it was something—a lot of something. "It is a mess, isn't it?"

Joseph recovered himself enough to agree. "A lot of mess, Missi." He glared at the man.

"You must let me take care of this." The other man raised a hand. "No, I insist. My driver is at fault. I will not allow you to disagree with me." He gave her a boyish smile and pulled a mobile from his pocket, flipped it open, and barked orders to someone Anita immediately felt sorry for. The driver Mahmud offered an apologetic smile before climbing back into the driver's seat.

"Please," she began when he finished his call, "the car will drive. My driver will see to it, and I will forward the bill to you."

"No, no, madam, you must let me manage this."

"Sar, I wish I could, but I must continue on my way." She reached into the car for her cloth bag and rifled through the pockets for a business card. "Here. There is my contact information. Have you a card?"

"You modern women make it so hard for men to be chivalrous." He pulled a card from his shirt pocket and handed it to her.

She read the card, Riyas Patel, Consultant. Several phone numbers were listed. "You will hear from me, Mr. Patel. The car will go at once to the repair shop, and the manager will inform you."

"I can only accept." Riyas Patel bowed with an amused smile and stepped away from the car. Anita climbed into the back seat and gave Joseph directions. With only a few new noises, the hotel car settled into its new form and moved onto the road. "Really," she thought, "a black BMW and enough charm to drown an unsuspecting woman. He must be quite a successful consultant!" All she heard from the front seat was a grumble.

Anita laughed. "You don't like fragrances on men, do you, Joseph?"

Another grumble.

"Neither do I. And I am certainly not used to being on the receiving end of so much charm."

The accident almost derailed Anita's plans for the day. Since Hotel Delite could not send guests out and about in a dented vehicle, getting the car repaired as quickly as possible became the first order of the day. Anita saw her time shrink. She left Joseph in charge of the auto repairs at their regular mechanic, and hailed an autorickshaw.

An hour later she pulled up in front of Nisha's little pink house. Gone was the white plastic chair where the guard had reclined in the shade the day before, and gone too were the pieces of rope cordoning off the house. Anita was relieved at the thought of not having to connive or cajole her way onto the grounds for a better look. But she also had no policeman to ask about the neighbor who had called in the report about something suspicious at the house. She climbed out of the auto and decided to go to the closest four houses, and inquire at each one.

At the first house the only person at home was an old man wrapped in a mundu, snoring contentedly on the front stoop. He blinked at her, seemed insulted at being asked any questions about anyone, and waved her off. At the second house two children sitting at a table studying peered at her from within the front room and ran for their mother. She came to the door in a bright red Mother Hubbard, its long flowing skirt flapping around her ankles. She insisted she barely knew Nisha and her family, resisting any suggestion that she would know such a family that came to such an end. And after a while, Anita believed her. The children standing behind their mother nodded enthusiastically at her every word, with not a single sign they were bewildered by her lies. Anita concluded the mother was telling the truth.

At the third house, Anita found the woman she was looking for.

"She is like a daughter to me." Mrs. Rentu looked distraught. "I have two sons—god has blessed me—but no daughter to listen to my stories, to rub my feet when I am old and tired, to bring me sweet lassi when I am thirsty. Will a son or grandson do this? She was a daughter to me." The woman sighed. "Of course, today," she said, glancing over her shoulder, "I would have to take her mobile away from her to get her attention when I ask for lassi."

Anita stifled a laugh. "Can you tell me what you heard?"

"Two nights there was shouting." The woman cringed, tightening her shoulders. "But we are used to this. There is much arguing in that place. He is not a good husband anymore. Once, yes; then, a change."

"What happened on that very night?"

"There was some noise. Then it was quiet."

"Was it an argument?"

"Not the loud shouting, but voices. When I did not hear more, I am certain it is over and they are not arguing this night." She lifted a hand in dismay. "A knife is quiet. I would not hear this. That is what happened, isn't it? The police told me this." Mrs. Rentu wrapped her arms around her chest as though chilled. "I cannot believe such a thing can happen right here and the world does not stop."

Anita agreed. "Did you ever see them outside together, talking to each other or to others?"

"Yes, I am seeing." The old woman didn't seem to consider the question important.

"How were they together?"

"How? Ah, I see what you mean. Yes, he is looming over her, scowling if she spoke with a neighbor, calling her to the auto or to follow him. He is stubborn when he is wanting something from her. How is it you have known her?"

"She worked for us at my aunt's tourist hotel. Sometimes a guest became ill, and we want to care for the guest adequately."

Mrs. Rentu waggled her head in approval. "Yes, it is your duty."

"But she never spoke of Panju except to say that she was married." Anita thought back to the few times she and Nisha had spoken of family matters. "Could anyone else have come to the house?"

The woman shrugged and pulled a face. "I saw no one."

"What about her child?"

"Ah, the boy? The police asked me about him, but he has disappeared."

"The boy disappeared?" Anita again wondered why Nisha had not spoken about the boy. "And the girl?"

Mrs. Rentu shook her head. "Nisha is saying the girl is on her way to stay with family. She is telling me this on the very day. Her little house is too upsetting for the child, she is telling me." She sighed. "But then . . ."

"What about the other child, the boy?"

Mrs. Rentu shrugged. "He is a peculiar child. Very serious and not playing like the other children. He kept apart, studious I am thinking."

"Do you know where he has gone?"

"To his great aunt perhaps? Mrs. Eappen is her name." Mrs. Rentu paused. "She is father's brother's wife, so she is same as grandmother. They are Tiyyars, you know."

Mrs. Rentu recited an address, which was the same one Anita had found. "She is a strange one too. She came here once and never smiled. There was something strange there."

"In what way?"

The woman grew thoughtful, brushing a wisp of hair from her face. "She greeted the little boy like both were robots. She said, 'We must live out our destiny.' That was all. Very cold I am thinking."

"If I may, Amma, is Mrs. Eappen the only family here? Does Nisha have any other relatives in the area that you know about?" Anita asked.

Mrs. Rentu frowned. "Once Nisha told me she had hoped to live closer to an auntie, but she lived too far away. I think there is the young cousin, but she lives in college and works also."

"I have met the cousin," Anita said. "I am thinking you were fond of Nisha."

Mrs. Rentu nodded, her face folding with sorrow. "You want to help her, isn't it?"

"Yes, I am also fond of her. It is troubling, isn't it? A murder and no one heard anything. A family who told their neighbors so little. An employee I thought highly of who has vanished. Two children left alone."

Mrs. Rentu listened and let silence fall. After a moment, she said, "Nisha entrusted me with her house key." The old woman held it up and then let it rest on her palm, staring at it. "Like a daughter to me. Perhaps you will find something to help her." She held the key out for Anita, who tried not to show her excitement at such good luck.

The little pink house looked even more forlorn this morning, with the weeds in the path turning brittle and dry, and crows pecking at the front stoop. The smell of Dettol hit Anita full in the face when she pushed the door open. The cleaning liquid was overpowering, and she knew it would have been effective in removing any trace of the murder, but she hoped she would at least learn something that would help her. Anita automatically reached out to flick the wall switch for the ceiling fan. When nothing happened she looked up. The fan was dead.

Anita pushed her way in against the smell of bleach and rough soap and looked over the room. According to Mrs. Rentu, the landlord had received permission to reclaim his house and had set about it with a vengeance, sending in a band of cleaners who scoured the floors, walls, and, as Anita glanced upward, even the ceilings. Yes, even the ceilings. They had worked long into the night, with the landlord pacing around the house and stopping to peer in periodically. He was terribly worried about the karma of a violent death in his house, and urged on the workers with threats and pleas and praise. And they had responded admirably. But even cleaners weren't perfect.

Anita walked around under the milk glass light fixture, trying to determine if what she was seeing was a shadow on the glass or something more. After a moment's hesitation, she found a chair, put it under the fan and light, and climbed up. Someone else had already loosened the tiny screws holding the glass shade in place, and restored it haphazardly. Anita unscrewed it again and looked inside. A shadow on the glass shade turned out to be nothing more than a build-up of dust. Disappointed, she started to reinstall the shade but stopped. While she was up here she might as well try to fix the fan. She could at least be cool while she rummaged through the house.

She left the glass shade on the floor and climbed back up onto the chair. She loosened the protective cap over the wiring, intending to see if the fault lay there. But instead of finding a wire slipped from its screw, something small wrapped in a white cloth hit her in the face and fell to the floor. When she was safely down again, she unfolded the cloth and found a small mobile telephone in her palm.

At first she couldn't understand how the police had missed

this. After all, this was a mobile where a mobile didn't belong. But if they were intent only on the glass shade and on conducting a search, she reasoned, they wouldn't have wanted to spare time to fix a fan for a house where they weren't going to spend any more time than they had to. The cleaners probably didn't have time either.

Anita let the mobile—small and purple, like a child's—rest on her palm. She turned it over in her hand, wondering what it was doing up there. It was possible that it had been a gift to a child who had misbehaved and it had been taken away. Or perhaps someone—Panju, an earlier tenant, maybe even Nisha—was having an affair and this was the way the lovers contacted each other. Perhaps someone had stolen it and was planning on selling it but moved out and forgot it. Unlikely, but possible. Even so, that was an odd place to hide it.

Anita slipped the mobile into her purse and turned her attention to the individual rooms. The little settee had been shoved into a corner. Its cushions had obviously been roughly searched and barely put together again, foam escaping from one corner past an unzipped zipper. She pulled the settee from the wall, ran her hands over the wood, held up the cushions, pulled out the foam, then replaced it.

She went through each room, repeating exactly what she guessed the police would have done. She knew it was a waste of effort, but she did it anyway. She told herself she was doing this because Nisha was an employee and therefore the business was partly responsible for her, but in truth, Anita was too convinced of her own good judgment to write off Nisha as someone whose life inexplicably went off the rails. No, Anita could not have been wrong about Nisha. The young woman was a victim. Furthermore, Nisha had left her daughter at Hotel Delite, in effect asking for help.

The bedrooms yielded as much as the sitting room—nothing.

All the saris, cholis, petticoats, and the little girl dresses were washed, pressed, and neatly folded; Panju's slacks, mundus, lungis, and shirts were also clean, pressed, and neatly folded. Nisha was nothing if not tidy.

The back room had received less attention, it appeared, because the pallet was left lying on the floor after the search rather than rolled up, tied with string, and propped in a corner. The child's clothes were neatly piled in the armoire.

Anita ran her hand down the stack of clothing, feeling the cloth beneath her fingers. She picked up the shirt sitting on top and unfolded it, holding it up in front of her. It was ready made, as most children's clothing was now, but it seemed unfamiliar to her—not the kind of shirt she expected a young boy to wear. She turned it around, read the label—unfamiliar to her—and began to fold it up again when the weight of the cloth struck her. It wasn't a child's shirt—it was a man's shirt.

There was something else about the clothing. She held the shirt up to her face and sniffed, breathing in deeply the odor of the fabric. It was clean—she could smell the soap, plain with no fragrance added. She replaced the shirt onto the pile but continued to stare at it. She smelled something else but she couldn't put her finger on it. The aroma was neither strong enough to be overwhelming, nor so strong that she would immediately recognize it. It was a lingering scent, as though someone wearing a certain kind of perfume had walked through the room recently. She leaned closer to the stack of clothing, holding her nose up, trying to capture the smell again, but no luck.

Anita headed into the cooking area. The kitchen room was simple, with the obligatory stone top counter and storage space underneath; a gas canister with a line running to the double gas burner sitting on the counter; tins holding sugar, rice, and other ingredients, a few onions and potatoes in a bowl, and some spices wrapped in newspaper. The kitchen was more than simple—it was bare, as though the family had only just moved in and hadn't finished setting up. The few pots and pans were clean, sitting on the counter, near a short stack of white plastic plates. She paced the room slowly, sniffing, looking for that aroma again. But however it came to be in the house, it hadn't made it all the way to the kitchen.

Anita returned to the sitting room. The house was clean, every trace of the murder gone. In the bare light, the home seemed desolate, the house of a family slipping into poverty. Nisha had never mentioned having serious financial problems, nor had she ever mentioned a second child, a boy who must be a teenager at least.

Anita found Mrs. Rentu waiting for her and the return of the key. The neighbor lady was just as intrigued by the boy's clothing as Anita had been.

"They called him Tajji," Mrs. Rentu explained.

"Odd name."

"Odd name for an odd little boy, I am thinking." Mrs. Rentu glanced over at the house. This small neighborhood, level and sandy, had few compound walls higher than an adult's waist, and many were scalloped so anyone could easily step over them. Only a row of recently planted bushes separated Mrs. Rentu's property from Nisha's.

"How was he odd?" Anita asked.

"He was very serious. Very serious." Mrs. Rentu screwed up her face to make sure Anita understood just how serious he was. "Neighborhood children are playing freely all around here—our low walls make it safe for them to run together and they are safe on this lane. As long as they stay within the confines of this settlement, they can run free. Little Tajji only played once with the other children, and never again. They did not get on, I am thinking. He is not from this area, and he is here only staying with his uncle Panju for a time. Or perhaps Panju is not wanting him to play outside. He is insisting that he be studying all the time."

"What was he studying that was so important?"

The woman shrugged. "History? Tajji is telling me once he knows all the history of his family and it is a great one."

"Did that seem strange to you, for a little boy to be so quick to brag?"

"Everything about him was strange—his name, his avoidance of the other children, his attitude to others, his pride in his family. Once I am asking him, where is his father? What has he done to make you so proud? The look in his face. I am thinking if he had a knife I would be dead." Mrs. Rentu gasped and clapped a hand over her mouth. "Oh!"

Oh, indeed, thought Anita.

CHAPTER 9

The autorickshaw driver found Mrs. Eappen's house on the far side of the Killi River. Her home appeared to be traditional, with six rooms behind a deep veranda under a weather-blackened tile roof, one of the last in this neighborhood. A number of apartment blocks had sprouted up nearby, debris gathering along their compound wall, in stark contrast to the well-swept ground in front of the old woman's high white-washed wall.

Anita looked through the gate and pressed the buzzer. An elderly woman sitting on the veranda lowered her newspaper and peered at the gate. She gathered a few loose strands of gray hair and tucked them behind her ear before pushing herself out of the chair. As she came down the steps she brushed away wrinkles in her white widow's sari, which looked to be newly laundered and well pressed.

In as few words as possible, Anita explained who she was and why she had come. This was met with a long silence until Anita mentioned the child, Theti. Mrs. Eappen narrowed her lips and unlatched the gate.

"Yes, I should have known you would come," the old woman said as she led the way to the veranda. She motioned Anita to a rattan chair and called into the house, ordering a cold drink—lassi—for her guest. Mrs. Eappen sat down opposite Anita.

"Nisha is not here," the old woman said. She sat stiffly in her chair, her hands clasped in her lap, her face rigid and closed.

The announcement came in a quiet emotionless tone.

"I am very sorry for your loss." In fact, Anita was surprised the old woman had invited her in; Anita had expected to conduct the conversation through the gate, to honor the family's death pollution ritual. The drink came, salted buttermilk with fresh ginger and curry leaves, and Anita accepted it and took a sip while trying to decide how to proceed.

"Why are you thinking she is here? Panju is dead and Nisha is missing, I know. But why do you think she would come here?"

Anita put the glass down. Mrs. Eappen wasn't at all what Anita expected. She was prepared to deal with an old woman overwhelmed with grief, but instead Mrs. Eappen seemed rigid with the effort of control. Anita said, "I have come looking for Nisha because this is the address she gave for emergencies."

"Ah, yes." The woman began to fidget, as though uncomfortable with her chair. "I am the family elder."

"Have the police been here?"

"They too are looking for her but I am telling them also, she is not here. Why would she be here?"

Of all the reactions Anita had prepared herself for, suspicion was not one of them. Despite how carefully she explained her business, the old woman asked no questions about Nisha or the house or Theti. Every now and then, as Anita described the scene at Nisha's house, as delicately as she could, or her encounter with the police, the old woman glanced over her shoulder and once Anita thought she noticed the old woman shaking her head no with such subtlety that if Anita had not already been suspicious she would have missed it.

"Is there anyone else she could have gone to—an aunt and uncle, cousins, perhaps? Friends?"

The woman shook her head. She shifted in her chair. "I don't know her friends. And she is working all the time, isn't it? When does she have time for these friends?"

"Quite right," Anita said, trying to fit this piece of the puzzle into place. "Do you know who any of her friends are?"

"No. She would not tell me that."

"When did you last see Nisha, if I may ask?"

"I do not see Nisha often," Mrs. Eappen said, her hands curled into little fists. "Young people are different today."

It was a common enough complaint, but still Anita wasn't sure what to say to this. She had never thought of Nisha as terribly modern, but perhaps because of her career as a home health aide it seemed so to the older generation. "I thought perhaps she might have mentioned something to you, or her husband did. Some difficulty they were having that might shed light on these horrible events." Anita leaned forward encouragingly.

Mrs. Eappen stared at her. "You are not knowing," she said, as though thinking this through for herself. She looked confused and studied her hands in her lap, letting them fall open and wiggling her fingers. "Perhaps I will tell you."

"What is it I am not knowing?" Anita asked.

"The shame is what you don't know, and how it has grown." Mrs. Eappen pressed her hands against her face. "The family owes a debt." The old woman paused, her breathing growing heavy.

"What sort of debt?" Anita knew that Panju's family came from a small village in the foothills, that he was the younger son and had wanted no part of farming. He looked up to his older brother, Girjan, but wanted a different life. Nisha had seemed so proud of him back then when she and Anita first met.

"A family debt, it has been called." Mrs. Eappen began picking at her sari skirt, pulling up little waves of fabric and twisting them into surges of cloth, like wind spouts in a tornado.

"I don't understand, Mrs. Eappen."

"There is a moneylender in the village. Everyone knows him.

Dipak holds the strings, chains, on everyone living there. He is cruel."

"How big is the debt?"

"It is not the size that is troubling."

"What then?"

Mrs. Eappen looked into Anita's eyes. "It is what the debt became."

"I don't understand," Anita said.

"It is like this." She seemed to have trouble getting started, but she smoothed out her skirt and rested her hands on her thighs. "Girjan is meeting a man who is telling him, I will give you loan at very good price and you will pay off Dipak, the moneylender of your village. Then you will owe me but you will owe me less. He is wanting to establish his bona fides, so he is willing to take less than the going rate." Mrs. Eappen's head swung away, as though she couldn't bear to hear what she had said.

"And Girjan accepted the offer?"

"Girjan is happy. He thinks now he can buy more seed, better seed. He can grow better crops and feed his family. He has wife and son. Father and mother are dead. Panju has gone to the city."

"What went wrong? Did the new moneylender not keep his word?"

"Ah, the new moneylender." Mrs. Eappen shook her head and sighed. "Girjan only knows the agent, but this is enough for Dipak."

"I don't understand," Anita said. Moneylenders were a fact of life in villages. When the bank said no, and the villager had no gold to pawn, then he went to the moneylender. Many went to the moneylender first, never even considering the bank. Moneylending outside regulated channels might be illegal but it had been part of the fabric of village life for centuries. It wasn't going to just go away.

"Dipak is enraged. He is like a mad man. He makes demands, terrifying demands."

"What demands? Tell me, please," Anita said when the older woman shut her eyes.

"Dipak refuses the money the new moneylender has given Girjan to pay off his debt. He will not accept. It is tainted, he says. Girjan's debt to Dipak stands. But the debt is not for money now. Instead he demands a repayment of a different sort." The old woman stopped to catch her breath. Her eyebrows worked as though to stop the tears building. "Girjan is to kill the new moneylender. It is his duty, Dipak insists. He is afraid, afraid he will lose his business to a stranger, an outsider offering better terms. He cannot allow it. He demands this act of loyalty from Girjan."

The house had a sheet of stillness over it when the old woman finished her story. Anita looked down at her hands, gripping her dupatta as though she meant to tear it apart.

"Did he do it?" she asked.

The old woman shook her head and tears began to fall. "Girjan was my late husband's brother's child, a good man. He refused to do this deed."

Anita sighed with relief and wiped the sweat from her face.

"Dipak sent his men to persuade Girjan, but still he refused. They left him to die by the paddy fields."

Anita murmured condolences.

"His son, Tajji, found him. The goondas beat Girjan but that wasn't enough." Her voice caught, but she swallowed and continued. "They chopped off his leg. He could barely crawl. They left him to die."

Anita gasped.

"And then the message came from Dipak. He was not satisfied with Girjan's death. This is a family debt. Panju must pay the debt and do what Dipak asked of his brother, or face the same consequences."

Anita gasped. "Panju? But . . ." Anita swallowed hard. "He had some part in the debt?"

"No part," Mrs. Eappen said. "But Dipak is a mad man. He is deranged with anger. He wants revenge against the new moneylender and he will have the villagers know he is still powerful, more strong than anyone else. He cannot be defied, he is telling them, us. All of us."

The ugliness of Mrs. Eappen's story turned the air acrid and heavy. The older woman leaned back in her chair, exhausted from the telling. The ugliness of Girjan's death was etched on her face and made even her glance painful for Anita.

"I understand now why she felt she had to hide her child somewhere," Anita said. "But at least the child is safe." To her surprise, the older woman started. She quickly recovered, but still looked troubled.

"You mean the little girl," Mrs. Eappen said. "I am relieved to know this, to know she is safe."

Before Anita could put it into words she noticed an odor, one she had encountered before. "That smell," Anita said. But now she knew what it was. "That's toddy."

Mrs. Eappen rose and waved her hand as though sending away an annoying dog. Anita turned and looked into the solemn face of a boy. Small-boned and intelligent-looking, he could have been anywhere from twelve to sixteen. He was wearing the navy blue shorts and white shirt of the schoolboy, but he looked uncomfortable in the uniform and in fact too old for it.

"And who is this? Tajji?" Anita jumped up and hurried over to him.

"Please don't press him. He has been distressed."

Before Anita could respond, the old woman stood to block her from entering or seeing the boy. "You are good to come, but

Nisha is not here. I have told the police I don't know where she is and I tell it to you."

"I believe you," Anita said.

"Thank you." Mrs. Eappen sounded as though Anita had relieved her of a huge burden.

"The boy," Anita said. "He was living there, wasn't he? I saw his room." And his clothes and that odor of the coconut harvester we often find with the farmer, she wanted to add. "Was he at home through that night? He must have seen or heard something. What did he say?"

"He does not know what happened. He did not see. He was living there but he did not see." Mrs. Eappan returned to her chair but she seemed weaker now. "This is the grandson of the family, the only male left in the line. He has suffered greatly. He knows nothing about what happened to Panju."

"Perhaps he heard something," Anita said, unwilling to be put off.

"He was asleep. He heard nothing." Mrs. Eappen shook her head.

"What about the neighbor? The one who brought him? Someone must have brought him here." Anita was clutching at straws and she knew it.

"No one brought him. He knew the way." Mrs. Eappen's fear was palpable. Even if the boy slept through the worst of it, he must have known something was going on in that house.

Anita pulled out the purple mobile. She reached past Mrs. Eappen and held the phone out to him. Even in the shadows, the plastic glinted in the dim light. "Do you know this phone?" His eyes widened and he gasped. He started to reach for it, but halted. "You recognize this," she said.

"No. I don't know this," he said, backing away when Anita's hand closed over the phone.

"Whose is it?" Anita asked, but the boy had already withdrawn and shook his head, looking away.

"He doesn't know this," Mrs. Eappen said. "You mustn't distress him." She moved to block the sight of him.

Anita stood at the gate, reluctant to give up on the household. She had learned a lot, but not enough. Resigned, she turned and climbed into the back of the autorickshaw just as her mobile rang.

"Where now?" the driver asked.

"Moment." She pulled out her mobile and checked the number calling. She glanced at her watch and groaned. It was well past three o'clock, and there was no way she could get there in time. In effect, she had just stood up Rahul, the gallery owner, and Anand. And he was about to remind her of that.

"Anand! I am so sorry!"

"You are not on your way, are you?"

"I can't get there in time," she admitted. She leaned back against the seat and listened to Anand's quiet voice reminding her of her promise to bring the proofs to the gallery today. She listened to his melodious voice gently reminding her of their conversation the day before, but she knew underneath was reproach. She was letting him down badly. Rahul was a friend, an important friend in certain circles of Trivandrum, and this exhibit was not a small matter. Yet here Anita was, missing appointments and behind in her preparations.

"I hope you are not involved in this business about the man who was killed," Anand said. "There are times when getting involved is not appropriate."

"You are chiding me, Anand." Anita tried to smile, to sound cheerful and upbeat. She couldn't remember Anand ever being anything but amused by her penchant to investigate murder. And he always offered to help. But something had changed. He seemed different this time, and his attitude made her defensive.

She found herself explaining the unnecessary. "The police came to Hotel Delite looking for the man's wife. Nisha Eappen has worked for us many times."

The blue-painted gate of the Eappen compound rattled as a bus drove by and banged into a pothole. Anita thought she saw a maidservant adding a padlock to the gate on the inside. It made sense for Mrs. Eappen to be in mourning, sorrowful and even miserable. Certainly she had a right to be uneasy after a relative died in such a violent way. Anita wouldn't have been surprised if she'd been hysterical. But she wasn't. She was abstracted, oddly distracted, not quite present, and afraid, as though she were waiting for the next attack, certain it would come. She had broken the rules of mourning by offering Anita something to drink, as though life had turned upside down again.

"Anita?"

"What? I am here. I am here."

"Surely you are listening to me." Anand sounded on the verge of snapping at her.

"I am having confusion."

"I can hear it in your voice, Anita." He paused. "When are you coming to show your selections?"

"Tomorrow. Early. Yes?"

Anand sighed. She could hear him consulting someone else. It had to be Rahul. She hoped he was a patient man. "We were expecting you today, but . . . Tomorrow then. Ten a.m." Anand rang off.

Anita didn't have to look at her watch to know how late it was. She was so engrossed in talking to Mrs. Rentu and then Mrs. Eappen, driving all over the city, from one end to the other and back again, that she'd used up an entire day. But as she sat in the back of the autorickshaw, her greatest worry was

Anand. He didn't sound like himself anymore. He was mad at her, and not in a caring way.

CHAPTER 10

Anita threw her cloth bag onto the settee and opened the doors to the small balcony. She needed to see the ocean, its smooth, steady surface and series of waves, to calm herself. She tipped her head back, closed her eyes, and welcomed the breeze. Her trip to Trivandrum had been disappointing and frustrating. What she learned from Mrs. Eappen had been informative but not useful enough. She felt like she was treading water, near to sinking. And on top of that Anand was annoyed with her, something that almost never happened. But she had to admit—he had good reason. She'd let him down badly, and she didn't have much time to redeem herself. She felt awful.

"But not nearly as bad as Nisha must feel." Anita addressed the crow that had just landed on the parapet, but it didn't seem to care. It squawked and lifted off, perhaps in search of more congenial company.

She had promised Anand and Rahul a full set of proofs, and she was only waiting to complete two more. One was the aborted evening photograph when her batteries had expired and she'd found the odd slip of paper wrapped around one. The second was still on her card. She had printed it out once, not liked what she saw, and decided to retake it. Since the site wasn't far from the hotel, she meant to get to it in the morning. To be certain she got the right location, she wanted to take another look at the proof.

She pulled open the closet door where she kept her photography materials and chose a box on the top of a stack. She rattled it and felt the satisfying heft of three dozen photographs. Some would be larger and some would be smaller for the exhibit, but she and Rahul could go through these and choose the best, or at least the ones Rahul thought would be the most interesting for his clientele. She rifled through the photos till she came to the one she didn't like enough, as she thought of it. It didn't feel right.

Anita turned on her computer and printer. She opened her camera, popped out the card, slid it into the reader, and slid that into the computer. She opened the folder, rested her cursor on the first document, and stared. She didn't recognize this set of numbers. She glanced at the list. She thought she'd taken more than these dozen or so shots. She scrolled down to the lower half of the shots, trying to estimate where the one she wanted would appear. She clicked on those she thought were taken about a week ago, before she'd taken her camera into Shiva's Emporium. The first shot had a date of a month ago. Other shots were more recent, and she didn't recognize the thumbnails that popped up.

She had left the card in the camera thinking she would have a comparison for before and after servicing, in case she had any questions, but she'd let that idea go. She'd been too wrapped up in Nisha's disappearance to focus on testing the camera. She trusted George implicitly. Now she regretted that trust. Somewhere along the line she'd lost the card, or rather, Shiva's Emporium had lost it. She leaned in toward the computer to be certain and began a methodical review.

On the screen in front of her four men stood in the gateway of a private home shadowed by large overhanging trees. Anita peered at the figures. She didn't remember taking this shot. She clicked on the next one. This was another shot of the same group but from a different angle. She enlarged one or two faces, but didn't know these people and she didn't know this place. Anita leaned back in her chair. These weren't her shots.

Worried, she went to the top of the list of images and clicked on the first one, then went down the list, examining each thumbnail. The photos recorded men getting into cars in a courtyard; a black car driving down a street; a tall thin man with his back to the camera and leaning on a cane, talking to two men standing in front of him; a tall stately man looking like an ambassador or important property owner; the gateway of a large private home; the grill of a car coming through a gateway; and a picture of several cars in a new office building in a district of the city Anita didn't recognize. She enlarged the face of the stately man, but she didn't recognize him. Randall had mentioned something like this, but he'd been vague, giving more of his impression than anything she could use to identify someone. She continued through the list of photographs, none of which she recognized.

Anita rested her head in her hands and swore. A crow squawked and she waved at it fiercely and hissed. "Rahul is going to be furious with me. And Anand. Anand will be hurt. He will be hurt." The crow squawked. "I have no food for you. Go away!" She glanced at the clock and reached for her mobile.

"I know it's late, George, but perhaps someone can wait for me," Anita said. She didn't try to hide the desperation in her voice. "I am just coming." She hung up before George could protest.

Anita raced up the hill to get an autorickshaw.

George pulled open the full-length glass door and held it for Anita. His head jutted forward, his dark eyebrows thick with disapproval. Anita went straight to the glass counter and set down her camera.

"My card." Anita popped it from her camera and placed it on

the counter. "This is not my card."

"Who delivered the camera to you?"

"Nirmala did."

George called Nirmala in the back room. She appeared a moment later and George motioned for her to attend to Anita. "The customer says she has found the wrong digital card in her camera. You are straightening this out for her." Nirmala nodded and approached the counter.

She rested her hands on the glass, seemingly unwilling to touch the small object. She avoided Anita's eyes and glanced left and right. Her posture was perfect but as Anita waited, the other woman's shoulders gradually hunched forward. "You are explaining the problem, madam."

"This is not my card," Anita said.

"Madam, assuredly it is yours." Nirmala reached for the camera and slid in the card. "May I?" She held the back of the camera toward Anita and slowly punched through each photo as it came on the screen. "You see, madam, very nice shading here. Of your sort. Color contrast here. Of your sort."

"These are not my photographs, Nirmala."

"Please to look closely, madam."

"I have no idea where these places are or who these people are."

"Madam, you are knowing. You are taking time to see, please."

Anita watched the images pass by, but she was no closer to agreeing with Nirmala than she had been when she first walked in.

"And here you are having family."

"Family?" Anita couldn't keep the disdain out of her voice. She knew George was watching, but she didn't care. She was wild to recover her original card. Nirmala glanced over her shoulder as she held the camera closer to Anita. After a moment he went into the back room, leaving the two women alone.

"Always having family portraits is a sign of lovingness, isn't it?"

"Those aren't family portraits, Nirmala." Anita was growing exasperated.

"If madam is looking just there." Nirmala tapped a corner of the screen. Anita glanced at it.

"That is not . . ."

"Yes, madam, family is there."

Anita grabbed the camera out of Nirmala's hands, and held it almost up to her nose. She peered at the hazy figure, turning the camera this way and that as though she could adjust the light and bring the gray image into the forefront. She stared at Nirmala. "Nirmala, where did this come from?"

"This is madam's card, I am assuring you."

Anita lowered her voice. "George is in the back; he cannot hear me. You can speak freely."

Nirmala gave her a warning look as another customer pushed open the glass door and wandered in. He stood politely to the side, waiting his turn, studying the contents of the glass display case as he did so. He tapped his finger on the glass top as he worked his way along the counter.

"You have come to collect a camera, Sar?"

The man eagerly moved closer to Nirmala and began inquiring about a new movie camera. When he balked at the price, Nirmala suggested he return tomorrow, when they would have new stock. Grumbling, he left.

"Nirmala, last evening I found a slip of paper wrapped around one of my batteries, a nearly dead alkaline battery." Anita leaned across the counter and hissed at her. "You must tell me how you got this card and what it means. And what does the paper and its numbers mean?"

Nirmala opened her mouth to speak, but at that moment the panel door swung open and George returned.

"The problem is not resolved," he said, looking worried.

Anita said carefully, "I am only a little confused." She forced a smile, and George returned to his own work.

"I believe the card is undamaged, madam." Nirmala pushed the camera toward Anita. "These photos will reproduce according to your high standards." She rested her hands at the edge of the counter, but Anita noticed she was pressing down hard, as though keeping herself from shaking.

"And the other one I purchased at the time I left the camera for servicing? It is still here?" Anita said. "I forgot to collect it."

"Please wait. I am looking." Nirmala disappeared into the back room.

When she returned, Nirmala handed Anita an apparently new packet for a digital camera card. Anita pressed her thumb down on the plastic bubble containing the card, noting it was a different size from that advertised on the package. She glanced at Nirmala, who now had beads of sweat along her hairline.

"Madam is satisfied?"

"I think so." Anita shut off the camera and slipped the package into her cloth bag.

"You are most observant photographer, madam, an excellent recorder of details. You have found lovely old mansions to record for posterity." Nirmala paled, swallowed hard, and waggled her head in thanks.

"Going." Anita lifted the camera strap over her head and pulled open the door. On the cement step she reached for her mobile and called Anand. If the information on the card was all that she thought it was, she didn't want to risk a ride with an unknown taxi driver. Anand picked up on the second ring.

Anand had been considerate. He picked her up, drove her the half hour to Kovalam, and promised to smooth things over with Rahul. But he did it all without his usual grace. He was angry, she could tell, and that made her angry. He offered no sympathy for Nisha's apparent plight, or support for Anita's determination to help her.

"She's an employee, Anita." Anand sighed with impatience. "She is not your responsibility. She works for many people, not only you. Let her agency employer attend to this. They can work with the police. You are paranoid about this sort of thing, as if you are the only one who can help."

"Do you mean to be callous?" Anita said. "It isn't like you."

"You have other responsibilities." He stripped the gears as he downshifted. The hill was steep and dark, the power gone unexpectedly for an hour or so. It irritated him; she could see that.

Anita had the feeling it was important to fend off the argument that was brewing just below the surface of their exchanges, but, counter-intuitively, she also thought there was something to say that she wasn't saying because she didn't know what it was. She'd never felt uneasy in his presence before.

"He likes your work," Anand said. "That isn't true for most of our local artists. He is doing this for you."

"I know, and I appreciate it," Anita said. But something about the exchange felt wrong.

The hotel guard slid open the steel gate, the large panel waffling like a sheet drying on a line, and Anand drove in. Anita made her perfunctory thanks and climbed out. She wasn't entirely surprised when Anand backed up and drove away without so much as a backward glance. He was at the top of the hill before she reached her front door.

"And I'm not paranoid," she said as she threw her bag onto the settee.

That comment stung.

Anita made her way in the dark to the balcony. Across the water the lights from the small fishing boats were sprinkled along the horizon, like stars fallen from heaven, not yet extinguished by the sea. A single pair of red and white lights passed the long line of boats, the coast guard checking on the fishermen. They no longer set off dynamite to bring up the fish, but the patrols continued just the same.

Anand's comment hurt because it found the grain of truth and rubbed it against a sore spot. Anita did feel a certain paranoia growing in her as she gathered bits and pieces of Nisha's life and saw them pulling together into a single image. But even worse, Anand didn't offer his usual overview of what these pieces might mean, a differing perspective that might nudge her in the right direction. He'd always been a help to her before, even if he didn't take her completely seriously. But tonight, he'd shown an edge and a lack of interest that left her feeling unsteady.

"Rahul won't wait forever," he'd said.

Tomorrow, she had promised, and she meant it. She was grateful, massively relieved, to get her own card back, and she'd show it. She would print out the last two shots she wanted to show Rahul, explain why she thought these were important enough to wait for, and hope for the best. He was a reasonable man, she was certain, because he dealt every day with unreasonable people—artists, patrons, major and minor buyers, salespeople of all sorts. He'd be open to a reasonable artist offering a reasonable explanation. And that would leave her free to focus on her real problem.

Anita slid into her desk chair and stared at the list of shots pinned to the lower edge of the white board. The night shot she'd been hoping for would be impossible for another month or longer, and she feared the morning shot wasn't going to be interesting enough. She tried to focus on an alternative, but her thoughts kept returning to her encounter with Nirmala.

Nirmala knew exactly what was on that card Anita had found

in her camera. She knew what to show Anita. The last shot on the screen had been one more of strange people except for the hazy figure in the corner. It caught Anita's attention, as Nirmala knew it would. Anita would recognize Auntie Meena anywhere, and she was right there, in the corner talking to a strange man.

The pieces of the puzzle of Nisha's life and Panju's death were coalescing around Auntie Meena, the one person who should have been an innocent bystander. The little girl Brij had found, Theti, with blood all over her dress, the purple mobile hidden in the ceiling fan, and the photograph of Auntie Meena on the unknown card. And that slip of paper tucked in among the batteries? After looking at those shots Anita had a pretty good idea what those numbers represented. Nisha was using Nirmala to deliver important information, counting on Anita to figure out what it all meant.

The lights came on, the fan whirled, and Anita stood up, ready for bed. She closed up the balcony and just as she turned out the lights she saw an envelope on the floor. Someone had slipped something under the door. She opened the door and looked out, but saw no one except the guard, Sanj, asleep in his chair.

Anita opened the envelope and read the note.

"Bartonskutty has called. Hotel auto is repaired and ready to be collected. Please collect. He is needing your approval. Elayamma."

How peculiar, Anita thought. *He usually takes forever, but he's done this in less than a day.* She added a visit to the garage to her list of things to do tomorrow in Trivandrum.

CHAPTER 11

Nisha lost all sense of time in the dirt cave, and occasionally no certain sense of up or down. But the slightest sound of activity started a confusing reorientation. She knew the door was opening by the way the wood scraped along the pebble-pocked ground, even if she didn't see light pouring in. After more hours than she could keep track of, she thought nothing could surprise her, but this did. An unseen hand pushed open the door, and it was as dark outside as in. Terror flashed through her mind like the sight of a rat in the kitchen, lightning in the dry season over an arid field, a road falling off a cliff. Had the sun died too? Had the world so changed that these men no longer had need for her and were leaving her to a worse fate? She felt panic rise like bile and her breath come in short, sharp gasps.

But the familiar voice came, and in another moment she was bound and gagged and shoved into the trunk of a car. Once again she set her mind to memorizing the journey, straining to hear or smell something that would reveal where she was. She listened and longed but heard only buses and cars and autorickshaws honking. She could be anywhere.

At the end of the journey she was once again dragged from the trunk. Hands pulled her over rough ground and then lifted and deposited her on a hard floor. Someone ripped the ropes from her wrists. Her wrists burned and she rubbed one and then the other. She braced herself against the floor. She felt the smooth stone beneath her hands and legs, smelled the fragrance of new leaves woven for a roof and of well water stored in a clay pot. She inhaled fresh air as she shifted to a squatting position. She knew any light would be painful, and when the mask was pulled from her face, she kept her eyes shut. As she let her eyes slowly open, taking in slivers of her new location, she saw the pot sitting in a doorway and a cotton curtain twisting in the light air. She kept looking at it, caught by the vividness, the aliveness of it. She had no idea where she was, but the pot and curtain touched her deeply. She knew this scene from her own childhood.

She heard a scratch on stone, heard a match flare, saw the wooden match fall to the floor. She looked across to the open doorway; a long brown arm reached out and a hand snatched the match from the floor. A command. Go away. Not now. The old woman's form unbundled itself and Nisha saw feet padding away deeper into the house.

"I am told I should have a lighter," Dipak said in his distinctive voice. "Something with a name people will recognize. I am told it will let them see I am important, a person to be reckoned with."

Nisha raised her head and looked about her. She saw smoke drifting around Dipak's chair as her eyes adjusted to the bright light, sunshine refracted by white-washed walls. She heard him inhale again and this time he sent the smoke up to the ceiling, where a fan whirred and chugged, as though choking on the smoke.

She glimpsed sandaled feet of at least two men. The courage she had summoned for the ride in the trunk and the rough handling from car to house began to flag, and she was afraid she'd lose herself to fear. She closed her eyes against the sign of her body beginning to tremble. In the hours in the darkness and again in the boot of the car, she'd focused her thoughts on her cousin Nirmala and the digital card left under her door.

Nirmala needed time. Anita needed time. Nisha needed time. She hoped time would be her friend.

"I do not need something silly like a cigarette lighter to impress people," Dipak said. "People know me. They know I am a fair man, an honest man. I work for the betterment of my people. Isn't that so, Manju?"

"Yes, yes, always." Nisha heard a voice behind her, and a pair of sandals moved at the edge of her vision.

He might have been ready to say something more but Dipak waved a hand, and the man fell silent. "You see. I always work for others."

Dipak sat far back on a deep veranda at the front of a small village house, with a fan churning overhead, a few wooden benches placed along the walls, and a clay pot of water in the doorway. The broad steps to the yard were swept and washed, and the yard recently swept as well, the swirls of the reed broom leaving delicate patterns in the sand. All of this Nisha gleaned with careful twists to one side or the other. In the distance she caught a glimpse of the gate, but it was little more than a formality, standing almost alone, like a sentry, with no wall on either side to confirm its authority. The wooden doors that would swing open to welcome guests were rotted and mismatched now, one hanging precariously on its top hinge. In the compound she caught sight of a freshly built palm-leaf hut.

"People here know me," he repeated. "They respect my devotion to them. Who else can they turn to if problems arise? Who understands their needs, their troubles? Am I not one who listens to their woes, sons who cannot wed, sons who cannot go to a good school, farmers who cannot buy seed or pay their workers? Do I not listen to their very hearts?" He spread his hands wide and tapped the ash from his cigarette, then began tumbling it between his fingers. He stopped to look at these acrobatics, admiring his fingers' skill, then dropped the dying cigarette in a tumbler of water. Nisha gave an involuntary gasp at the wanton waste.

"Ah! You are a sensitive creature. You think I waste not only water but cigarette?" He smiled, but it looked to her more like a grimace. "I like that."

Nisha lowered her eyes and chided herself for showing any emotion whatsoever. She would have to do better, keep her feelings and emotions secret even from herself. She began to recite a small prayer, letting her eyelids flutter closed as she did so.

"Are you listening to me?" He leaned forward.

She looked up.

"Hmm." He leaned back in his chair. "You see, I give attention to others, so I expect it in return. You understand?" He smiled with a twist of his mouth. Nisha swallowed and nodded yes. "Mmm. Good."

The silence was broken by distant sounds, soft murmurings of work being done, people attending to their duties. She noted there were no sounds of children running off to school, and she listened for that because the sun seemed to say it was another morning. How long had she been kept in that cave? How many times had she crawled and felt her way to that hole in the ground to relieve herself? How many meals had she been fed? Had she been hungry each time? Had her body told her, yes, it is time for another meal? Or had one or two meals come too soon, before she was ready to eat again? Was it the confinement that confused her body, or were her captors playing with time? Or was this a cruel game her mind played with her, a perverted way of fighting the darkness to keep it from entering her soul?

Nisha felt her legs begin to ache. How long had she been sitting at his feet, like a pathetic supplicant? Were his servants used to seeing people come crawling to him? Is this what he insisted on? She had heard about the moneylenders in the rural areas—she had heard how they could be. At first they pretended to help, but once trapped in the cycle of debt, no one escaped. The moneylenders grew rich and lived in fine houses, little palaces, while the farmers and laborers died in poverty. The moneylenders' business was illegal, but no one could stop them. They were as old as the mountains, as resilient as palm trees in a monsoon.

She glanced around at the old house, well cared for but small, and she knew he didn't live here. He might own it, use it, but he didn't live in it. He would have a fine compound and a yard with rows and rows of potted plants in bloom all through the year, and a gardener who did nothing but tend the flowers and a vegetable garden in the back. Yes, this moneylender would have a fine house. All of a sudden, she felt an enormous rage that he should live so well and she should struggle, but she swallowed this unexpected feeling and tried not to breathe so heavily.

"You are growing anxious," he said. "Perhaps you know why I have sought you out."

Nisha lowered her eyes and shook her head.

"I was betrayed." There was nothing of the playful pretense of the kindly village benefactor in his voice now. His words were cold and his voice colder. He bolted forward. "Do you know what it feels like to be betrayed?" When he said nothing more, she looked up into his eyes. "Do you?" It wasn't a rhetorical question.

"No." She shook her head.

"No, of course not. How can you know? You are a young woman, some would say beautiful. You are protected, at least so far." He leaned back in his chair and pulled out a cigarette pack from his shirt pocket. He was wearing a mundu and a well-ironed and starched white shirt. It looked new and had the folds that signified it had only recently been removed from its packet. She glanced away and noted that the water glass with the doused cigarette was gone, somehow taken away without her even noticing. It gave her a chill and she shivered involuntarily.

"Ah! You sense your vulnerability now, don't you?"

Be careful, Nisha, be careful, she repeated to herself. He sees everything—he has eyes like the leopard.

"No one has ever betrayed me before. Think of it. I am not a young man, though I am still vital. Am I not, Manju?"

"Yes, yes—"

The man stopped his minion before he could elaborate. The moneylender wanted nothing from his goondas but agreement; they could keep the flattery. "Who would have ever thought someone would try to betray me, after all I have done? Did he not think I would be injured and hurt? Did he think I would take betrayal as a little mistake? No matter, just go to the temple and make a little puja, some flowers, no worry. Did he think that?" He frowned and shook his head, as though pondering the question. "What sort of man betrays his greatest benefactor and walks away? Eh? I ask you?"

Her breathing grew heavy; she felt the sweat on her upper lip, and fear pricked at her insides.

He shook his head with a look of sadness. "Girjan was my friend. So I thought. A man I could trust. I knew him and his brother, Panju, as boys. I knew the whole family. Did you know that? I knew them better than you did. You only met them when your marriage was arranged." He shook his head, heaved a great sigh, and stared out across the yard to the jungle beyond. It wasn't thick here, and he could look down into paddy fields and see a small stream winding its way to the channels dug for irrigation. She wondered if the house belonged to a debtor who hadn't been able to pay and gave up the house as forgiveness for the loan.

He had a way of twisting words that threatened to pull her

off a cliff of lies and distortions. She wanted to scream out the truth of what sort of man he really was—a murderer. But she knew that would cost her and bring her nothing. He was who he was. He was Dipak, the moneylender, and everyone in this district knew and feared him.

"It was such a little thing I asked of him, so little." He threaded the cigarette through his fingers and tapped it on the chair arm, admiring his own dexterity again. He leaned to one side, and Nisha glimpsed a coconut knife hanging on the wall. It made her sick to her stomach.

He put the cigarette in his mouth, pulled out his match box, and struck a match. He lit the cigarette, began to shake the match, then stopped. He leaned over and held the match close to her face. Nisha began to pull away but the man behind her put his hand on her head, his fingers splayed over her skull like a medieval torture device. "Why do you pull away, Nisha? Have I hurt you? I would not hurt you. You have not betrayed me. Have you?" Her eyes grew large as the match moved closer. Slowly she shook her head no. "No, you haven't." He watched the match burn closer to his fingers. "I don't want my fingers burnt. Blow it out, Nisha."

She could barely get enough air into her lungs but she managed, just one second before the flame singed his fingernail. She hung her head in relief, trying to recover and calm herself.

"Thank you, Nisha. That was kind of you." He leaned back in his chair, tossing the match to the ground. A scrawny brown hand reached out and snatched it from the floor.

CHAPTER 12

Early the following morning, Wednesday, after flute music had awakened the deities from their sleep but before the muezzin's call to prayer drifted up the coast, Anita made her way to the back of the hotel, where some of the employees lived during most of the month. On the headland two foreigners sat cross-legged in meditation, and on the beach a group of five foreigners practiced yoga facing the rising sun. Along the lanes men and women walked to their jobs at hotels or restaurants. A single truck could be heard turning into a driveway.

Brij sat on the grass with a plate in front of him. Beside him sat Theti, also eating her breakfast. The little girl glanced up at the sound of approaching footsteps. Her smile disappeared and she jerked her head toward Brij. "Look!" Theti poked Brij in the leg. Anita crossed the path and felt a pang for having taken the smile from the little girl.

Brij at once welcomed Anita, and waved her to a seat. The child looked to Brij for a sign and after he smiled broadly at her and Anita, the child visibly relaxed. He began telling Anita about his plans for the day.

"Look, Theti," Anita said. "I've brought a *theti* for your hair." She held out a brilliant orange flower she had plucked on her way down the stairs. The girl's eyes widened and she reached for it. Brij helped her tie it into her braid. After a few minutes of enjoying the ornamentation, she offered a shy thank you. Brij explained how the child had spent her time the day before, taking care of the goat and helping him gather in the laundry.

Anita judged the time right, or at least as right as it would be. She pulled out the purple mobile and placed it on the ground in front of her. Theti's mouth fell open, her color turned ashen, and she cringed, pulling away from both Brij and Anita.

"Amma?" Brij looked scared.

"She recognizes this mobile," Anita said. Indeed, she feared she had frightened the child beyond speech. Anita picked up the mobile and slipped it back into her cloth bag, hoping that would calm the girl. Theti relaxed, but she kept her eyes on the bag.

Anita leaned forward. "Does this mobile belong to someone in your family? Your amma or acchan?"

Even this question seemed to distress the child. Her food was forgotten and she quietly changed her position so she could jump up quickly and flee. Anita leaned back in an effort to re-assure her.

"I found this in your house," Anita said. Theti scowled at Anita's bag, as though she could see through the double layer of red cotton and its colorful embroidery. Anita slipped the bag from her lap and opened the mouth, as though she were going to reach in and pull something out. Theti stiffened.

"Do you know this thing?" Brij asked with naked curiosity. He put his hand on the child's back and spoke with a comfort-ing tone. She looked up at him and gave a nearly imperceptible nod.

"Whose is it?" he asked.

"Acchan had it."

Anita silently repeated the answer. She could read it several ways. Panju brought it into the house as his new phone, as a gift, as a borrowed article, or as something he found. He could have stolen it, traded his own for it, or picked it up from someone else by mistake.

"Where did he get it? Did he buy it?"

Theti shook her head. "No, not buying."

"Was this the one he used every day?"

Theti shook her head.

"This was not for your acchan. Was it for your amma?" Anita rested her hand on her bag and felt the phone inside. "It is a pretty color. Was it for you?"

Theti's eyes widened and she shook her head. She gaped at Anita. Clearly the phone was not for the child. Theti stared at Anita's bag. The fear the mobile had first incited in the child was giving way to a deeper impulse to reveal something. Anita sensed she was on the verge of learning something if she could just keep the child calm and trusting. She held as still as possible. Brij rested his hand on Theti's back.

"Tell me, Theti," he said. "There is no problem here. I am here."

Theti peered at the bag, her head bobbing forward. She looked up at Anita. "Amma saw the mobile. She was angry. Very angry. Crying."

"I'm sorry your amma was angry. Thank you for telling me." Anita paused. "Do you know where I found it?" She expected the child to shake her head no. Instead, Theti looked slyly at Brij before turning to Anita and nodding. "Where?"

"Amma took the mobile and hid it in the fan."

"You saw her do this?"

Theti nodded.

"Did she say why?"

"It is bad," Theti said. "Amma is crying but pretending she is not crying."

"You saw her?"

"In the night she is getting up when we are sleeping. I saw her take the mobile. I could see her through the doorway. She opened the fan and put it in there. It is being there. Hidden."

"Did she see you watching?"

Again the child nodded. "I am to promise to never speak of this to Acchan."

"Did you keep your promise?"

The little girl's chin trembled, but she nodded yes. "Acchan is very angry with Amma. This is great power, he is saying. She must give it back. Shouting and crying."

"Your acchan is shouting and crying?"

"Yes."

"This has great power?" Anita repeated the child's words.

The child nodded again, her expression set.

Anita decided to change the subject slightly. "Did you ever see your father with a camera?"

"Yes," Theti said with some reluctance.

"A big one? This size?" Anita held up her camera. Theti nodded. "How did your amma feel about that?"

"She told him to give it back and he said he would." Theti lowered her head as though ashamed of admitting this.

"How long did he keep it?"

"Not long." She shrugged. "Maybe a day. And then it's gone." She sighed.

"Only the one time?" Anita asked, remembering her conversation with Dhanu and Randall.

Theti pursed her lips. "Twice, three times," she said, correcting herself.

"How did your amma feel about that?"

"It is a bad thing, she said. It cannot be good, she said." Theti sighed like an overburdened householder.

"What do you think she meant by that?"

The child shrugged. "They are arguing all the time and Amma is saying this is the wrong way. The wrong way."

Anita heard herself repeating the child's last words.

"Now she is gone." Theti sounded almost philosophical, like

an adult steeling herself to carry out a difficult task.

"It is only for a while, Theti. I'm certain of it." Anita hoped this would not turn out to be false comfort. "Did she say when she would come back?"

Theti shook her head. "If she does not come back, I am to ask to go to Auntie's house."

"Who is Auntie?" Anita asked, hoping this would lead to more relatives and more resources for locating Nisha.

"Mrs. Eappen. She lives that side." Theti waved her hand, as if to take in all of Kovalam and half of southern Kerala.

Anita headed back to the hotel dining room. She still had an hour or so before guests began clamoring for breakfast and asking about day trips around the area. She had time enough to sort through some of what she had learned. The mobile was clearly the key to some of this trouble, and she wanted to examine it more closely. She took a table by the window, where she could hear Brij and Theti finishing their breakfast and chatting about the goat. Their conversation sounded so normal, so homey and comforting, so at odds with the terrifying reality it concealed.

"Why are you here?" Auntie Meena stopped in the doorway, glanced at the empty tables, and stared at Anita.

"Resting, Auntie."

"Oooh." Auntie Meena waggled her head, as if resting in an empty dining room before the start of the day made perfect sense, and trotted off. She always had an air of worry about her, but it seemed to Anita to be intensifying, almost to the point of blinding her. Instead of pouncing on Anita for sitting and lounging when there was so much to be done, her aunt had accepted it and hurried off.

"Perhaps I am imagining it," Anita thought. "Perhaps it is just the usual worry about business. Perhaps I am attributing to her all the worry I feel about Nisha and Theti." Anita turned her attentions to the mobile.

"Peculiar," Anita said, flipping open the device.

"What?" Auntie Meena appeared in the doorway again. "What is peculiar? Brij's child?"

Anita stiffened and slid the mobile into her lap. She had warned Brij to keep the child out of sight, counting on the other employees to help him keep her secret, but she should have known that was naive. "You think the child is peculiar?"

Meena frowned. Her look said that Anita was being deliberately obtuse. "Not the child, Anita. Why is he bringing her here? Where is the child's mother? Has she run off?"

Anita opened her mouth to say something but nothing came out. She was struck by how close her aunt had come to the truth. But even worse, she had no idea what Brij had told Auntie Meena, if anything, and that meant Anita was in danger of compounding the problem if she came out with the wrong lie. Instead, she shrugged.

"Is there no one dutiful anymore?" Meena shook her head and dragged herself back down the hall.

Not feeling very optimistic about the future herself, Anita flipped open the purple mobile and began to run through its features and content. All she found was a list of phone numbers, but no names, only first initials. This seemed a risky way to keep track of people, especially since all the numbers were local ones. She scrolled to the first one, highlighted it, and pushed to call. The phone rang.

"Yes, yes, ready." The voice spoke rapidly. Anita heard a click, and the call was ended.

"Well, that was interesting if useless." Anita scrolled to the second number and called.

"Tomorrow, yes? Tomorrow." The caller again ended the call peremptorily without waiting to hear a reply or a question.

"Hmm." Anita paused to consider. She called the next three numbers and got almost identical responses, quick, abrupt, and agreeing. Each person called seemed to know who was on the line, who was making the call. No one said, "Hello? Hello? Who is this? Who is calling?" Anita continued down the list. At the next call she managed to break into the terse reply.

"Wait, wait," she said. "Who is this?"

The voice on the other end fell silent. She heard breathing and then a click. The recipient had disconnected. Whoever it was, he or she had not expected anyone to speak. Anita tried the next number, and when she again broke into the call, the speaker on the other end fell silent. She could feel the tension coming through the phone. And then a click and the sound of a call dropped.

"One more time," she said to the sugar bowl sitting in the middle of the table. She hit the next number and waited. Farther away in the hotel she could hear a mobile ringing. She held the purple mobile closer to her ear, so as not to miss a syllable.

"Not this week. You are calling last week already. You are mistaking." The phone disconnected. Anita didn't have to break into the speaker's reply to ask who it was. She'd know that voice anywhere. Auntie Meena was Auntie Meena, regardless of where Anita heard her voice. Anita leaned forward to look through the doorway into the office beyond. There, she could see Auntie Meena replacing a purple mobile phone in her purse, clucking and shaking her head as she did so.

Anita stood in the doorway and bent over to arrange her sandals. The cloth bag fell against her side; she could feel the purple mobile knock against her hip. That little device had to be the key to what had happened to both Panju and Nisha. And if her aunt was on the other end of that phone, Anita was in a different kind of trouble. She would not be able to run ideas past her aunt, ask for help, or even let her know what was going on. Since Meena had a purple mobile of her own and was listed on Panju's mobile, she was part of the circumstances that had led to Panju's death. Anita wondered if her aunt knew the danger she was in, and if she did, why had she said nothing about it to Anita? She had never had to consider her aunt a suspect before, but that's what she was now—one more person involved in a death who chose to withhold information rather than tell Anita or the police.

"Why are you looking at me in that way, Anita?" Auntie Meena pushed her purse farther under the desk with her bare toe. "I am very busy. You are having question, please to be asking." Meena slid into Malayalam, her English breaking up into odd phrases interspersed with the noncommittal verbs of her native tongue. She wandered between English and Malayalam, with neither one making much sense. Anita knew what that meant. Her aunt was on the verge of hysteria. She was too brittle for even a gentle probing. Anita would have to take a different tack.

"You seem less worried about Padma today," Anita said.

"Why do you say that?" Meena looked ready to lunge at her.

"Because you have not mentioned her today," Anita said, surprised at her aunt's reaction to even these mild comments. "Your worries must have settled down."

"Oh, yes, of course." Meena turned again to her desk. "We have not spoken today, isn't it?"

"Perhaps when I return, we can chat and you will tell me what Padma is doing these days, other than traveling to Washington." Anita pulled her dupatta from her shoulder and draped it over her head. "I am going into Trivandrum again."

"Again?" Auntie Meena looked on the verge of speaking but her thoughts seemed to drift away and she blinked absently at her niece. "I have no need. No errands are requiring your assistance. Go." She waved her hand in dismissal and returned to her stacks of paper, preparing bills for guests checking out the following day.

"Have you forgotten the note you left me about the Hotel Delite car? Bartonskutty sent word last night that all was ready," Anita said.

"Oh, I did?" Auntie Meena looked up. "Yes, yes, of course, I am leaving this note. And you are standing here?" She turned a stern expression on Anita. "You are going to collect the auto at once, yes? We have much need, much need for this."

Yes, thought Anita, *we are definitely going to have a chat, just as soon as I discover more about this purple mobile business.* She nodded to the guests passing through the hall on their way to the dining room. As she climbed into the taxi, with Joseph in the front seat with the driver, it occurred to her that Auntie Meena hadn't once objected to her taking the car or told her to stay away from the investigation into Panju's death or Nisha's disappearance. Whatever Auntie Meena had on her mind, it had to be huge.

CHAPTER 13

Anita directed the taxi driver to Bartonskutty's garage. Joseph sat in the front also, hunched over and scowling at every turning. He'd had no say in where the auto was repaired and acted like someone had put him out of his home. To every one of Anita's directions he added, "Just here, just here," as though Anita didn't know what she was saying and the driver couldn't be trusted to follow directions.

The taxi turned down Piper Lane. Before the driver could reach the garage, however, two motorcycles, one car, and a small van pulled onto the lane and began the artful ballet of too many vehicles in too little space. The jostling and nudging and swerving and stalling reached critical mass until all of a sudden all the vehicles were on their way and Anita's taxi pulled up in front of the garage. She climbed out feeling sticky and irritated, and it was only eight o'clock in the morning.

Anita scanned the rows of vehicles and spotted the Hotel Delite car. Joseph headed straight for it, as though it were a long-lost relative. She walked around it, ran her hand over the repaired fender, marveling how quickly the work had been done and how solid it seemed. She was impressed, but apparently she was the only one. Joseph scowled at the car, still angry that someone had dared to run into him.

"Ah, you have arrived." Bartonskutty came up behind her and stopped to admire his handiwork also. Even though he owned the garage and at one time had been its only mechanic, he rarely worked on cars now. He kept the books, cultivated the best customers, and ranged around the yard checking on his employees' work.

"Very nice job, Bartonskutty."

He waggled his head. "Very little work. Soon done."

"Very soon done," Anita said.

"Our head man is diving right at it!" Bartonskutty smiled like a proud parent.

"Have you contacted the other driver yet?" Anita stopped when she saw his expression change. "Oh dear." This didn't look good. "There is a problem?"

"Hmm, no, not a problem." He squinted as he tried to find the right answer for her.

"If not a problem for you, then a problem for me. You have not been paid or he has refused to pay. Yes?" Anita avoided looking at Joseph, knowing he would be gloating over her naiveté in trusting a stranger. Really, she should have known the man's offer was too good to be true. No one got rich by being generous, at least not in her experience, and he was obviously very well off. She shouldn't have been so easily seduced. She should have taken his particulars and plate number and gotten all the details for a claim, even the names of witnesses.

"No, he has not refused."

"Then tell me. What is it?"

"He insists on paying when you tell him you are satisfied."

"Oh!" Anita smiled. "Well, that's very nice of him, isn't it?"

The garage man continued to scowl.

"It is very nice, Bartonskutty." She leaned toward him in emphasis.

"I am not to release the car to you until he is here and hears you say you are satisfied. I am to call him to tell him you are here."

"Oh." Anita leaned back against the car and crossed her arms.

She frowned and pushed away the image of a scowling Rahul and sternly disapproving Anand. "Just how long will this take? I have things I must get to very soon."

"Yes, yes, I am understanding." Bartonskutty looked miserable.

"Then tell him it is all correct and I am going."

"I cannot, Missi. He is promising to pay only under certain conditions." The garage owner looked away, then closed his eyes for a moment. "He is holding me hostage and he is holding you hostage and he is holding the car hostage." Bartonskutty's voice softened as he looked at the vehicle, as though it were another human equally unhappy at the loss of its freedom.

"Well, then, I guess you'd better call him." Anita settled back to wait. It was one thing to have another driver not balk at paying for the damage he caused, but it was another thing entirely for him to hold the Hotel Delite car hostage.

Anita didn't hear the car arrive, and she didn't see it drive in. She didn't know anyone else had entered the office until she smelled his cologne. Bartonskutty had taken her to wait in the small room, offering her tea and biscuits. If it were not for the other man's peculiar and particular request, Bartonskutty would have given her the keys and happily sent her on her way, knowing in the end he would be paid. But this man was very particular, so Anita and the garage man waited, their conversation desultory and of next to no interest to either of them. Joseph wandered the yard, inspecting everyone else's work.

Anita held a cup of tepid tea in her lap. As she was about to take another sip she recalled the moment immediately after the accident when she had looked at the dent in the car and felt a ripping frustration. The fragrance of a man's cologne, sea air and winter breezes and something woody, enveloped her. As the fragrance grew stronger, she recognized it. She stood up and there he was.

"Ah, Mr. Patel." Anita nodded in greeting. He extended his hand and she shook it a little awkwardly. She didn't really like shaking hands—it seemed an unnecessary, sometimes even unpleasant formality.

"Have I made your life so very difficult?"

"Not at all, not at all. My garage man has done his usual excellent work and we are eager to have the hotel car back." She avoided looking at Joseph, who hovered in the doorway. She knew he wanted her to speak more forcefully and lodge a complaint about Mr. Patel's insistence on her waiting for him, but she wanted to get moving without an argument or unnecessary discussion. "I'm sure you know that in business mobility and flexibility are key."

"Indeed, madam, indeed. Very true." He smiled, and then seemed to realize something more was expected of him. "May I see your auto and know that you are satisfied?"

They walked across the yard to a line of cars. Joseph followed them, looking put out. He bounced from one foot to the other, barely able to contain himself, as he watched the two examine the car. Riyas Patel peered at the damaged fender and examined it by running his fingers gently over the repair, murmuring appreciatively at the workmanship. Bartonskutty stood nearby looking sullen and impatient.

"As long as you are pleased," Riyas said.

"Yes, yes, I am well pleased." *Really,* she thought, *why should this be such a big deal?* But she looked around to nod at Bartonskutty, as if to say, "See, isn't he a nice gentleman to work for?" But Bartonskutty looked like a smile had never split his face, and today would not be the first time.

"Then, it is done." Riyas waved at an assistant, who gave a nod to Bartonskutty, and with some reluctance the garage man followed the other man's assistant into the office.

Really, thought Anita. *Life is so easy for some people.* And then she noticed his car.

"What about your car? It wasn't damaged at all? I distinctly heard the crash. Your car must have been damaged also."

"My car?" Riyas smiled. "A minor scrape here and there. Nothing to worry about."

"But not repaired already." She nodded to the small white car. "This is a different car."

"There is only a minor delay. Of no concern."

"So, perhaps your other car sustained more damage than you have admitted." Anita paused. "I would be remiss if I were not concerned also. Even if this car is nicer in some ways."

"You like this little one?" Riyas said.

"It is compact, is it not?"

"I do believe that is how it is called." He pulled a stiff smile, but Anita's attention was still on the car, specifically on the registration plate. She strolled closer to it, pretending to admire it.

"I was thinking of getting a car of my own soon," she said. "May I?" She asked but didn't wait for a reply, and instead walked around the car examining it closely. She tapped the trunk as she took a turn around the back and came to the other side. "Very nice."

Of course, she thought. She tried not to stare at the registration plate, but she was careful to memorize it. KL 11 CH 2004. No wonder the number on the slip of paper made no sense; part of it was missing, the KL, for the state of Kerala. She should have recognized it at once. She should have known it was important, a link to whoever was involved in Panju's death and Nisha's disappearance.

"So, you have two cars," she said when she noticed Riyas watching her.

"Only one. I borrowed this white one."

"Ah, good friends are invaluable, are they not?"

Anita listened to Riyas's replies while casting around in her mind for a way to extract more information from him. He deflected every question, and insisted on reassuring himself that she was truly satisfied with the car repair. After that he managed to segue into questions about her parents in the States, the people she knew there, and the business world in Trivandrum. She feared the situation might grow awkward until she spotted a man lope through the yard carrying a metal basket holding glasses of milky coffee. The normally busy yard fell into the quiet of late-morning coffee time. Mechanics took their glasses and chatted; some handed around a newspaper.

"Ayoo!" Anita straightened up and twisted her watch around on her wrist. "The morning is passing and we are standing and doing nothing." She expected to see Joseph napping in the back seat of the hotel car but instead he was sitting bolt upright at the steering wheel watching her.

"Nonsense." Riyas smiled, but Anita could see the effort he made at exuding charm.

"We have guests at the hotel who will be clamoring for transportation," Anita said.

"Are they so rude?" Riyas asked.

Anita was just about to open her mouth to comment when she thought better of it. "They do have a right to expect a car if they've booked it."

"Agreed." Riyas nodded like a European gentleman, reminding her of a movie she had seen once but whose title she couldn't remember. She found it unsettling to have been maneuvered into such a casual intimacy with him over the matter of a dented fender. She thanked him again as she backed away, opened the car door, and climbed into the back. Ensconced in the front seat, Joseph looked like a man once

123

again in charge and he revved the engine, tipped his chin up, and drove out of the yard with the dignity of a chauffeur to millionaires, instead of an old man struggling to keep a rattling secondhand heap on the road.

CHAPTER 14

Anita dropped her cloth bag on the table in the office and exhaled loudly. She was somewhere between feeling deeply ashamed for having missed her meeting that morning with Rahul and relieved that she had managed to call only a few minutes late to explain her absence. Well, confirm her absence. There really was no excuse that would do for Rahul or Anand. But when she saw that license plate, Anita knew she had to get back to Hotel Delite at once.

Anita called Anand and explained that something had come up, and in her voice she heard a tone she had never used with him before. She heard the warning that she was no longer accommodating, giving him the benefit of the doubt when he pressed her. She would be ready for the exhibit but on her terms, not his. With both Nisha and Meena involved in Panju's death, and with apparent strangers circling her and turning out to be part of the mystery, she would not drop the investigation. Anand would have to understand. She would meet her obligations to him, but on her terms.

"Is it done?" Auntie Meena looked up as Anita began rummaging in her cloth bag.

"Done, and quickly too." Anita still found the alacrity with which Bartonskutty fixed the car surprising.

"Then Joseph can return to ferrying guests," Auntie Meena said, "and I to my work." She leaned over the ledger, but it was obvious to anyone watching that she wasn't looking at the pages

125

lying open before her, the neat blue letters and numbers drib-bling down the lined paper. She was staring at her hand, which was doing a poor job of concealing a small scrap of paper with notes scribbled across it. She looked tense and forlorn. Overhead the fan spun with its incessant hum, and just beyond the parlor windows waves crashed. The high-pitched whine of the refrigerator in the hallway added another layer to the incessant pounding of noise against anyone working in the office.

"Oh! You are still here!" Meena slid the scrap of paper into her choli and pulled the folds of her sari over her blouse.

"I am still here." Anita pulled out a chair and sat down, keeping a relaxed smile on her face. She wondered if she should have confronted Meena earlier this morning when she'd punched in a number and heard her aunt's voice answer the call. But she hadn't. And now, no matter how she went about it, she had to be gentle. She knew that. She called out to a passing waiter and asked tea to be brought.

"At this hour?" Meena said. "It is so late. Meals are coming soon."

Anita shrugged. "At this hour, Elayamma. I feel the need of some comfort."

"The car is not correct? The damage repair is not satisfactory?"

"The car is all correct and damage repair is paid for." Anita leaned back in her chair. "We are always rushing here and there. Sometimes I want to be still." She paused. "And count my blessings."

"And you have many, Anita. Many." Meena folded her arms on the table. "I wish others felt as you do."

"Anyone in particular?" Anita tilted her head to one side, inviting her aunt to share confidences, but instead Meena's face sagged. She looked like she was ready to cry and instead studied the pages of the ledger. Years ago Hotel Delite had instituted credit card payments and international banking arrangements, and yet every transaction, no matter how small or how it was made, was recorded by hand in one of the old-fashioned ledgers that continued to fill shelves in nearly every business or government, and even personal, office in the country. It seemed incredibly redundant and wasteful to some, but it meant that every transaction could be traced, and Meena could see at a glance where the money was going to or coming from. She compared computer printouts with her ledger every week, and was more likely to find an error in the computer information than in the handwritten accounts.

Meena shook her head as she murmured no.

"What more have you heard from Padma?" Anita asked. Meena blanched but she quickly sat up straight and shook her head. "Has she told you anything more about her adventures in Washington and the senator?"

"No, nothing." Meena pushed her chair away from the table. "I am weary, Anita. I must retire. Forgive me for not sitting with you while you have your tea." She glanced at the tray with the small pot and two small cups as Moonu placed it in front of Anita.

Anita nodded. "I heard that Panju was taking up photography before he died."

Meena glanced at her and shrugged, seemingly uninterested.

So, Meena was listed on the purple mobile Nisha took from Panju, but didn't know about Panju's photographs, Anita concluded. She reached into her purse and pulled out the slip of paper she had found wrapped around the camera batteries. She laid it on the ledger.

"I found this on the floor," Anita said. "Is it yours?"

Meena reached for the slip of paper, squinted at it, and began to shake her head no. But at the last minute, she reared back and took a quick in-breath. "Why are you having this?"

"I found it. What is it?"

"It is nothing. Throw it away."

"It is obviously not nothing if it upsets you," Anita said.

"I am not upset. Throw it away." She started to take it from her niece's fingers but Anita withdrew her hand and slipped the paper back into her purse.

"Meena Elayamma," Anita said softly, using the traditional form of address, one that could be relied on to soften Meena's heart.

"I must rest. I am weary."

Anita grabbed her aunt's wrist before she could escape. Meena lifted her face and managed to look determined, but Anita held on. She said nothing, kept her expression neutral, and waited.

"I can't, Anita. I can't." Meena slid back in her chair, and this time she did cry. She rested her head in her hands and let the tears run down her cheeks and fall to the table. The little drops soaked into the wood, like little gray flowers opening up. She reached for her pallu and pulled it to her face, wiping away the tears.

"It cannot be so bad, Elayamma."

"You do not know how bad things can be." Meena reached for a box of tissue and began blowing her nose and muttering to herself. Anita waited for her to launch into her standard lament about the fickleness of husbands who die just when they are needed, the thankless daughters who run off to America, the foreigners who quibble over a few paisa and then pay thousands for a fake Ganesh statue, the climbers who will not come to harvest the coconuts in a timely manner, the drivers who leave the tourists stranded at a strange hotel while they return to their home village for a wedding, the ones who tip not at all and the ones who tip too much. Anita waited, but Meena offered none of this; she remained silent, staring miserably at the tabletop.

Anita grew worried. "Just how bad can things be, Elayamma?"

Meena had little lines fanning out around her eyes, and ripples flowed away from the corners of her mouth. This day, Meena was old.

"I think you'd better tell me, Auntie."

"Yes. Perhaps I should." Meena licked her lips and pressed them together. "When you hear what I have to say, do not bother chastising me, Anita. It is too late for that."

"I love my daughter," Meena said.

Anita's heart sank. This was not a good beginning, an apology for a mother's love. "You'd better tell me everything, Elayamma."

"I took out a private loan," Meena said, avoiding Anita's eye.

"You went to a moneylender," Anita translated.

Meena nodded.

"Even though they are illegal and we have excellent credit." Anita closed her eyes for a moment. "Go on," she said.

"Padma has contracted a few small debts and asked for help. She sounded so helpless, so . . . She is my daughter, is she not?"

"Sometimes I wonder," Anita muttered to herself.

"Ayoo! Anita!"

Anita patted her aunt's hand. "I only mean she is not like you, careful and frugal, Elayamma."

Meena tried to smile but instead her face pulled into a grimace. "I sent her money."

"How much?"

"A lot."

Anita shook her head. "Well, it's not the worst thing that could happen." She looked up to see Meena watching her. "You have done this before, yes?"

Meena started to say something and then changed her mind,

closing her mouth and turning to the open door. No guest came to rescue her from her uncomfortable talk with her niece.

"There's something more, isn't there?" Anita waited. "Elayamma, you must tell me. I cannot help if I do not understand."

"Yes, yes. Why do you have to be like this?"

"Like what? Persistent?"

"Like your father."

Anita had to laugh. "Just tell me what else I need to know."

"I am getting very good terms." Meena straightened her back as if to emphasize there would be no arguing about this.

"But?" Anita said, knowing the signs.

Meena sighed. "You will be angry."

"Perhaps, but probably not with you. Tell me."

"I dislike anger," Meena said, trying to look philosophical.

"If I am angry it will not be with you. It will be with Padma for burdening you."

"You are such a good daughter to your mother and to me."

"You're stalling. Tell me."

Meena watched her fingers pleat themselves in her lap. "I pledged Hotel Delite."

Anita gasped. Her mouth fell open. She had been wrong. It was the worst that could happen.

Once Auntie Meena had managed to get the truth out, Anita was the one who was plunged into despair. Her aunt wrote down the amount owed. Anita stared at the row of numbers that represented the rupees borrowed, and watched the thin blue lines swim and reshape themselves, but every time she blinked and looked again, the numbers were unchanged. They did not swim or fly away, or reform themselves into a lesser amount. Something inside them, like steel reinforcing rods in a building surrounded by adobe walls, would not let them change.

On top of this was the interest. She couldn't have said how long she stared at the figures.

"This is your home, Elayamma," Anita said, trying to come to grips with the loan and its consequences. "This is Hotel De-lite! This is where we live. Our family owned this land for centuries. It was ours always, before the foreigners, before the British, before the maharajahs. It was where our people came for sea bath, to offer thanks for good health or pray for one who was ill. War was never fought on this land. Through war and poverty and upheaval and storms we held onto this piece of land. We lost power and we lost wealth and we lost plantations, but this piece we kept." Meena nodded as Anita spoke. "This is everything you have. It is everything I have."

"This is what I have done for my thankless daughter," Meena said.

"You have already sent her the money, isn't it?"

Meena nodded.

"Ayoo!" Anita took a deep breath. "All right, then, Auntie, you must help. We will do this together."

"Do what?" Meena said. Anita couldn't miss the tone of contempt. "It is paid, Anita. Taken and given."

"Who is the moneylender? How did you find this one for such a large sum?"

"It is such a large sum, isn't it?" Meena began. "No one would give. The bank would not give and the small moneylenders around here would not give. I could not go to other family and I could not go to family village lender." Meena leaned forward in her chair and held her arm against her waist, as though she had a stomachache. "I saw Panju in the city talking to a man and I idly asked him who he was. He said he was a moneylender."

"Who was he?"

"He is new to the area." Meena took a deep breath. "I approached the other man and asked him if this is what he does and he is saying yes. So I am taking loan that very day."

"Did you get a paper?"

She nodded.

"And I can see this?"

Meena studied Anita for a moment and then went to the desk. She unlocked a small drawer and struggled to get it open. Meena pulled out a folded piece of paper and handed it to Anita, who read it.

"But, Auntie, this is such a small amount. Not what you showed me. It is large, but not devastating."

"See the second page."

Anita turned to the second page.

"Oh!" The second page listed the full amount. "Why?"

Meena shrugged. "I think he is having black money and this is one way to use it without attracting attention from authorities. If I fail to repay, he buys Hotel Delite for a small amount, it seems. No one would pledge a hotel for such a small amount, isn't it?"

Anita returned the forms. "I don't recognize the signature. What name is that? It looks like Varadajana."

"What does it matter," Meena said. "It is enforceable. The man who gave me the money is the agent for a big lender."

"Moneylending is illegal, Auntie."

Meena gave her niece a look of contempt. "So it is made to look like a purchase."

"And this?" Anita pulled out the slip of paper she had shown her aunt earlier. "You recognized this. Where did you see it?"

Meena glanced at the paper and read out 11 CH 2001. "It is the license plate number of the man I met. KL 11 CH 2001. I saw him drive away in the car with that plate."

Anita pulled out the purple mobile phone. Meena blanched but said nothing until Anita ran down the list of numbers and punched in one. Meena winced when she heard another mobile ringing.

"It was you this morning, wasn't it?" Meena asked. "The man only calls the day before, not the week before. I wondered if something had gone wrong."

Anita nodded as she gazed at the phone.

"Where did you get it?" Meena's expression changed from curiosity to shock. She gasped. "Not you too?"

Anita laughed. "No, Auntie, not me too. I have no debts. Can't you guess where I found this?" Meena shook her head. "I found it hidden in Nisha's house."

"Hidden?"

"Nisha took it from Panju." Anita shut off the mobile and slipped it into her purse. "I do wonder, though, why did the moneylender give you one?"

"To remind me I can never escape," Meena said.

"He didn't say that," Anita said.

"He didn't have to." Meena wiped the pallu over her drying tears.

CHAPTER 15

The purple mobile sat on the table between Anita and Auntie Meena while they listened to the hotel guests laughing and chatting as they came up the stairs. They had lingered on the terrace long after breakfast, drinking coffee and gossiping, and watching the sun rise high in the sky. The guests wandered through the reception area and out into the lane.

"How did you get that?" Meena asked when quiet returned. She hadn't taken her eyes off the phone while the guests were in earshot.

"I told you I found it," Anita said. "It was hidden."

"You could not have found it. Lender would not have let it be lost."

"But he did."

"You cannot keep that, Anita. These are not foolish men. These are dangerous men. They will not care that you are beautiful or young or half-Amrikan. You must give it back."

Anita's eyes widened. "Give it back?" she repeated. The idea had not occurred to her but immediately it captured her imagination. She repeated her aunt's words. "Oh, Auntie, what an idea!" She leaned forward. "That may be a good idea, Auntie, a very good idea. Give it back." She let the idea twirl in her brain. "When did you get your purple phone, Auntie?"

"After I signed the document, I began to understand what I had done. These are not ordinary moneylenders. They are much bigger. Lender is giving me this phone and telling me he is calling regularly to make sure my payments are on time. Not only interest but also principal."

"Hmm. Also principal. A little different, isn't it?"

"I argue, but he says he is only agent. This is the way."

"So someone new to the scene, or someone with another purpose." Anita considered this.

"A heavier burden. He gives me this little phone. I am to use it for nothing else but to speak to him. It is programmed. He will call. I may call. Nothing else."

"So everyone who takes a loan from this man gets a purple mobile," Anita said. She picked up the phone and felt its lightness in her palm.

"I don't know anyone else who has one," Meena said. "I am thinking he doesn't trust me. I am a foolish old woman to him."

"Everyone is foolish to him," Anita said. She turned on the telephone and pulled up the list of phone numbers. Auntie Meena gasped. She leaned forward and then pulled back, both fascinated and repelled by what she saw.

"It has many numbers, Anita."

"This is the lender's mobile, Auntie." Anita shut off the phone. "The man puts much power in this device."

"Power?" Meena screwed up her face in disbelief.

"The idea of programming each individual mobile is interesting, yes?" Anita said. "Direct connection, yes?"

A look of distaste spread over Meena's face as she watched the mobile in her niece's hand. "It is like carrying a snake in your pocket," Meena said. "It will kill any threat, but you must always be afraid it will awake and bite before you want it to." She pulled her arms tight against her chest as though in pain. She shut her eyes and turned away. "Put it away, Anita. Please."

"I have something else to show you, Auntie," Anita said. She had left the unknown card in the camera for lack of a better hiding place. She didn't know yet what she should do with it, so she kept it where no one could get at it without tackling her first. "Take a look at these."

Meena opened her eyes. She looked more tired than Anita had ever seen her, even after the death of a relative or friend, when she mourned deeply and sincerely.

"I have not been adequately enthusiastic for your new program, isn't it?" Meena said. She had all the signs of someone slipping into rote behavior, doing what she was supposed to while her soul wandered elsewhere. "Perhaps you are forgiving me and I am finding this opportunity to be cheerful another time."

"I appreciate the sentiment, but this isn't about my gallery exhibit, Auntie. These are not my photos I am showing here." Anita held up the camera and began to click through the shots. Meena leaned over to watch, but it was clear she wasn't paying much attention. Anita kept the commentary to a minimum until the last one.

"Hmm. I am not knowing these."

"I said the same to Nirmala, Nisha's cousin who is working at Shiva's Emporium. You remember her, yes? I am telling her this is not my card, these are not my shots, and I am returning this. She insists. She says the proof is here in the shot I have taken of my family." Anita tipped the camera so Meena could see more clearly. "And she is correct. There. Do you see?" Anita pointed to a figure in the corner. It took a moment but Meena did see. She groaned and Anita rested the camera in her lap.

"Oh, Anita! My life is all tumbling about my toes. I am crushed beneath this evil of greed. I am a fool and an old woman and I shall die begging on the streets."

Anita smiled. "Now you sound just like your old self, Auntie." Anita leaned over and gave her a kiss on the cheek. "We shall defeat this problem. You will help."

Meena rolled her eyes. "I am the problem."

"True, but first we deal with this one." Anita tapped the camera screen. "Where is this place? Why are you there? And these other mansions? Where are they? And who took these photos?"

"I am only going to each place once. I go to one place to meet a man, to another place to sign a paper, and to the third place to collect the money. That one." She tapped the camera screen.

"How did you find them?"

"Lender is giving me the name of an autorickshaw stand. I am to go there and take a certain auto. The driver is knowing the way. I am going."

Anita listened to this recitation, marveling at her aunt's desperation that led her to place such trust in strangers.

"Oh, Anita, I am terrified. I do not ride in autorickshaws. I do not know these drivers and here I am careening about the streets going to places I do not know with strange men. I do this only to save my daughter. I am arriving at this one," she said, with a nod to the camera screen, "and the driver is nodding to the gateway. Stand there, he says. I stand under the tree. I know this is the correct place because I am seeing lender's automobile. It is this very plate you are having."

Anita placed the camera on the table. "I can hardly imagine you going to an unknown place and then standing under a tree with all those strange men, but there it is on the card." Anita shook her head. *We are all foolish over something,* she thought. "Then what?"

"Lender comes out of the gate and passes the men. Some nod, some do not. He comes to me and hands me another document and I sign. You have seen these two documents. He hands me a packet. I take it. He goes away. I stand there, unable to move. What am I to do? Should I go? Should I stay? The auto driver decides. I hear his engine. I get in and I leave. And I am lost from my life."

Anita went over this story.

"Is it true in America people say they give their souls to the devil for money?"

"They do say this," Anita said. "You have read it yourself in literature classes."

Meena nodded. "This is true. But I am never understanding the feeling before this. I have created very bad karma this time."

"We shall balance it with good karma, Auntie. Now you must tell me all you remember about the drive to those houses. All those trees, Auntie. These cannot be new places in a new development."

"No, very old mansions. And this last one, with a fine gate. Did you not notice in the photos? Such a lot of money the owner is having."

"And most of it is probably not even his," Anita said.

"Did you see Panju there?" Anita asked after Meena had offered the worst possible description of her drive to the last house. She couldn't remember where she got the auto, who the driver was, how long the trip took, where the driver went, on which side of the city the address was. She might as well have been blindfolded during the entire trip. She probably kept her eyes shut.

"No, Anita. I am seeing no one I am knowing." Meena relaxed in her chair, almost sprawling, as though the worst were over, as if she had been knocked flat and now she could only sprawl. She had spoken honestly to Anita, told her all, it seemed, and had gained from this a sense of true relief, as though Anita had somehow magically shouldered the burden. Meena waited for questions, looking less worried, more resigned.

"What about someone with a camera?" Anita prodded her

aunt to remember something, anything, that would help.

"A camera? I would not allow anyone to take my photo in such a situation, would I?" She sat up, then paused, glancing at the camera. "But someone did, isn't it? I did not know anyone was there."

"No, of course not." Anita slid forward in her chair. "What sort of men were there?"

"Patient. They are waiting as men do."

"Did they know the lender?"

Meena shook her head no, and then changed her mind, so her head wobbled up and down and side to side. Anita felt seasick. "They are nodding to him. He is not speaking to them, but I think all are knowing one another." She pursed her lips. "Hmm, perhaps not knowing the person and his name and his family. But knowing that this one stands here as do I. This one is known to the ones who decide who can stand here. That kind of knowing."

"That kind of knowing," Anita repeated.

"It is poor, is it not?"

Anita smiled. "We must find this lender. First, you must lock up the documents, Auntie."

Meena began to smile for the first time in days. Anita noticed the change, which only increased her own anxiety. The debt was large, the mode of contact through an anonymous mobile awkward at best, and the lender completely unknown. The possibility of losing Hotel Delite was real. And they wouldn't discover who the new owner was—if it came to that—until it was too late.

CHAPTER 16

Nisha could not guess what was going to happen moment to moment. When she was dragged away from the veranda, she began to panic, but the terror subsided when she realized that Dipak meant to confine her in the hut she had glimpsed nearby. She was still a captive, but at least she wouldn't be buried alive. Not just yet, anyway.

From the dim interior of the hut Nisha inhaled the smells of the new leaves. The light filtering through the leaves dappled the ground. She lay on her side and folded her arms beneath her head. She could hear the sounds of workers passing by and their cheerful voices—sometimes raised in debate, sometimes dropping to a soft, almost whispery sound, then rising again farther down the lane. She guessed their easy conversation came only when they were away from the house. They knew this place, its occupants, and perhaps even that she lay tied and trussed inside. The flowering plants and shrubs might shield most of the hut from view, but not its roof, not its existence; the villagers knew it was here, and probably knew what it was for. Nisha wondered who else had been confined here, too afraid to shove the walls away and simply stand up and flee. Except that she couldn't stand and flee—her ankles were bound with coir rope, as were her wrists, though not behind her back.

The meals came regularly, every few hours, which again made her wonder. They were being so much less violent to her—aside from confining her—that she was growing increasingly confused.

She had expected to be beaten at the least, and she kept waiting for the intimidation to begin. When the man she later learned was called Manju had grabbed her pallu on that first night, yanking her back and knocking her to her knees, she had prayed desperately for an escape. But she knew the only escape was by her wits. She had to keep the men at bay, persuade them she knew nothing and could do nothing—which was almost the truth. As she thought back to that moment, before Dipak emerged in front of her, she'd calculated how she might escape. But when she saw him, her mind went blank. She understood how he had terrorized this region for so long, why she could lie tied and terrified almost in full view of the villagers and no one dared lift a finger to help. As this reality grew sharper, her calculations took a different turn.

I cannot be afraid, she told herself again and again and again. I can let them think I am, but I must think behind that veil. If they think I am afraid, they will work to use that fear and I can slip farther and farther away, seemingly too terrified to do what they want, too frightened to even understand what they are asking. I cannot let them know I understand.

Nisha closed her eyes and at once the image of her daughter filled the golden light. Her daughter, Theti, was her treasure, her only reason for living. As Nisha grew into adulthood, she had watched her birth family die and her own life move away from them. She stood by helpless as her dear husband turned into a stranger. Only her cherished daughter remained. But now her child was in mortal danger, and Nisha would rather give up her own life than see anything happen to her. Stalling Dipak had become her reason for breathing.

The light did not blind her, but the swiftness with which the man opened the door startled her. He motioned for her to stand. She scrambled to her knees, then rose to her feet. She began to teeter, dizzy from lying still so long in the cramped space, but the man did not reach out to steady her. She fell against the bamboo post and slid onto her knees, watching the ground rise and spin below her face. She closed her eyes and waited for her brain to settle in its basket. She wondered if the meals had something added to them.

"Come on, come on!" The man stepped away from the door. He was an old guard—his posture still that of a soldier, his chest caved in, his beard grizzled and patchy. He had grown up wearing shoes—she could tell from the way his toes ranged side by side, not splayed the way villagers' feet developed. He had been born into a family of substance. "Come on, come on! He's waiting."

She didn't have to ask who *he* was. She took mincing steps, jumped a little, and awkwardly followed the old guard, but when she began moving to the front veranda, he waved her in a different direction. She followed him to the back of the house.

"My poor woman," Dipak said as soon as Nisha rounded the corner. He waved from his seat on the veranda for the old man to remove the rope around her ankles. As soon as the guard had done so, he pushed her to the ground. She fell onto her knees and felt the bile rising to her throat. She pressed her lips shut and stared hard at the ground. She half-crawled, half-walked to the edge of the veranda.

"Do you like this chair?" Dipak ran his hands over the smooth teak chair arms with the fold-out extensions almost two feet in length. She had seen plenty of these chairs over the years, though she had never owned one and never expected to. "A leftover from the Raj." He rubbed the wood, admiring it. "Superior workmanship. You agree?"

Nisha nodded and managed to mumble yes.

"Of course, no Indian would be so crass as to use something like this. We designed low platforms, so the maharaja could see his subjects better." He shifted in the chair, still running his eyes and fingers over the furniture. "No Indian would raise his bare feet to rest on these boards. We learn early never to sit with our feet facing our teacher or our parent or any elder. Uncouth. Yes, uncouth. You agree?"

Again Nisha nodded and mumbled a reply.

"Yes, I thought you would. You are a good girl." With that, he paused to look directly at her. She could see him tip his head as if to get a better look at one side of her, then tip it back the other way. He settled into the seat, resting his head against the back, just looking her over. "It's surprising really, when you think about it." He looked around him. "It was so easy for so many to look down on us, on me, on my family. Do you know where we come from?"

"You are from this place. This is your native place," Nisha said.

"Ah, yes, this is our native place. But what would others say is our real place?"

Nisha shook her head. She'd never heard anything about Dipak except that he had risen from obscurity to become a successful and feared moneylender.

"Night soil." He leaned forward and spat out the words. His look seemed to dare her to respond. "Untouchables. Gandhi's Harijans." His gaze wandered as his mind drifted over the names and all they conjured. "I swore when I learned what was expected of me that I would never again—no matter what—touch anything that had ever touched night soil. I would die first." He looked directly at her. "You can understand that?"

She nodded. Her mouth was dry.

Dipak lifted his hand to his pocket and pulled out a pack of cigarettes. He slipped out one and ran it under his nose. "I wonder if I should notice the smell is different with each brand, but I don't. I fear my olfactory sense is compromised—by age, perhaps. Or perhaps by my family history." He let the cigarette trip among his fingers, rolling it one way and then the other, like a magician rolling a dime along his knuckles. "I had to fight my way to where I am today. Hard work every step." He held the cigarette between thumb and forefinger, straight up, like a candle in a dark room. "You understand hard work, to feed your family, care for them. Hmm?"

"Yes," she mumbled.

"Of course you do." He turned his head to the left, closed his eyes, and lifted his chin. Immediately, skinny feet on skinny legs beneath a worn mundu appeared behind his chair. When Nisha looked up she saw a long thin brown arm dab the sweat from his brow and upper lip. She glanced down at the ground and saw a dark brown spot, her sweat. Another drop fell, sank into the dirt, and barely changed the color; but another fell, then another. It was hot. This was one of the hottest times on record, and most people had gotten used to it—what else was there to do?—but seeing her own body melt reminded her. She wished she hadn't noticed. She was afraid she'd feel woozy and grow faint. The thought caught her. Could she feign illness to hold off his terror? Would it be enough of a distraction? Or would he simply dispose of her? Would her death be enough to protect her child? Her heart leapt at this solution. Her own death—it would be so easy—and so certain. The little girl would disappear into another life with Anita Ray and her family, safe and sound and gone. But Nisha's heart ached at the thought.

Nisha's mind raced over every image of defiance, distraction, confusion, anything that could deter Dipak and his goondas. He would be moving on to the next phase soon, she knew. She had to decide.

"It is hard for someone to work their way up and then have it all fail in the end. Can you imagine how I might feel?" He looked from the cigarette to her and back to the cigarette now balancing on his knuckles. He tipped his hand so the cigarette rolled down and then back, then flipped his hand and caught the cigarette in his palm. "I have worked hard and always I have helped my fellows. Hmm?" He glanced at Nisha, to see if she was still paying attention. "And then to have this happen." He sighed. "You understand?"

Nisha nodded, the rest of her body stiff with anticipation.

"It was terrible," he said. "I was betrayed." He looked at her. She nodded. Why couldn't she control her breathing?

"To be betrayed is a terrible thing. Terrible." He placed the cigarette on the teak chair arm, uncrossed his legs, and leaned forward. "I was betrayed by someone I helped. Think how that must feel."

Yes, she thought. It is coming. A decision. I have to make a decision.

"I extend myself to help others and when one of them betrays me—well, no one ever has. No one. Isn't that right, Manju?"

"That is right," Manju said, stepping forward. "Never, no one—" Whatever he was going to say next was lost when Dipak waved his hand and the other man stepped back into the shadows.

"How can I forget I was betrayed? Hmm?" He shook his head, as though finding the whole thing inexplicable. "I never thought Girjan would do something like this to me. Never." He shook his head again in apparent disbelief. He peered down at her. "Oh, I know what people are saying. I can imagine the gossip inside the houses in the village, when only the cooking fires light up the back rooms, when people are falling asleep and they are careless in their talk. I know. But I did not kill him. No, I did not take such revenge." He stared at her. She knew what was expected of her.

Nisha nodded dumbly, trying to get her limbs to ease, to relax. She needed to think. She had to be prepared.

"I give him so much to save his farm—the family estate he

has pledged and borrowed against and misused for so many years. And his father before him. Do I lecture him? Do I tell him, Girjan, this is ancestral land? You should be careful with it? Do I demean him in this way? No, of course not. I understand his needs. I want to help him. I do help him. And he promises to repay me. I am of the same stock, am I not? I am of this village." He waited.

"Yes, yes, Sar." Nisha could barely whisper, her mind running from one idea to the next.

"And what does he do? Does he come to me at the time his loan is due and say, Sar, I don't have it? Does he tell me this? No, he waits and waits and waits. He gives me a little. What am I going to do with a little bit of money when I have given him so much? I have given him my trust, my friendship. Money is nothing. We are like brothers, and yet he lies to me. He says he has no money." He hung his head, then snapped forward. "And then he betrays me." He shook his head from side to side. "This cannot be. I cannot allow it."

"No, Sar." She could only hope he'd draw out his story so long that he would eventually grow tired of talking to her. That would give her time, more time. She needed more time to think.

"He promised to pay me. I gave him a way. And what did he do? He failed me. He took my trust and he failed me. He betrayed my faith in him." He pressed his lips together as though in danger of saying something vile. "I had to punish him. But I did not kill him. No, not I."

Nisha stared at the ground, too anguished to even try to speak.

"It is humbling, is it not? I only punished him. It was others who killed him. The villagers and even his family left him to die. I took his leg, a clean cut at the thigh. But the others took his life. The villagers left him to die, to bleed to death, by his paddy field. No one came to help him, no one came to save him, no one came to call others for help. No, they left him to die."

Nisha pressed her eyes shut. She had to control herself. She had to. That was all she had left.

"It is terrible to know in the end that no one cares for you. Girjan died alone—abandoned by his family and the villagers who were his friends. I did not kill him. All those others who pretended to care for him killed him. A terrible thing. He must have suffered greatly." Dipak seemed to take satisfaction from this, and leaned back in his chair.

The sweat trickled down her ice-cold back. How could it be cold when she could feel the sheen of sweat like a coating of cake icing all over her, thick and slippery? New patches of wet appeared on the ground, her sari folds clung to her legs, her blouse to her back.

"Your husband, Panju, understood." Dipak leaned forward again, pushing his face close to hers, speaking into her ear. "He was going to restore the family honor. He was going to fulfill his brother's obligations. He understood that a debt is a debt until it is repaid. There can be no honor until it is repaid. He knew he had benefited from my generosity—he knew all this. He was a man of honor." He leaned back, then lifted his foot and nudged his toe under her chin, lifting her face.

She did her best to nod. He dropped his foot. She thought about Girjan, only a few years older than her husband, lying with his leg chopped off at the side of his paddy field, a man who longed only to hold onto the family land despite their deepening poverty. She thought about her beloved husband who had changed before her eyes in ways she couldn't comprehend—becoming secretive, aggressive, angry, and finally violent. She blamed Tajji, Girjan's son, for poisoning Panju's mind. She knew there was more to it than that, but here her heart failed her.

"I looked to Panju to make this right. And now, Nisha, little Nisha, you have cheated me of what was rightfully mine. You tell me you killed Panju. How will I be repaid now?" He sprawled in his chair, another mood flickering across his face.

She opened her mouth to speak, but her throat was dry, her tongue stiff. She pushed air out and tried to speak, tried again. "Money," she whispered. "I can get the money."

"Money?" Dipak began to laugh, first a little chortle, then a loud raucous cawing. "Money!" He turned toward the men standing behind her, to the workers in the garden, looked up into the trees as though even the birds were his minions. The laughter rippled around her. Then, just as suddenly, it faded. "No, no, little Nisha. Girjan promised me much more than that. And Panju also. Both promised me and failed and now both are gone. Tajji is a child, and I can't wait for him to grow up."

"I . . ."

"Let me explain it to you," Dipak said, shifting in his chair. He picked up the cigarette and held it between his first two fingers, took a match and lit it. He smoked his cigarette, inhaling deeply.

"Panju," Dipak said, savoring the name. "Panju promised me two things. He would give me something—it was valuable to me—and he would do something for me. For these two things I would forgive the debt." The moneylender sighed and looked around. "I have lost my chance at both, it seems. All I have now is you." He took a long pull on his cigarette and glanced at the still-burning match. He stretched out his hand and held the wooden match in front of Nisha's face. She could smell the sulphur, hear the flame lapping at the wooden stick, see the golden fire thinning as it grew taller and taller, reaching to the dark dirty curls hanging over her forehead. Her mouth was dry, her lungs frozen. She swallowed, closed her eyes, opened them.

"Nisha? This match . . ."

Nisha nodded. She made her decision. She prayed. She shaped her lips. A wattle of spit hit the match. The fire hissed and sizzled and died. She never saw the fist that hit her.

CHAPTER 17

Anita worked long into the night printing photos, trying out possible arrangements for her meeting later that morning with Rahul, and praying the gallery owner wasn't so disenchanted with her and her delays that he'd drop the whole idea of a solo exhibit. She managed to sleep for a few hours, and rose early. Her plan was to escape Hotel Delite before any other disaster could befall her and delay her trip to Rahul's gallery. She'd be pathetically early, but she'd wait in a nearby coffee shop until Rahul arrived. It was early Thursday morning, a quiet time in the city.

Anita made it all the way to the bottom of the steps, her prints neatly packed in a sturdy box. To her surprise, the gate was already unlocked. Before she could go out, Auntie Meena appeared in the hotel doorway.

"You had better come, Anita." Meena turned away, assuming Anita would follow. And with a summons like that, she had no choice. She slipped her bag over her shoulder and followed Meena into the office.

Mrs. Eappen sat at the round table. The silver streaks in her black hair curled and frizzed and flew free around her face, as though she'd not brushed her hair after sleeping. Her sari was wrinkled and stained; she looked like she had left the house in her work clothes, right after preparing and serving a meal. The old woman ignored the cup of coffee placed in front of her, and pressed both hands flat on the desk, leaning over as though trying to catch her breath.

Surprised and worried at finding the old woman here, and at this hour, Anita pulled a chair up beside her and gently greeted her. Mrs. Eappen seemed not to notice. With effort, she composed herself, her glance wandering around the room.

"You must help me," Mrs. Eappen said. She was no longer the ice-cold matriarch who would have nothing to do with Anita. She was an old woman, distraught and frightened.

"I will do whatever I can." Anita waited. "Just tell me what has happened."

"Promise me you will help me. You will find them."

"Them? I will do whatever I can, but you must tell me what has happened."

Mrs. Eappen grabbed Anita's arm and hissed at her. "Promise me. The boy is all I have. He and the girl . . ." Anita cringed at the woman's naked desperation.

"Yes, I promise." There was nothing else to say.

The old woman closed her eyes and let her breathing slow. She opened her eyes and looked around her, as though seeing the office for the first time, taking stock of where she had landed and who was there with her. "Yes, you will help me."

"What has happened?" Anita felt the old woman's fingers unclench. She saw the bracelet of reddened skin encircling her arm—Mrs. Eappen might be old, but she was strong.

"He is gone," Mrs. Eappen began. "This morning I went to wake him but he wasn't there. He sleeps on a mat on the floor beside my mat. Sometimes he gets up early and goes into the kitchen to talk to the servants, but I went there and he was not there. The maidservant said she had not seen him. I went through the house—into every room—and I did not find him. I searched the grounds. He was nowhere. Nowhere." She took a deep breath to calm herself.

"Where would he go?" Anita asked.

"He has no place to go." Mrs. Eappen began to shake her head and little spurts of keening erupted from her. "He has no one. I am looking everywhere and he is nowhere."

"It's all right, Mrs. Eappen. We'll find him."

"You don't understand. I went looking everywhere. Everywhere. I went back into the sleeping room thinking perhaps he is playing a game, hiding, being just a silly boy. But he is not there." From her choli she pulled a handkerchief and held it crushed in her hand.

"I'm sure he is all right," Anita said. "We will find him."

"He is not all right. I searched the house a second time. And then my maidservant tells me there is a man on the veranda. It is not even time for the early tutors and already someone has come to my house."

"Who was it?"

"A man from Girjan's village, Tajji's village." Mrs. Eappen paused.

"What did he want? Did he threaten you?"

She nodded. "In the way he looked at me, the way he said things."

"What did he say?"

The old woman began to rock back and forth. "He said he came to give me a message."

"Yes?" Anita tried to keep her talking, but each word seemed to be harder for her to say than the previous one. "What was the message?"

"He said it was there in front of me. Then he left." Her eyes began to shine with tears.

"What was there in front of you?" Anita leaned forward. She frowned. "What did you find?"

"This. I found this." Mrs. Eappen laid the handkerchief on the desk as though it were delicate china, and lifted up one corner and then another, unfolding it as though it held the finest diamond. A little finger, caked in dried blood and black with dirt and bruising, rolled onto the white tablecloth. Mrs. Eappen pressed her hands together and started sobbing. Auntie Meena gasped and covered her mouth. "It is Tajji's."

"Tajji's?" Anita pulled the handkerchief closer, to get a better look at the digit. She examined it carefully, taking a pencil from the desk to turn it over, around, lifting it up. After a moment, she shook her head no, as she reviewed each knuckle and wrinkle.

"I don't think so, Mrs. Eappen." Anita spoke slowly, trying to sort out in her own mind what this meant. "I think this is Nisha's."

Outside the hotel, a single autorickshaw revved and ground its way up the steep hill. One man called to another. In the distance the occasional hello melded with voices singing. This was how it must feel to be walking to your doom, Anita thought, while everyone else went on with their lives. Anita stared at the tablecloth where Nisha's digit rested. Little bits of dried blood flecked the embroidered white fabric, a single smear drew a line over the threads of a green flower leaf. She felt sick. She leaned back in her chair and heard a little prayer leaving her lips. To her surprise Mrs. Eappen repeated it.

"I must go there, to the village." Anita looked at the handkerchief as she spoke.

"No!" Mrs. Eappen turned from Anita to Meena. "It is not safe. This is not a good place."

"I think it is where Tajji has gone. Unless you know more. Perhaps Tajji has gone some other place?" Anita said.

The old woman clapped a hand over her mouth and shut her eyes. "No, no, no. I told him never go there again. Never go there. It is only bad things for you. Trouble is there, only trouble. I order. I beg. He promised." Mrs. Eappen appealed to Anita like a calf deprived of its mother. "He is the only one left—his mother is gone, his father, his uncle, his aunt; it is only me and Theti, his cousin-sister."

"I hope not his aunt too," Anita said absently. "But we will find him. Tell me anything that will help."

Mrs. Eappen squirmed in her chair, but in the end she hunched over and began to talk.

"Girjan's father, Tajji's grandfather, took on debt to keep his farm, but things got worse and worse. All around small farmers were leaving their land, some were drowning themselves, others were abandoning their families. The old man held on as long as he could but when he could not pay, he was beaten to death; he left a huge debt for his sons. Girjan took over the farm and he worked so hard. We thought he would be free of this debt. But one day, he came to me and told me something had changed."

Mrs. Eappen struggled to find words. Anita murmured what comfort she could. The old woman opened her mouth to begin, closed it, wiped away tears, and sought Anita's hand.

"The moneylender Dipak is from this place, the same village. He considers it his place. But another man, another moneylender, was offering to lend money to farmers at lower rates. Dipak was furious." Mrs. Eappen's voice grew thin and squeaky. "At last he refused to let the farmers repay him with money they got from the new moneylender. But most of them owed him small amounts, and he couldn't take their property for so little without the authorities learning of it. Moneylending in this fashion is illegal. They could go to the authorities and complain."

"But Girjan was different," Anita said aloud without realizing it. "His debt was huge."

"Exactly." Mrs. Eappen nodded. "He offered Girjan a choice—his farm or a task."

Anita frowned. "What was the task?"

"He was to kill the new moneylender." Mrs. Eappen whispered the words as she shut her eyes.

Anita could guess what happened.

"In the end he couldn't do it," Mrs. Eappen said. "Dipak took his revenge. Girjan died by the edge of his paddy field. Dipak sent a man to take his leg—he cut it off and left Girjan to die. It was Tajji who found him just at the end." She began to weep quietly. "Dipak has declared this a family debt. It was up to Panju, Nisha's husband, to take on the task."

"What did Panju say to this?" Auntie Meena asked. Anita had almost forgotten she was standing there, and now wished she had sent her away. She didn't want her aunt to hear this.

Mrs. Eappen looked up. "He said he would. He told Tajji he would do this and take revenge against Dipak for what he did to his father and brother, but he died before he could do any of it." The hard exterior Mrs. Eappen had first shown Anita began to reappear.

"Panju is dead, and the police think Nisha killed him." Anita saw the pain gather in Mrs. Eappen's eyes.

"If she did, she had reason." Auntie Meena crossed her arms over her chest. Mrs. Eappen and Anita stared at her.

"I think I assumed, Auntie Meena, that she didn't kill him, that someone else did." But even as she said this, Anita knew there was merit in Meena's point of view. "But I suppose you could be right." Anita tried to imagine, without success, Nisha—sweet, kind Nisha—having the physical drive to kill someone, especially her own husband.

"Please find him," Mrs. Eappen said again.

Anita sent Mrs. Eappen home and turned to the problem of finding Tajji. Anita believed there was a slim chance that the boy would seek refuge in Nisha's house. After all, no one would expect to find him there, and he knew the area well. She set out for Chakka. She had spoken to only three neighbors during her first visits, and there were in fact four. She would begin with the fourth house.

She climbed out of the autorickshaw and walked around the small pink house. The landlord had not rented it yet, and it looked as forlorn as a house could look. She peered in the windows, studied the ground and windows for any sign that someone had entered or tried to get in, but found nothing suspicious. She headed to the house on the other side, the only one she hadn't visited. She had just an hour before her meeting with Rahul.

The plaque on the door said N.V. Vasu, and beside it sat a house bell. The door was open and Anita could see through to the back yard. She pushed the bell and waited. An old man shuffled to the back door and peered at her through the dark interior as though through a tunnel. Pushing his shoulders back, he made his way slow step by slow step to the front door. Anita pressed her hands together in anjali and introduced herself.

"I know who you are." He nodded and stepped out onto the veranda. He tapped the sign and that was all the introduction Anita was to get. But he seemed willing to be cordial. He pulled a chair forward and motioned her to it, then disappeared inside, returning with a second chair. "We have no servants during the day. I alone manage the daytime living." He lowered himself into the chair. "I saw you the first time you came. You went to each house except this one."

Apologies were in order.

"You were lazy, stopping at the last house because they gave you answers you wanted." He managed to offer this scolding without a single offensive tone or look, and Anita had to agree he was right. "Others have been smarter."

"I did miss some information, I know. This is why I am returning." She wasn't surprised if the police had been smarter; that was their job. "I am wondering if Tajji has come back. Have you seen him in the area, today or earlier?"

"Ach! He will never come back here!"

"I thought if something frightened him, he might come here for safety." Anita knew it was unlikely, but she hoped for a reply that would open the conversation.

The old man shook his head. "He has no fear." He pulled a face. "And it is good he is gone. He brought the poison into the house. He changed them. Changed him, the uncle, anyway."

"I don't think I understand," she said, though she was pretty sure she did.

"Tajji was twisted by the way his father died." The old man smacked his lips as if savoring being right. "Panju and Nisha took him in. But it was no good. His father's death poisoned him."

"Yes, it would, wouldn't it?" She stopped to consider the trauma visited on the boy.

"Not everyone would be twisted the way he is," the old man continued.

"How do you mean?"

"Wants revenge. It is set in his heart." The old man leaned forward, his eyes shimmering in the light, spittle forming at the corners of his mouth. "Talked about it all the time. How he would get his revenge, what he would do when he could. It was a matter of honor. He talked a lot about honor—talk I've never heard from a boy—it rattled out of him like a school recitation." The old man snorted, wiped his nose on the end of his mundu. "A serious boy but he didn't get good grades. Always studying but not showing anything for it. Then he stopped going to school." The old man paused, jutted out his lower lip. "The other boys probably made fun of him, mocking him, the way boys do if someone's a little different."

"This desire for revenge," Anita said, trying to bring the conversation back to the subject. "Tajji's desire for revenge poisoned Panju too?"

"Course it did! It was his brother who died, and before him, his father." The old man looked at her as if she were crazy for not understanding this. "The father dead. His brother killed that way? The son left an orphan? And the way the boy talked—it would turn anyone. All those plans he had."

"These plans. Panju told you about them?"

"I told him about the boy not being right, and he said he'd take care of it. After he'd finished with what he planned, the boy would be all right."

Anita could feel her heart sinking. "What did he mean? Did he tell you?"

The man continued to look at her as though still uncertain about her, but he seemed to come to a decision, and grew reflective. "One morning, after the both of them had left the house, the boy came over—he is lonely, I am thinking—so he saw me sitting out here and he came over and started asking me things. Had I ever seen anyone die? How did I know when he was dead? Did I know the person was going to die? What was the surest way? How long did it take to bleed to death? How long did this or that poison take? What was the most painful?" His voice broke and he struggled to finish his words. "I told him he was too young to be talking like that."

"Did he mention anyone specifically?"

"He didn't have to." His eyes glimmered, then faded. He turned to Anita. "Said he knew one way to do it for sure, but he had to be strong. To do his duty, he said, a man had to be strong."

"He's just a boy!" Anita said, shaking her head.

"He's no boy," he said. "Here in the city perhaps he's a boy. But he's fifteen and in a village that means he is nearly a man."

Anita considered this. "What about Panju? You said he told you about the boy's plans." *Please, please,* thought Anita, *tell me something that will help me find Nisha. Tell me she is innocent in all this.* "Did you tell Panju what Tajji said?"

"I told him about the boy, the way he talked." The old man turned his attention to the quiet lane in front of his house where a number of goats wandered untended, foraging or seeking a shady place to rest.

"Was he upset? He must have been terribly concerned." Anita leaned closer, trying to call him back from his reverie, from whatever it was that had captured his imagination.

"Do you know what he said?" The old man swung around to face her.

Anita shook her head.

"Hatred. Terrible poison." He sighed. "Panju told me he admired the boy's courage and would be his father now in every way." He paused. "I knew then it was too late. They had their plans. All I could do was watch."

Anita leaned forward, going over his words. Like a lot of people, he knew something, and he wanted to tell and he didn't want to tell. Holding back information was, for him, a source of power. "You mean you saw something happen, didn't you?"

"I will not talk to the police," the old man said. "They are fools. Looking for Nisha." He shook his head in disgust. "She is not the one they want."

"Who do they want, Sar?" Anita spoke softly, trying to enter his reverie as a companion in his journey of painful memories. He looked at her with his rheumy eyes, bloodshot and brown with thin blue borders.

"He hired someone," the old man said.

"Hired someone? To do what?"

"Panju hired someone to kill Dipak, of course. I saw him."

Anita frowned. This seemed so unlikely, so far-fetched as not to be credible. "How do you know this? Who did you see?"

"We all know the secrets. All that shouting, the boy talking,

Panju talking. They think we don't understand, but I do. They hired a killer. That's who I saw. The one he hired." He leaned back and smirked, confident in his secret knowledge.

"What happened exactly? Please, this could help me find Nisha."

He snorted. He sat forward as though imparting a secret. "He came late one night, driving down that lane over there, the one that runs parallel to this one. His car parked just there between the houses. He walked across, through the brush, to the back of Panju's house. I saw him." His eyes glistened and his mouth worked in and out of a smirk. "Tajji saw him."

"Tajji saw him? You are sure of that."

"The boy came out of the house an hour before this man arrived and hid in the bushes, waiting." The old man worked his lips, running his tongue from corner to corner, smacking them together as he grew excited. "The man fell, tripped on a liana." The old man wheezed as he tried to laugh. "He got up. Went inside. Panju was at the door to greet him."

"And Tajji?"

"Ah, Tajji!" The old man wheezed as he laughed. "He saw where the man fell and went there and rummaged in the ground. He found something. I saw him pick it up. He went back into hiding until the man left. I wonder maybe he planned to trip him. Maybe he set the vine to catch him."

"What did Tajji find?"

The man shrugged. "Perhaps a torch. It had a light. I could see it from my back stoop."

Anita studied the man. He could be lying, she thought. "If you were sitting on the back stoop, did Tajji see you?"

"He did." The old man hunched his shoulders.

"Did you say anything to him?"

"Of course not. He has chosen his path. It is not my duty to interfere." He was angry, indignant, at being caught out idly watching a crime happen.

"When the man came out, did Tajji give him what he found?"

The old man laughed, coughed, and laughed some more, shaking his head the while. "He came again," the old man whispered, "a second time."

He's enjoying this, she thought, doling out tidbits of information that could be important, but which for him are merely gossip, little pieces of the story to keep me here. "When?"

"One, maybe two nights later."

"When was this exactly?" Anita asked.

"The second time was the night Panju died." He glared at her, defiant. "That very night."

"Are you certain? You didn't tell the police this, did you?"

"I will never tell the police. It is not my duty to do this. If I tell you, who will believe you?"

Anita decided to let that go. "What about Tajji? Was he here also the second night?"

"Oh, yes, he was here. He is outside watching, but this time he is not watching the man arriving. He is watching us, the neighbors."

"You?" She paused. "So there are no witnesses," Anita said more to herself than to him.

"Shrewd fellow but for karma. It recoils upon us all." He grew philosophical, once again an old man sitting on his stoop watching the world move on without him.

"That first time must have been one of the nights the other neighbors heard fighting," Anita said absently.

"Loud fighting," he said. "The wife is defiant of her husband."

Trying to save his life, is more like it, Anita thought, *by hiding the visitor's purple mobile in the ceiling fan.* "What did the man, the stranger, look like?" Anita held her breath. This could be everything she needed, everything that would lead her to Nisha.

The old man shook his head and scowled. "It was dark. I

could not see him." He spat on the ground. "You ask all these questions. Nosy woman."

Anita found the old man unpleasant, but he had been clear about what he saw and equally clear about what it meant. If Panju and Tajji had indeed decided to hire someone to take revenge on Dipak, she had to find that man, whoever he was. She drove back to the road and took the lane that ran parallel to Nisha's.

At the first house backing onto the section where Nisha's house stood, she came up with nothing. No one in the household had seen a car parked late at night, and neither had anyone else in the neighborhood, as far as they knew. Anita continued her trek from house to house, even asking if she could walk through the backyard, to get a sense of what it looked like from this direction. No one said no, but neither did anyone offer any help. No one had seen the car, seen the man coming at night, seen Tajji outside watching, or seen anyone driving away, with or without blood on his hands.

Anita walked along the side of the house directly behind Nisha's. As she drew closer to Nisha's house and deeper into the trees and undergrowth, she tripped over hidden vines, flailing her arms in an effort to keep her balance. She felt ridiculous, as though she were walking a high wire without a balance bar. No wonder the man had lost his mobile in this mess.

Tree branches framed the back of Nisha's house. To her right was another thick clump where anyone could hide safely, even in daylight. Tajji would have had no trouble at night. Beyond she could see the back of Mr. Vasu's house, and she could easily imagine him sitting there in the dark, a smirk on his face as he watched.

The purple mobile. The visit two nights in a row. The camera and practice shots recorded on the card. Anita ran through what she knew, and what she knew for certain was that Panju didn't have a plan, only a passion. He and Tajji put together their plan, if you could call it that, one step at a time, improvising at every turn. Panju must have been mad with grief, and Tajji no better. Neither one of them should have survived, thought Anita, knowing what she did of the men they were up against. And yet they might both have survived, if not for the man who came in the dark, walking into a trap he turned to his own advantage.

CHAPTER 18

Anita sat by the window of a small coffee shop in a new hotel. She'd left Nisha's old neighborhood uncertain of her next step, but determined not to miss her appointment with Rahul. She lifted the coffee cup to her lips just as a motorcycle swerved around a bus and pulled up in front of the Bourne Studio. The driver parked, climbed off the cycle, and lifted the helmet off his head. Rahul had arrived at his gallery at exactly five minutes before ten.

She was surprised he was so prompt; she had half expected an assistant to open up, giving him the freedom to meet clients elsewhere and to arrive when he pleased. But he was a businessman, and it seemed he took his work seriously. She forgot her coffee and dashed across the street, her box of prints clutched to her chest.

In a matter of minutes Anita had spread her photos out on a table and stepped back, ready to answer questions and offer explanations, but that wasn't what happened. Rahul nodded and stepped forward. He touched each photo in turn, moving one aside as he examined another. He kept his eyes on the images, and after a while Anita stepped away to let him think at his own pace. He didn't seem to notice.

Rahul was shorter than she was by two or three inches, slender, with graceful hands and long fingers. He had a neat mustache, like so many men his age, and kept his hair relatively short. He wore sandals, unlike the newer class of businessmen who wore tie shoes, but he kept his blue shirt tucked into his gray slacks. He looked like he'd put on his clothes that very minute, so perfectly pressed and cool were they.

After an hour, a young woman came in with a tray holding two cups of milky sweet coffee. Rahul nodded to her to place the cups at the end of the table. Rahul never took his eyes off the images until he had gone down the full length of the table and back twice, pulling out some, pushing others aside. After another half hour of this, he held his cup of tepid coffee and examined the layout he had created. He sipped and then ran his tongue over his lips, lowered his cup to its saucer, and leaned on one leg and then the other.

Anita finished her drink much sooner. She stood quietly, to one side, her arms crossed, wisps of hair brushing against her forehead in the breeze from the overhead fan. She waited for Rahul to speak, but the only sounds were an occasional hum and the chafing of paper against wood as he moved photos around on the tabletop. His assistant sat at a small desk in a corner by the door to the office. She moved papers on her desk in near silence, and when the mobile rang she reached for it swiftly, to silence its ring. She never looked at Anita, and rarely at her employer.

Without turning around, Rahul began speaking. He lifted one photo and turned it perpendicular to the others, letting its end hang over the edge. "This one," he said. "This one is special. You must enlarge this. It will be the center of the exhibit. Don't sell the rights to it." That said, he shifted his weight to his left leg and leaned toward the other end of the table.

Anita stepped forward to get a look at which one he had identified as so special. It was a photo of the sunrise over Vilingham, a nearby fishing village, with the bright orange-red orb burning off the gray morning thickness. She'd liked the photo when she took it, and kept a copy pinned up near the desk where she worked, next to a collage composed of bits and pieces of a photographer's life—old Polaroids, crushed camera cards, a couple of dime batteries, pages torn from magazines. There was something about the photograph that held her, but she hadn't thought anyone else would be drawn to it. Nor had she thought it was special. She tried to see it now through Rahul's eyes.

He raised a question she had struggled with for years, and wondered if she'd ever have an answer for. If she created a great photo, would she recognize it, or would she have to rely on the chance comment of someone else to tell her that, yes, this one was special? The question made her uneasy, as though she weren't good enough to understand her own work or to receive the inspiration for a great photograph, as though whatever good work she created was an accident, something she wasn't entitled to call her own.

"These." Rahul shuffled together a number of images he had set aside, and waved his hand lightly to indicate that the others should be put away. Anita slid the rejected photos together into a separate pile. As she cleared the table Rahul took the selected ones and spread them out. "These," he said again.

Rahul gave her his ideas for the arrangement, his eyes straying to one or another photograph as he talked, and she listened, no longer feeling the need to take notes. His vision was so clear, so congenial to her own thinking, that she didn't worry she'd forget or misconstrue later what he'd said. As she listened, she felt an enormous and deeply intimate gratitude for the way he talked to her. There was no posturing, no effort to impress or manipulate—he was all ideas about imagery, the audience, the impact of art on viewer.

Anita would never have believed she could feel the way she did as she listened to Rahul talk and plan. He never gave her a compliment, but she knew how he felt by listening to him, the ideas he shared and the plans he offered. She didn't think she could be any happier, and then Anand came through the glass doors—lovely, handsome, generous Anand who had made this possible through his friendship with Rahul. Life couldn't get any better.

In the afternoon, after three hours with Rahul, Anita stepped out onto the wide sidewalk feeling like she had just met herself for the first time. She hardly knew if there were words for the experience. She looked up at the canopy overhead in a moment of joy, and felt a rush of affection for the rain tree and its feathery pink blooms. She was about to hail an autorickshaw when she stopped and again looked up at the arching branches. She took the measure of the neighborhood. This was an old area, and the rain tree too was old and well established. There were trees like this in the photos she'd found on the card in her camera, but no trees like this in Nisha's neighborhood.

Yes, trees, she thought, *old trees.* She glanced back at Rahul's gallery and then down the street. She saw more old trees and began walking, taking note of each one, its type and age. After a mile or so, she spotted a coffee shop and headed for it. She was hungry and wanted time to think.

All the outside tables and chairs shaded by trees and umbrellas on a raised terrace were occupied, but the inside café was less populated. She found an empty table near a window and ordered a sandwich and coffee. A few minutes later the young waitress deposited a plate on the glass tabletop along with her coffee. Anita thanked her and picked up the sandwich.

"That looks very good. And I've not had a meal. I rushed out without eating." Riyas Patel smiled down at her. "If I may, I'll get something and join you."

Anita greeted him and put down her sandwich. She was surprised to see him, but her session with Rahul had left her with a sense of deep calm, and seeing Riyas did not unsettle her. She knew there was little chance his appearance was entirely accidental, so she decided to make use of it. She gathered her thoughts, deciding how to approach him. A moment later Riyas pulled out a chair and sat down across from her with a mango smoothie.

"Is that your meal?" Anita asked.

"Alas, yes. I should be on the other side of the city in five minutes. Think I'll make it?"

She shook her head.

"Your meal doesn't look very substantial," he pointed out.

"I was starving and not willing to wait," she said. "Besides, I like the area. It has so many old trees. Not many areas have any left these days. Everything's getting cut down for new high-rises and parking lots."

"Your car is running well?" he asked.

"Oh, yes, of course."

"I'm glad to hear it. You never know what these mechanics will get up to if you don't watch them all the time."

"Bartonskutty is known to me and my family. We trust him." Anita tried not to sound snippy. "He has been our mechanic for years." She smiled and wiped her hands on a napkin; she had to stop herself from looking around for a sink but decided this wasn't that sort of restaurant. This menu offered only Western finger food.

"Ah, forgive me." Riyas pulled a face as he responded to a ring tone. He extracted his mobile and glanced at the number. "One moment." He stepped outside and tapped in a text message, followed by a long conversation during which he bobbed his head and shrugged his shoulders.

Anita tried to spot his white car, or even the black one, parked along the curb, but just then her mobile rang and she opened her cloth bag and rummaged inside for it. "Oh," she said aloud when she realized it was the purple mobile. After struggling with the temptation to answer the call, she flipped it shut and shoved it back in the bag just as Riyas returned.

"It is Auntie Meena. I have been so remiss of late in meeting my hotel duties that now she has taken to tracking me down," Anita said. It seemed a reasonable lie, but she wondered if he'd caught a glimpse of the device.

"I am one who understands." Riyas sat down again.

"Always more work," Anita said as she set her bag aside. "Is your business going well?"

"My work is dull. What brings you to this neighborhood?"

"I had an appointment with a gallery owner." Anita nodded in the direction of the businesses down the street. "It went on longer than I expected and I was famished at the end of it—partly nerves." He offered a generic compliment on her success-ful art career, and the conversation veered into recent changes in the city, the upcoming monsoon—which couldn't come soon enough for him—and the erratic government policies to deal with inflation. She tried several times to bring the conversation back to work, but the talk veered off again.

"Good galleries in this area," he said. "An alternative career if you give up the hotel?" Riyas leaned forward and gave her a half smile.

"I can honestly say that I never considered that idea," she said. "My art career sometimes interferes with my work at Hotel Delite, or is it the other way around? I don't know, but I certainly don't want to give up either." She pulled back in her chair and crumpled up her napkin. "And my family has owned Hotel Delite and the land it sits on for generations. We would never let it go."

"Of course not," he said, standing up.

"So perhaps I should get back to work." Anita stood up too.

"Time for us to be on our separate ways." He nodded to Anita as he pulled open the glass door. The midday heat sucked them onto the terrace.

Anita watched him jog down the steps and turn down the sidewalk. *He knows I'm suspicious of something,* she thought as he disappeared. She pulled out the purple mobile and checked for missed calls. There was only one, and the number was blocked.

As soon as Anita returned to Hotel Delite, she spread out the studio shots Rahul had selected and tried to study them as he had. Over the next hour or so she began to see what he had seen, and felt a small thrill of anticipation. She had eighteen photographs to refine and print. His workmen would do the matting and framing. It was late in the evening before she remembered she hadn't eaten a substantial meal all day. Time for a break.

An hour later Anita opened her laptop. She slipped the found card from Shiva's Emporium into her computer and opened the first photograph. This was the scene that the rain tree outside Rahul's gallery had brought to mind. In the photo the compound wall was old, judging by the design, and the trees surrounding the house were at least a hundred years old. She focused on a small area of branches hanging over the inner courtyard and magnified this. She went in closer. A tulip tree, with its yellow flowers thick among the canopy. She magnified another area and thought she saw the branches of a second tulip tree. There weren't that many left of that age and size in Trivandrum.

Old compound wall. Tulip trees, at least two.

Anita clicked on the next photo and enlarged it. She ran her cursor over the image, looking for some detail that might tell her something. With a few clicks she brought up a partly defaced name etched on a thin piece of brass set into the old wall. She opened the photo in another program and began to enlarge and enhance the inscription. After several efforts she thought she discerned the remnants of a house name: Suryanivas. House of the Sun, or of Surya.

Anita clicked on the next photo. Several cars were visible in this one but parked in such a way that Anita couldn't read the registration plates; no matter how she focused, enlarged, or enhanced the scene, she couldn't bring up a clear plate. She turned to the general scene.

A group of men seemed to be waiting for someone, almost as people did outside the office of a dignitary or official who was the only one who could sign or authorize or approve a certain action. As well dressed as most of them seemed, they were still petitioners. In the usual situation, people clustered closer and closer to the doorway, to ensure they were the first ones into the office, sliding into the two or three chairs placed in front of the desk.

Anita enlarged each face. Only one was turned away from the camera, so she tried to discern something significant in the view of the man's back. Nearby one woman swung a broom and two women stood apart chatting with each other. In the background Anita found a detail of the tile roof. From this she could conclude that at least part of the house was of South Indian design. She added that to her list of identifying features.

In the fourth photo Anita again enlarged each face. On the edge of the crowd stood Auntie Meena looking frightened and awkward. Anita winced. Seeing the figure clearly and enlarged seemed to make the whole thing worse. Anita was deeply ashamed for her aunt. Meena seemed to be backing away, and Anita could easily imagine her embarrassment at finding herself at such a location, as well as her confusion and uncertainty. Three men seemed to be looking directly at the camera, but perhaps that was only because they were looking toward the street. Anita moved her cursor and started to enlarge the three faces, enlarging and sharpening, until she thought the features

171

began to make sense. She turned her attentions to one of the three. She studied the face.

CHAPTER 19

Anita wasn't one for jumping to conclusions, but she was certain she had found the key to the whole mess Auntie Meena was in. She stared hard at the photo on her computer screen as she continued to refine the image. It was grainy in areas, blurry in others, but the face was recognizable to one who knew it. She knew there was a chance she was seeing what she wanted to see, so she closed her eyes and opened them. She turned away from the screen, let her eyes and mind focus on something else, and then turned back. Yes, the image really was there. She hadn't superimposed her memory over the mass of pixels. She printed the photo, and hurried down the stairs to the main building.

Anita found her aunt in her own room. Meena opened the door wearing her night shift, her hair falling about her shoulders. It was rare for Anita to see her like this and she slipped into the room before Meena could object.

"You must answer one question," Anita said.

"Do you not know how late it is, Anita? You should be asleep." Meena sat down on the edge of her bed, sagging as though she were nearly asleep again. "I should be asleep. Can this wait?"

"Auntie!" Anita shook her aunt's hand and startled her fully awake. "One question."

"All right, all right. What is it? Ask."

"What is the name of the lender?"

"This is not a question you can ask."

"Of course it is."

"I do not know," Auntie Meena said.

"You borrowed money from someone and you don't know his name?" Anita said.

"He is saying I am not needing to know the name of the agent or anything more."

"What about Panju?"

Meena blanched. "I am too ashamed. I do not ask."

"And the money? Whose is it? Where did it come from?"

"The agent wouldn't tell me where the money came from," Meena said. "He is protecting the important man, he is saying to me."

"Whose name is on the document you signed?"

"Another agent, perhaps," Meena said.

It made sense, Anita had to admit. If the moneylender could hide himself behind layer upon layer of agents, there was less likelihood of getting caught or being prosecuted. "Did anyone ever talk to the agent in your hearing? Perhaps you heard part of a name."

Meena shook her head. "Most particular this man. But I am hearing this is expected. He is protecting himself. Understandable, I suppose." She continued on in this fashion, talking more to herself than to Anita.

"I think I know who it is."

"You can't know, Anita. I am not telling you."

"Auntie, listen to me. You are risking Hotel Delite for an outrageous loan that is illegal. And you are going to do what a lender tells you?"

"I . . ." Meena frowned and swayed where she sat. "He was most insistent."

"I do not doubt this. But still you must tell me."

"It is dangerous," Meena whispered.

"Not nearly as dangerous as what you have already done."

"Oh, Anita! What am I to do?"

"You are to trust me."

Meena offered Anita the saddest, most pathetic plea. "I don't know what to do. If you already know . . ." Anita sat down on the bed and put her arm around her aunt.

"I must be certain. If I make a mistake, I won't get a second chance. You must trust me. I cannot help you if I am not certain who we are dealing with."

"Everything you say is true." Meena sighed and rubbed her hands over her face. "You are always so logical," she said.

"Auntie?"

"If he finds out?"

"We have bigger worries, Auntie. By the time he finds out, the situation will be very different." Anita looked at her aunt. "I promise you. Now, tell me."

"Do you know, Anita? You said you knew."

"I think I do. His name. It is Riyas Patel, is it not?"

Auntie Meena shut her eyes and cringed.

"I knew there was a reason I kept running into him," Anita said.

"What? You have seen him?"

"Yes, but never mind that now. Go back to bed, Elayamma," Anita said. "I have to think about my next step."

Anita settled herself at her desk again. Through the open window she could see the flickering lights of the fishing boats far out on the horizon. The lanes nearby were still, quiet. A dog growled. She went to the balcony. Below her, on the terrace, the hotel guard dog trotted along the fence sniffing and nuzzling and searching for the chipmunks that tormented him in his kennel during the day. He scratched at the sand, sniffed some more, and headed back around the building. Brij had taught him to circle the hotel along various stairways and openings in the fence near the kitchen, and the animal went along wagging his tail and growling at the shifting moonlight. Anita left him to his duties and returned to her own problems.

She had a list of identifying features of the house where Auntie Meena had gone to collect her money. After reviewing all the photos of the three mansions, she found fewer details in two of the houses compared to where Meena was photographed in front. She decided to focus on that one.

She had the name of the house, Suryanivas, but few people knew the names of houses anymore, or could locate one in the city. Besides, Suryanivas was a fairly common name. More to the point was the location, and that she could narrow down by the environment.

The house was located on a wide street, which was clear in one of the photos taken at a distance, and the old trees would seem to confirm it. Anita scrolled down to a broad view of the front of the mansion and zeroed in on the trees on the left of the entrance. The first one seemed to be a copper pod. Anita enlarged its lower branches and thought she recognized the early yellow five-petaled flowers of the first flowering. The lower branches were perhaps twenty or thirty feet from the ground, which meant the tree was probably over sixty feet tall.

Anita moved her cursor to another tree. This one was a tamarind. Not surprising. They made wonderful shade trees. She moved the cursor again. That had to be a tulip tree, and the way the branches turned and looped over each other, there was a good chance there were two of them rooted close together.

An old house lot with a copper pod, two tulip trees, possibly a rain tree, and a tamarind. All old, well-established growth. She had the house name, some identifying features, a little architectural information. Now all she had to do was locate the property.

Anita made a list of her personal contacts who might know where the house was. An amateur horticulturist might recognize the trees, a domestic architectural buff might recognize the gateway, and a news reporter used to tracking down famous or important people in the state capital might know the house and who lived there. Anita glanced at the clock. Almost one-thirty in the morning. Surprised at the hour, she tucked her contact list under the corner of her computer and shut it down. Anita thought she knew just how her aunt felt. She was exhausted, and it wasn't entirely from lack of sleep.

CHAPTER 20

Nisha heard the music first, the drumming, perhaps five or more drummers in the distance. She didn't think anything of it, but the music comforted her. Then, to her confusion and surprise, a rough hand grabbed her in the dark and tied a cloth around her eyes. Someone dragged her out of her hut and across the yard and around to the back. Someone else tied her wrists together. Another tied a gag over her mouth. One of the men struck her on the side of the head, knocking her to the ground. She heard their coarse voices laughing as they walked away and left her lying there.

Nisha knew they hadn't dragged her far. The blindfold had been loosely tied, and her hands were tied in front of her. She could see the bottom of the pillar, part of the yard and the steps to the back veranda. It was dark but the waxing moon sprinkled light across the land, and for once Nisha could see her own limbs, the pleats and folds in her ragged and filthy sari. For the first time, with her hands tied in front of her, she could tie the end of her sari tighter, gather her folds, and redress herself. As she pulled the fabric across her waist she felt the absurdity of what she was doing—protecting her modesty when she could be moments away from dying.

She settled back onto her heels and listened. The night was quiet, almost silent, as the music faded. But in a moment the sound of drumming returned. She heard a *nadaswaram*'s mournful sound and imagined the musician taking a deep breath and gathering in his soul as he played. She heard another sound she couldn't identify. It suggested a temple elephant being led from house to house through the night, according to the donation each householder could pay. For a moment she drifted into the quiet pleasure of imagining the elephant at the door with its mahout, the big animal garlanded and reaching out for the bananas being offered. She turned her head one way and then another, trying to catch a sense of how near the celebrants might be, but it seemed they had moved on. For a moment she thought she caught an odor on the light breeze drifting down from the hillside, the fragrance of toddy. She sniffed but the aroma was gone.

Nisha listened hard for some sound that would give away the presence of another. There had to be someone else nearby. But she smelled no beedis, no coffee or tea, no rice or vegetables cooking. She smelled no dirty feet, no laborers whose sweat changed with the seasons, no oiled hair needing to be washed. She heard no radio blaring—only the drums—no voices low in the distance, no maidservant chatting to her employer, no murmurs of a cowherd talking to a calf. She knew she was still at the same house—they hadn't dragged her far—but she heard not a single sound that could tell her anything.

The rope reaching to the pillar lay slack in her lap, falling between her knees, dragging along the dirt, before rising to the cement pillar. She tipped her head back to see beneath the blindfold and saw the rope rise as far as the base on the veranda, losing sight of it as it rose in the air to, she imagined, a hook on the pillar or perhaps the eaves. If she tipped her head to one side she could glimpse the floor of the veranda. This was where she had listened to Dipak—and where the knife had come down on her hand.

She shifted her legs and the rope let her turn a few inches, so she could scan the veranda for the guards. All she saw were steel pots lying on thin cotton towels, left to dry in the evening air—she was surprised they hadn't been taken in before night fell. A row of pink and yellow and green and red plastic water buckets lined the far end. But however she looked, wherever she looked, she saw only cooking utensils and equipment—no maidservant or night guard lay on the veranda asleep on a mat. She was alone as far as she could see.

Nisha pulled down the blindfold and went over the sights again. She looked over every inch of the veranda, stretching to see the far end, then working her way back to where she knelt. She began with the plastic water pots, a few clay pots, a stack of kindling, some small steel water pots, a rag tossed against the sill of the locked back door, a red plastic stool tipped up against the wall, a square flat basket for sifting and picking through the rice, and the last item. Sitting there, at the end of the veranda, as though forgotten in mid-cleaning, with an oily rag covering most of it, was a gun. A small black gun.

She had never seen a gun before, not a real one, and certainly not like this, lying outside as though someone had just gone off and left it. She glanced away. It couldn't be—there couldn't be a gun sitting outside on the veranda, just sitting there. She looked back at it. It was there, beneath its rag. She couldn't take her eyes off the weapon. She inched closer, checking the rope as she did so, but it continued to give her leeway, dragging in the dirt, swinging in the hot night air. She twisted her wrists against the rope, but the knots held, giving her no leeway to slip out her hands.

Farther down the lane she heard the drummers coming closer, their drumming getting louder and louder. That must be why they moved me, she thought. Half the village will be passing by and if I screamed and knocked down the walls of the hut someone would have to notice me. It wouldn't be safe to leave me out there.

She began to breathe more deeply, more rapidly, excited yet distressed that help could be on the other side of the house, just a few feet away, but lost to her because no one would hear her cries over the sound of the drumming. And then the horns! She heard the *nadaswarams,* their high-pitched wail rising into the night sky, and after them the cymbals. Her head fell forward onto her chest; she wanted to cry.

Nisha looked again at the gun. She could reach it—she knew that—but could she use it? She leaned over to study it and saw a gun that looked like something out of a movie. It made her stomach churn and her body grow cold and her breath come in shorter and shorter gasps. Near the rag lay a stack of old newspapers neatly tied in string waiting for the paper man who came on his bicycle once or twice a week. Neatly tied in string, thought Nisha. She looked along the rest of the veranda, at all the neatly and appropriately placed tools of a well-functioning home. The gun was the only discordant note—that and the way she was tied, with her hands in front of her.

She began to move away from the gun. For whatever reason it was there, it was not meant to benefit her, she was certain of that. If she reached for the gun, any one of Dipak's men could come out of the darkness and shoot her, telling the local constable she had a gun and threatened him. If she reached for the gun and fired it off to warn the villagers passing by in the temple procession, they might not hear her but the gun might explode in her hand. She would kill herself at no risk to Dipak.

If she took the gun and kept it, she might find herself forced to use it, and this act alone would trap her. But no one here would ever let her get that far with it—she was sure of that. It probably didn't even have bullets in it. No, this was a trick, some kind of trick, an obvious trick. She should have seen it right from the start. All she had to do was pick up the gun and that would tell them she could kill. She would be trapped, betrayed by her own behavior.

Until that minute, it hadn't occurred to Nisha that Dipak didn't know what to do with her. He had kidnapped her, tried to force her to complete the task her husband's family had either failed or refused to do, and now he was stuck with her. The mighty moneylender whom everyone feared and obeyed had put himself in a corner and didn't know how to get out of it. Murdering her was not the same as murdering someone who owed him money. The police would look away at some things, but in the city someone would ask the right questions and the investigation would begin. She was a problem. By refusing to do anything, she had frustrated Dipak's plans.

Nisha rocked on her heels, swaying in the night, the sweat dripping down between her breasts and down her back. She had seen herself as too naive, too trusting, too simple in the ways of the world to know how to escape this labyrinth of evil. She assumed Dipak was in control, able to make her do his bidding, but there was more to the situation than that. Her determination thwarted him. She eyed the gun and tried to move even further away, inching along the dirt.

Maybe she was just afraid, she told herself. Maybe she was turning away from her only chance to escape, to free herself, to either die on her own terms or escape and flee to the police. She tried to get a glimpse of the gun again as the moon emerged from behind a cloud. A mere wisp of white moved across the sky. She remembered when she and Panju sat on the veranda and watched the monsoon roll in. She ran out into the yard and felt the first few drops large and succulent slide down her face. Theti followed her, jumping up and down, throwing out her arms and spinning in a circle until she collapsed in a pile of giggles onto the ground. Panju picked her up and swung her around in his arms like a fish swimming through the monsoon waters.

"I know where everything I care about is at this moment," Panju had said, looking over at Nisha. She knew too, and she could imagine the rest of his family standing at the edge of their paddy fields with a smile spreading across their faces and a look of relief in their eyes. Even though the monsoon came every year and had done so before there was rice to plant or farmers to plant it, Panju's father marveled every year and offered a special puja in gratitude.

Nisha dropped her head onto her chest. The deaths of all three men of the family, leaving only Tajji, had to be the end. Whatever happened to her, she decided, she would not be maneuvered into adding to the violence. She could better understand now the change that had come over her husband, the way he turned from a man of reason and quiet strength to one desperate to end the violence, to one in whom the poison of revenge had tainted his soul. She understood, but she would not follow him. She pushed the blindfold into place and settled back on her heels to wait, knowing Dipak and his men would come soon to put her back in the hut, perhaps with a beating for not giving in to temptation, or perhaps with a beating for no reason at all. She listened and waited. Then she smelled it. He was coming back.

CHAPTER 21

The moon filtered through the curtains, but it was hardly bright enough to wake her up, Anita thought. Then she heard the buzzer. She found the clock and squinted at it. Could it only be five-thirty?

"Amma?"

"Sanj?" At the sound of the guard's voice, Anita crawled out of bed and opened the door.

"You must come." Sanj turned and hurried down the steps. Anita grabbed a robe and followed him to the top of the steps leading down to the lower compound. He pointed to the scene below.

Light from an open door washed far enough along the ground for Anita to see Brij crouched on the dirt. He turned. As he did so, she saw what he'd been looking at. There in front of him lay the black guard dog. Brij's face was streaked with tears. Anita ran down the steps and knelt by the animal.

The dog lay perfectly still. He seemed smaller, too small to be threatening, as though his life had drained away. A few flies buzzed around his head. Anita pressed her hands along the dog's neck and head and chest. His body was warm. As she moved her hands along she felt a weak pulse. Enormously relieved, she said, "He's alive."

Anita looked up. On the other side of the dog's body stood the child Theti, her eyes riveted on the animal.

"What is this?" Auntie Meena appeared on the back steps.

"Auntie!" Anita said. "Take the child." Anita turned to Theti and said, "He is sick, Theti, but he will be all right. Go with Auntie." Theti went dutifully, looking back as she climbed the stairs. Anita heard their voices fade.

"Amma?" Brij knelt down in front of the dog. He was quick to love, quick to sorrow. "What is happening?"

It would be light soon. Already workers were readying for the day, walking along the lanes to their first jobs, householders waking their children for early-morning tutorials, tourists rising early for yoga on the beach or meditation on the rocky headland. Anita and Brij and Sanj would have to pull the dog out of sight. The dog lay just beneath the guests' balconies and bedroom windows. Even now anyone could peer over and see it lying there, and the hotel staff kneeling over it. And if she didn't hurry, plenty of curious guests would do just that. She instructed Brij to bring rope and canvas sacking. She helped him drag the body over to the kennel, and sent Sanj to the village for an animal healer.

"Brij, we have to take stock now," Anita said. The sun was making its presence known along the horizon. "A very bold thief has come in the night, with a purpose." She looked down at the dog. "The animal was poisoned, I think. We have to figure out what the thief wanted. Is anything missing? Are there signs of a break-in?"

Brij shrugged. "Sometimes a little food is missing from what I have set aside for myself."

"I'm not talking about pilfering," Anita said. She wrapped her robe tighter around her, retied the sash, and turned back to the house. "We must look for the reason for—for this."

Anita paced the perimeter of the hotel, looking for signs that someone had come over the compound wall or gate. The ground was well swept, too well swept. Other than the footprints of the household discovering the dog, no others were to be seen.

Whoever had done this deed had swept away his tracks.

"Amma!" Brij called to her from the wall where the potted plants were lined up. She waved him away but he called again. Reluctantly, she went and looked where Brij was pointing. A mobile was lodged in a crack in the blue trim that capped the compound wall. Someone had dug out enough concrete and pebbles to make a place where it could stand up and be noticed. Anita pulled out the mobile and looked it over—it was an ordinary mobile but an old one. It looked vaguely familiar. She flipped it open but it wouldn't turn on. She opened the back and saw there was no sim card.

Anita entered the hotel through the main door. She scanned the registration desk, unlocked the office and examined it, checked the dining room, the pantry, the back bathroom. She found what she was looking for when she came to the front parlor.

There, lined up on an old mahogany sideboard that once showed off the family china but now held magazines and forgotten books were three outdated mobiles. They were old and no longer able to hold a charge, and Anita had stored them away, planning on returning them at some point. At some point. It was one of those tasks she knew she'd never get around to because she didn't really have to. They had lain forgotten in the top drawer, with other odds and ends, and now they were lined up on the well-polished top of the sideboard, for anyone to see. Set in a line—black, gray, black—they looked like hand grenades ready to go off.

Anita sank down on the settee, her eyes riveted to the sideboard. Whoever it was had been inside this room while Sanj and the guests slept, while the night guard was napping in the parking lot, perhaps even while Anita stared at her computer wondering how to locate the lender, Riyas Patel. What if she'd gotten up to go into the hotel for something to eat? What if one of the guests had gotten up, unable to sleep, and come downstairs looking for something to read? What if . . . Anita felt a chill ripple down her back.

Anita thought about the purple mobile sitting in her purse. She thought about the card still sitting in her camera. She thought about the enlarged photos cluttering her desk. She had to bring this terror to an end.

Anita gathered up her notes on the house and trees and headed into Trivandrum. She found her aunt's friend Chandra Moni at home in a small house in one of the developments along the railway line. The lanes were narrow and quiet, with old trees leaning over dirt paths as though tired of their years. Chandra greeted her warmly, as though she were used to having people drop in on her at all hours. They settled on the veranda with coffee, and Anita immediately began telling her about the trees she had identified in the photos.

"I want to know where they are located," Anita explained.

"Oh! The grid! You want to see if we can track them on the grid!"

"That's exactly what I'm hoping," Anita said.

Chandra's eyes sparkled and she sat up at once in her rattan chair. She was a warm, agreeable woman who expected surprises in life, even relished them, the result of living a quiet and dutiful forty-plus years. A woman of purpose, Chandra was always pleased to see a friend but even more pleased to have something to do, some way to help.

"It is finished, isn't it?" Anita said. For the last year or so the environmentalists in the city could talk about nothing else but the plan to map all the heritage trees in Trivandrum. The powers that be had laid a grid over the city, sought volunteers among the people, and sent them out into their particular squares to record every tree. The result was a stunning and thorough record of the city's horticulture.

"It is exquisite. So many volunteers working so hard. I thought the size of the grid and the extent of the project would daunt many a volunteer, but it was not so. The people embraced the task with enthusiasm and energy, and the volunteers scoured their assigned areas. They worked with a will, and finished even before the deadline. We are now knowing every heritage tree in the city. We know where they are located, we have all the proper names, and we know their condition." Chandra leaned forward with her palms pressed against her thighs.

"You mean how healthy they are?"

"Exactly." Chandra smiled politely without showing any teeth, but anyone could see she was ready to burst with enthusiasm.

"I am looking for a few particular trees in a particular setting," Anita explained.

"It is a test, isn't it?" Chandra clapped her hands and grinned. "We can test how accurate and useful the grid is. Come." Chandra bounded to her feet and waved Anita to follow.

The interior of the house was dark, with curtains over tinted windows and dark heavy furniture. Chandra led the way to a small room beside the kitchen and opened the door. Inside was the room of a busy, creative woman, with books and papers stacked on chairs, tables, the floor. She cleared a long table underneath a window, turned on a light, and unrolled a large map of the city overlaid with a grid. In each square were a number of small green circles with names in English, Latin, and Malayalam alongside. Some had four names, the fourth being Sanskrit. Anita was mesmerized.

"Oh, Chandra! This is wonderful."

"It is wonderful, is it not?" Chandra gazed fondly at the map. No grandchildren ever saw greater affection in a grandparent's eyes. "My husband cheered me on, but even he did not expect such success. Saving our trees is extremely important. This is our heritage. Without trees our city would be unlivable—no oxygen, no cooling breeze, no healthy nature, no place for birds or small animals, no seedlings. No history." She whispered, as though the last were especially shameful. "It does not bear thinking about." She grinned. "So I don't."

"It is truly an achievement." Anita gave herself over to admiring the detail of the report. She recognized certain trees in specific grids, appreciated the care in labeling, and remarked on the number of students and schools participating.

"Do you see what you are looking for?" Chandra asked.

Anita pulled out the list of botanical features she had catalogued from each photo, and handed it to Chandra. "Do these names mean anything?"

Chandra studied the list. She wasn't yet ready to give up and shake her head. Anita turned on her camera and punched to one of the photos on the suspect card.

"Take a look at this. Do you recognize the gate or the trees or the neighborhood in general?" Anita asked.

Chandra tapped the small screen. "There are three neighborhoods I have seen. I have gone there because they are having the old heritage tulip trees and others as well. The houses are old, and the people who live there like the older ways. They have enough money to keep them too. This photo might come from there."

"And where are these places?"

"Here and here and here." Chandra pressed her index finger on a square and tapped the map three times. "It is one of these squares behind that new hotel. The neighborhood is very exclusive and protected. I think you will find there the house you are seeking. The streets are broad even though they have little traffic. It was the way they were laid out almost one hundred years ago when only a few people had homes there. It was an old village."

Anita leaned over the map and studied the three areas. She scanned the trees listed in each square, comparing those with the ones on her list. "This one looks most promising," she said.

Chandra also compared Anita's list of trees with those noted on the grid. "They are very fine trees, and such a fine area, to have so many old ones still standing."

"Do you know anyone who lives in the area?" Anita asked hopefully. Chandra was one of those rare creatures whose genuine enthusiasm for life drew all sorts of people to her—she could befriend just about anyone without sacrificing her true character. If Anita had Chandra's personal connection, it could make a big difference, but instead the other woman shook her head slowly and gave Anita a look of deep regret.

"I wish I did." Chandra stepped back and again gave Anita a wildly enthusiastic smile. "The trees are beautiful. You will be transported as you walk among them. But to live there!" She sighed. "To live among such beauty is truly a blessing."

"They must have lots of visitors," Anita said. "People just driving by to enjoy the beauty and the breezes."

"Oh no, this is a very exclusive area, Anita. Even I with my credentials as a horticulturist would not dare go there without an invitation. It is most exclusive." With a furrowed brow, she handed the list of trees back to Anita.

The wide tree-lined street stretched out in front of the autorickshaw. The sidewalks were wide but unpaved, offering only soft feathery sand to the walker. Trees stood in the middle of the sidewalks, shedding leaves throughout the year. A cooling breeze drifted along the street.

Anita put on her best look of innocence and befuddlement, to persuade the autorickshaw driver to take his time driving through the neighborhood. At each gate or driveway, Anita ordered the driver to slow and then stop. He did so, and turned to look at her while she studied the image on her camera and compared it to the live one in front of her. She shook her head after the first gate. The driver grumbled and drove on.

The rain trees sagged under their leaves, and the copper pod dipped low, teasing the chipmunks scurrying below. A lone bougainvillea covering one part of an old compound wall was so thick with red flowers that half a dozen children could have hidden behind it. By another gate a red hibiscus tree dangled its blooms almost to the sidewalk, its thick dark leaves offering welcome shade. She ordered the driver to slow and halt, and once again she compared gate and photo. This was it, the house she was looking for. She ordered him to drive up to the gate when she saw a guard turn and stare at her.

"You are lost, isn't it?" The guard addressed the autorickshaw driver. He was being polite, Anita knew, because she was wearing enough gold bangles to buy a fleet of taxis and therefore her arrival in an autorickshaw was merely a quirk of personality rather than an indication of financial status.

Anita climbed out of the auto and stood back to stare up at the trees. She took a few steps in one direction and then the other, as though she was looking for something in particular up among the leafy branches. Anita read the brass nameplate on the wall. She looked up at the house, noted the construction of the roof and the parking area inside. She added these features to her list of items to match up with the photo on the card. So far, she had a one-to-one match for every feature. She tried to get a look at any cars parked inside, but all she saw was an old jeep, the kind that had gone out of fashion the minute the government opened the market to imports. The trees, of course, were the feature that mattered, and she had to admit she admired the owner's commitment to maintaining the copper pod tree, the rain trees, and others that required care as they aged.

"You are looking for some place, isn't it?" the guard said after watching Anita. He waggled his head and smiled, but Anita knew he was using the opportunity to get a good look at her and count her gold bangles. No one else was about, and that was the only difference between her view this day and the image on the card.

"This is a very fine old house," Anita said. "The owner is most fortunate. What is the name? Perhaps I know the family."

The guard's expression changed from curiosity to annoyance. "No one is living here, madam. Guards are present to deter hooligans. People are curious. They come to look. Security must be there."

"Very wise," Anita said. "The owners must live overseas then?"

The guard shrugged. "Only the bank officers know."

"The student volunteers have come and gone, making notes of all the heritage trees," Anita said. "We are undertaking random checks to ensure quality."

"Ah!" The guard nodded, his mouth turned down in a knowing frown. "Ah, students."

"But it seems they are most accurate in this area of the city," Anita continued. She strolled closer to the house, her eyes on the canopy overhead, until she reached the gate, which she intentionally bumped into. She pretended surprise and confusion and took the opportunity to grab hold of it. It only took a second to recognize that if anyone wanted to get inside, they would need a key. That meant Riyas had a key, or access to someone else who did.

"Now, the owner," Anita began, staring at the list of trees in her hand.

"Not known," the guard repeated.

"Ah, yes, you did say that." She frowned. "Who is caring for these heritage trees?"

The guard's eyebrows went up. "No one. I am seeing no one coming here for such business."

"Oh, but you must be seeing someone," Anita said. "The trees are well cared for, and the grounds as well." She peered through the gate. She pointed to the pots with thriving flowers while also noting two windows on the ground floor with half-open shutters. No one might be inside now, but someone was coming and going.

"I am not seeing," the guard said. "Perhaps at another time of day or night."

"Yes, perhaps." She turned away from the gate. She'd learned all she could here. "You must compliment the gardeners when they arrive. Caring for such old growth is difficult and they are doing a fine job. All the city benefits." She offered a fatuous smile and received a grim nod in return. Anita climbed into the auto and the guard saluted. With that he stepped away from the auto, signaling the driver to go, but not before Anita got another good look at the badge of a small private bank sewed over his breast pocket.

The driver zipped down the drive. He pulled onto the road and when Anita told him to pull over, he shook his head. He didn't stop until he pulled up in front of a café.

"Guard would have heard us." The driver turned around. "He was listening."

"You think he was suspicious?"

"I think he is one who is always suspicious."

"Why? Why do you think that, and why do you think he was suspicious?" Anita valued the opinions of people who worked every day below the radar. She could see he was thinking about what to tell her, and she did her best to be patient, not one of her strong suits. "Just tell me what you think."

"You do not know this place," he said.

Anita shook her head. "Should I?"

The auto driver shrugged. "People say the owner of the house is K.K. Varjen. He is very powerful. He owns much in the city and even outside in other parts of India. When he decides to build, no one stands in his way. It is said he got his start when his wife inherited a piece of land along the new highway farther north. He threatened to break it up and sell pieces of it to thousands of people if he couldn't negotiate what he wanted."

Anita winced. "That would have been quite a mess."

"He got what he wanted." The driver watched her. "Why are you going there?"

"I have seen at other times there are many people there," she said, avoiding his question. "But today there is no one."

Anita leaned back in her seat. Few cars or autos passed by, and occasionally she saw the dark-panted legs or the waving silk sari skirt of another autorickshaw passenger through the open sides of the auto.

"One more stop," Anita said, and gave him directions to a municipal office building in Vanchiyoor.

"Waiting." Anita climbed out. The driver didn't seem to mind and settled back in his seat. He was probably calculating his fare, Anita thought as she ran up the short flight of steps.

India government offices were notorious for their sloth, but they were also notorious for confounding some applicants with their celerity in accomplishing certain feats. Anita entered prepared to wait, fill out forms, redo forms, prod, cajole, and shut her eyes in frustration while she waited and the auto driver grew richer. But instead, she spent half an hour sitting on an uncomfortable wooden bench and then another half hour staring down at a book of deeds.

Mr. K. K. Varjen's name did not appear anywhere on the deed to the property graced with some of the city's finest heritage trees. Suryanivas, House of the Sun, so shaded that

Surya rarely had a chance to drape his golden beauty over the tiles, belonged to one M. Akhil Baseer. After looking at a few more books of records, Anita found Mr. Baseer listed as the owner of another home only a mile or so away. She wrote down the address and headed back to the autorickshaw.

The address wasn't difficult to find. Mr. Baseer lived on a small lane in Thycaud. The auto sputtered up the hill, turned at the top, and turned again. The driver pointed to a narrow lane as yet unpaved. A goat wandered across from one house to another. Anita climbed out and started down the lane. When she reached Mr. Baseer's address she began taking photos of the goats. An old woman came to the compound wall and watched her, suspicion etched all over her face.

"Photos for tourists," Anita said, lowering the camera.

"Hmm." The old woman scowled at her, looking unconvinced. "No goats in the West?"

"Not in the streets."

"Ahh." She twitched her eyebrows, as if to say there is no accounting for foreigners.

"You live here?" Anita nodded to the house. "My family has a worker who lives here in this neighborhood." She made up the name of a family of several brothers who painted Hotel Delite one summer several years ago, and waited for a reaction.

"Not here," the old woman said, pulling her mouth down. "Not here."

"Baseer was their name."

"No, no." She shook her head vehemently. "This house is Baseer, but no brothers living here, no painters here. Wrong street."

"Oh!" Anita put on her best expression of confusion and scanned the neighborhood, as if the intended house were there, just out of sight, perhaps hiding from her. "I was sure the Baseers lived here."

"We are Baseers," the old woman said angrily. "But no painters."

At that moment an old man wobbled to the door, his white mundu and white vest well worn with age. He seemed to see nothing of interest and turned around and went back inside. Anita heard a television grow louder and a chair scrape along the concrete floor.

"Husband?" Anita said. The old woman nodded. Anita noted the new tile roof, a good tile roof, on a house that looked like it might collapse in the next strong rain before the tiles had a chance to grow black with mold. But the old woman wore no jewelry, not even a nose ring or toe rings. Anita offered another smile and backed away, taking a few photos as she went, including one of the Baseer house after the old woman turned her back.

"Wrong house?" the driver said when she climbed back into the autorickshaw.

Anita shook her head. "Do you know what *benaami* is?" she asked.

"Illegal." The driver gave her a reassessing look. The practice of hiding property behind fake owners, called *benaami,* had been illegal for some time, but that didn't stop people with huge amounts of money from using it to protect themselves. The straw owner got forgiveness on a loan, perhaps a new television, or maybe even a chance to live a few more years. It hardly mattered. Few straw owners were willing to risk taking the case to court, revealing their participation in a *benaami* transaction and asserting the right of full ownership. The law was written to protect them, but few had the courage to take advantage of it. Mr. Baseer was certainly a case in point.

Anita glanced back at the narrow lane and the crumbling compound wall. Mr. Varjen had no fear that the teetering old man Mr. Baseer would try to claim Suryanivas as his own. He wasn't even strong enough to push open the gate.

CHAPTER 22

Anita returned to the hotel and went straight to her flat. She didn't stop to say hello to Ravi, on the registration desk, or Sanj, who was pacing the parking area and looking grim. Nor did she tell Auntie Meena she was back. Anita had spent the long drive out from the city absorbing the calamity that could at any moment overtake Auntie Meena and Hotel Delite. Anita wouldn't even know who to go after to fight back—the lender had insulated himself well. And then there was Nisha's situation.

Anita cleared off her desk and set out the purple mobile and the found card. Next she spread out the photos she had printed from it. After staring at the three piles, she popped the card back into the camera and deleted the two photos that included Auntie Meena. She also removed the same photos from the wall where she had posted them to study more easily. She knew what the new technology was capable of. She had once deleted an entire card, over one hundred shots, inadvertently. Once back in her flat, she'd searched the Internet for a solution, found a software package, and retrieved her photos. But she was able to do this only because she hadn't added or deleted any more photos.

Now she wanted to be certain no one could recover the photos of Auntie Meena or any she had taken that might identify her as the photographer. She sighted her camera and began taking shots of the blank wall, well over four dozen, and then deleted them. The photos of Auntie Meena were now unrecoverable.

Anita left the remaining photos on the card untouched. The faces were blurry, and almost indistinguishable one from the other. No one would be able to identify anything more than the guard, who was ever present, Riyas Patel, and the plaque on the compound wall. If anyone who knew the other men looked at the shots, he (or she) might be able to identify them, but on her own Anita didn't see enough clear features to think she could identify anyone. If anyone else wanted to find the house, even with the house name, Anita concluded, they'd have to know about the heritage tree grid or drive up and down every wide street in Trivandrum. Anita popped out the card and put it back on the desk. Once again she stared at three piles.

Sunlight glinted on the card and the mobile, and a light breeze lifted the corner of one of the photos. These were her bargaining chips, she thought, these flimsy pieces of paper and bits of cheap plastic and metal. They hardly seemed worth the price of a paltry meal let alone a life or a hotel. But to her and, she hoped, to two other men, these were worth lives, walking breathing people. She felt the first rush of adrenalin-fueled excitement. She was betting her life too. If she chose one of the items to offer to Dipak or Riyas, and it was the wrong one, she had no way out, no other option to tempt the man and rescue herself.

The purple mobile held the names of other victims, other men and women carrying excruciating loans that were both illegal and onerous. If she gave the mobile to Dipak, he would get nothing out of it but more victims, and the people whose numbers were listed in it would continue to be haunted. If she gave the mobile to Riyas, who had originally lost it and who seemed willing to take big risks to get it back, she might be doing nothing more than assuring his position with his boss, who might or might not be the man whose name was on the document or the man behind the loans, K.K. Varjen. Anita could feel her heart pounding.

Anita turned her attention to the photographs. Anyone could take a photograph of an old unoccupied mansion and pass it off as the property of a moneylender. There was no one to say otherwise. Even the guard didn't know whose property he was protecting.

She began to wiggle the corner of the photograph on the left, where Riyas Patel smiled as he extended his hand. She wondered how much money was concealed in the folded newspaper. She had to admit, the lender's boldness paid off. The true owner of the property, if found, could easily claim he had nothing to do with what went on outside his gate, and it looked like nothing went on except a few supplicants sharing a newspaper. Nothing illegal there.

Anita dropped her head into her hands and shut her eyes. What did Dipak want more than anything? What was worth Nisha's life? And what did Riyas want more than anything? Did he want the same thing as his boss? And was Varjen, the document signer, truly his boss? Was there any chance Riyas was an independent player? Did he have another job with Varjen while he ran his own moneylending business on the side?

"I'm getting a headache," she said. "I can't even think clearly anymore." But she knew one thing for sure—she couldn't delay. Today was Friday. Nisha had disappeared on Sunday night, after Panju died. How long would Dipak hold her before he decided to use her to send a message to the rest of the village?

Dipak and Riyas didn't get where they were today by standing on the sidelines and thinking things over in a leisurely manner, and she couldn't sit here waiting for them to make their next move. They were cobras who knew when to strike, stalkers who knew the habits of their prey. She had to move or she would be that next prey.

Anita pushed her chair back and stood up so quickly her chair almost fell over. She tidied up her desk and slipped the photographs into an envelope. She called the hotel desk and asked Ravi to send Brij to her. As she stood at the door, she had the awful feeling her home might not be the same on her return.

In the back of her mind Anita knew she must look slightly ridiculous, driving along in the hotel car with Brij sitting in the back seat. He didn't sit unobtrusively, modestly in the corner of the right or left side, but instead sat in the dead center, bolt upright, as though he were giving darshan to the teeming multitudes, except that he was peering out the window with undisguised curiosity and the holy men who offered darshan were steely faced and somber. She had rented a car and refused Joseph's offer to drive, which meant Brij, who otherwise would have sat in the front seat with Joseph, was relegated to the back seat while Anita drove.

Panju's family village lay in a small cleft of the rising western Ghats, a sheltered valley where farmers had struggled for years to make their fields pay, and where just as they got on their feet, the monsoon grew selfish and took its rain elsewhere, only coming back when it was too late to save the farmers from heartbreak. In less than an hour Anita felt the road rise without leveling, twist without straightening, and she knew they were close to the village.

"Look, Amma! Tea shop." Brij leaned over the seat and pointed to the little clearing up ahead. "The village must be near."

"I must find Tajji's farm without delay, Brij." She handed him a few rupees, and he clambered out of the car. Anita picked up a fan from the front seat and began waving it. This produced a rough hot breeze that did nothing but remind her of how hot she was, and she eventually gave it up. When a car sped by, she turned her head to avoid the sand it churned up and quickly raised her window.

"Fresh lime soda. I watched him make it." Brij handed the glass in through the open window. Anita thanked him and sipped it. To her pleasant surprise, it was quite good.

"Finish up, Brij. We have to find the farm. I think there is a post office up ahead at the cross roads." She started the engine.

"It is only there, over the rise, down the road on the left. Then along to the pond, and just after that." Brij climbed into the back seat as Anita turned around to stare at him.

"You asked?"

"We are going there, isn't it?"

"But now everyone knows we are going there."

"They are knowing before I am asking."

Anita was torn between anger at Brij's lack of discretion and concern that all her movements were known before she made them. If she had underestimated Dipak or overestimated her bargaining chips, she was in trouble.

"The tea wallah is saying we must have come for the dead farmer, isn't it? No other family members have come, so we must be the family."

"Oh." Anita leaned back and thought about this. She had taken the trouble of renting a car that didn't have a tourist license number painted on the fender, or a hotel logo painted on the doors. She should have known that villagers would expect her to have some identity, and if they didn't see it announced, they would fill in the gaps for themselves. "And what did you say?"

"I am poor cousin come to see the house." He leaned forward. "I told him I owe you money and you want the house." When he saw the look on Anita's face, he grew pale. "This is a bad lie? I'm sorry."

"He might think I am another moneylender," Anita said, feeling a sudden chill. But after a moment she thought this might give her more leverage, of a different sort. She turned her attention to Brij's directions.

Anita drove down into the village, following the directions until they came to the pond, once attached to a temple and now a crumbling pool with stagnant water. The road opened to a view of paddy fields spreading out into the distance and a hillside covered with thick growth. Half a mile down on the left was a small farmhouse. The road curved off to the left, disappeared into the jungle, and reappeared on the other side of the valley. After they passed the pond, there would be no one in sight. Anita could easily, too easily, imagine how a man could be left to die out here and no one might know for hours, even days.

Anita parked and climbed out of the car. She stood by the door, waiting for someone to come around the corner of the house, listening for the sound of farmers and villagers in the distance, straining for the smell of farm animals—the cows and goats and chickens that usually went with the same paddy fields. But there was nothing. It reminded her of a scene from a war movie, where everyone abandons the village before the advancing army arrives. Well, she and Brij had arrived and there was no one, no creature of any sort, to meet them, not even a curious child.

The small house sat on a gentle rise with the forest growing up close behind it. She caught sight of a cardamom bush, a pepper bush, the expected mango tree grown tall and full, something old that had been left. Someone had replaced a few of the roof tiles, so the blackened ones were punctuated by a few bright orange ones, the tiles themselves a sign of an earlier period of prosperity. Across the front of the veranda, hanging just above the main door and spreading out on either side were

203

a number of framed portraits of the gods—Vishnu, Rama and Sita, Krishna, and others. But they looked neglected, and most of them had fallen askew, hanging crazily from their hooks, the glass cracked, the thin wooden frames moldy and damaged. The only garland hung dried and brown from the main image over the door, a few of its dead blossoms lying flat on the doormat.

Anita walked around the house to the back. She realized she was giving it a wider margin than she had out front, perhaps afraid of what might suddenly jump out at her. Brij followed along closely behind—she could see him out of the corner of her eye, watching the house, watching her. She scanned the woods. Had she seen a flash of color? Had she seen someone duck behind a tree? She gave herself a good shake; she was frightening herself. Time to stop it.

The back veranda was broad and empty—the pots and other implements of a working household were nowhere to be seen, a few rags hanging from pegs high up in the eaves.

"Empty," Brij said, breaking the stillness. He sounded alien, out of place, and Anita felt they had invaded a world they weren't part of. She was trespassing and anyone could drive them off. But he was right—the place was empty.

Anita went up the steps to the veranda and rattled the back door. The lock held. She peered between the shutters—they were the old windows, with wooden bars to keep out animals and birds (and the occasional thief) and shutters on the inside that could be closed in the cold season, or when the house would be empty for some time. Anita rummaged in her cloth bag for a pen and slipped it between the shutters, looking for a latch to release. Then Brij took over and in a few seconds one shutter fell open. He pulled on the bars, but they held. He was quicker with the next pair of shutters and worked on the wooden bars until they loosened and gave way. He pulled them out and helped Anita climb in.

"What are we looking for?" Brij said when he landed on the floor beside her.

"I don't know." She looked around, noting the paucity of furnishings. The house had only two rooms, one at the front and one at the back.

Anita believed that any occupied house or room took on the feel, the character, of its resident, that you could sense what sort of person lived there. It wasn't the choice of furnishings, or art or books or the lack of them; it wasn't the quality of the materials or the quantity. It was something else entirely—a residue of character, the same thing that left you feeling better or worse after an encounter with a particular person. She walked through the house, trying to get a feel for the family that had lived here. She knew and liked Nisha, and because of that she had assumed she would like her husband, Panju. And she had, the few times she had encountered him. But she had not known him well, and she had been shamefully inattentive every time.

The house was a typical village home, a dearth of furniture—one chair, a table, and a simple wooden bed frame in the front room—and images of deities and ancestors on the walls. A few books sat in a pile in a corner of the front room. Anita picked up the top book and read the title—a Marxian title from a local political party. A page from an old ration book served as a bookmark. She dropped the book onto the pile, feeling the sense of helplessness that must have overwhelmed Girjan during the days before his death.

In another corner sat an old crate, with a few items tidily arranged—two plaid lungis neatly folded and stacked; two vests, worn but clean. In the corner of the room stood a thin, well-worn sleeping mat rolled up and leaning against the wall; on a stool sat a flat iron pan for cooking, along with an aluminum plate and a steel cup with a flat-bottomed bowl as a saucer. Anita looked up and saw a cloth bag hanging from a rafter, which she suspected contained a few provisions, perhaps rice and dhal and some vegetables. This was the final proof that someone was living here. Tajji? Was this where he had disappeared to?

Light fell through the cracks in the shutters and she peered out at the paddy fields. What must it have been like for Girjan to struggle day after day to bring in a crop that would give him enough to live on and repay his debts, only to have his payment turned down for a demand that must have been anathema to him? And then to lie dying by his fields, unable to crawl to safety, to stop the bleeding to save himself. She only hoped he had been in shock, unable to feel the torture his body was going through. And then there was Tajji. What must it have been like for him to find his father and not be able to save him? Anita pushed the thought away.

She took a deep breath and straightened up. She opened her mouth to speak but before even a sound came out Brij waved her to silence and pointed. She turned again to the shuttered windows. She looked through the crack and studied the landscape, but when she saw nothing but what she expected, she turned back to Brij. Again, with a fervor and anxiety she hadn't seen in him before, he clapped his hands over his mouth and motioned with his head to the window. Once again she peered through the cracks, running her glance slowly over the lane, the fields, the jungle. She saw nothing.

"You are overexciting yourself, Brij."

"No, Amma." He peered through a corner of the window. "There. A yellow lungi."

"Just a flower. Here is very beautiful."

"No, Amma. Not a flower."

Anita was growing exasperated. "If there is something there, Brij, it is only a farmer passing by on the way to his fields."

Anita learned early on from her mother that to manage

servants one often had to exhibit a confidence one did not feel, or lose control forever; now was one of those times. "It's just another villager, Brij, probably someone who was asked to guard the house and does not want to confront a stranger unless forced to."

But Brij would have none of it. He kept his hand clapped over his mouth and shook his head, his eyes wide with fear. Anita turned to look over the room one more time. She refused to consider—at least aloud—that it could be one of Dipak's men come to watch them. The mere thought of coming face to face with Dipak before she was ready sent a flood of adrenalin through her

"Well, I think we've seen enough. Come along." Her voice was loud and commanding, and Brij hustled to obey. She climbed out the window and waited while Brij closed the shutters and reinstalled the wooden bars. She walked around to the front. Before she could reach her car, however, a man emerged from the woods in a blue and green plaid lungi.

"What are you doing?" Anita listened to the sound of her own voice, imperious and arrogant.

The man let his hands hang loosely at his sides. "You are seeking to buy property?"

A smile of relief spread over Anita's face. Really, how could she have been so suspicious? He was just another village farmer.

CHAPTER 23

"I am interested in the house," Anita said. The man had emerged from the trees and walked toward her car so casually that she was at once disarmed. "You know the family?"

The man smiled. His expression made her feel like she was under a microscope but not uncomfortable. "Did you find anything inside?" he asked.

Anita glanced back at the house, gathering her thoughts. He'd been watching them for some time, it seemed. "Nothing of value. Someone is living there, I think."

"You saw evidence of this?"

"We did. A bedroll, some items for daily use." She wasn't reluctant to tell him that. "You must already know this. Everyone here must know if someone has come into the village. Villagers are aware of their surroundings, isn't it?"

Now it was the man's turn to look up at the house. He was of average height, with the usual build of one who worked in the fields or climbed coconut palms—all muscle. He wore no shirt, only the clean and recently pressed lungi. He wore a thin string bracelet on his left wrist and another on his right, but no watch. His mustache was trimmed short, his hair neatly combed, his face worthy of a Rajput painting. He reached for the fold of his lungi and slipped his hand along the edge of the fabric, pulling up the hem and flapping both corners to create a breeze. He turned back to her with a sad smile.

"The family is beset by tragedy," he said. "Each one, Girjan and his father, then Panju, and now the son has fallen into the clutches of the moneylender of this area." It seemed everyone knew about the moneylender's demand and the family's descent into misery, a state even worse than the usual dire poverty. "Do you know about this?"

Anita nodded. She had the sense he was trying to tell her something, or perhaps deciding if he would. He seemed enveloped in a calm that set him apart from the usual bustle of village life.

"I have met the family." She paused. "They are dead, I understand."

"Not all of them."

"You mean the son, Tajji."

"He has come to try to save his land," the man said.

"Is that what you meant when you included Girjan's son as one who has also fallen into the hands of the moneylender?" Anita studied the man and his steady gaze. He was different from what she expected of a villager. He didn't seem to fit. "I have met him," she said.

"I have heard he has returned to live here, and follow in his father's footsteps."

"He seems much too young to manage alone."

"He is in his teens only," the man said. He settled his gaze on her, and she wondered how long they would avoid saying the obvious.

"I think he means to avenge his father's death," Anita said.

"He might do better to bide his time."

"I believe he feels a sense of urgency," Anita said. She was no longer waiting for him to share what she suspected he knew, to decide she was acceptable and worth helping. She had a task ahead of her, and he was not part of it.

"Because of the moneylender?" The man tipped his head to one side.

Anita shook her head. She started to turn to look at the house again. "I think his uncle's death has bolstered his desire for revenge. And he knows they have taken Nisha, Panju's widow, hostage for the debt."

"Ah! He is driven by a sense of justice." The man smiled.

"She is not responsible for this debt." Anita closed her eyes to calm herself. She had not meant to speak so passionately.

"Not responsible?" He gazed up at the house. "You may think so. I may think so. The entire village may think so. But if Dipak does not think so, how is it important what anyone else thinks?" He held the edges of the lungi again, like a man afraid to let the hem touch the dirt, and turned to walk down the little hill.

"Do you know where can I find Nisha?" Anita asked, taking a step after him.

At the bottom of the slope he turned around to face her, folding his draping lungi again, so that his sarong-like dress fell only to his knees. His lungi was still clean, and it made her wonder who he was, what sort of villager he was.

"The woman Nisha?" His eyes were kindly, set into the sharp planes of his face.

"Does anyone know where she is? I am thinking she is with Dipak. We have had a warning," Anita said.

"A warning?" The man lifted an eyebrow. "So unlike him," he murmured. "Dipak is not patient."

Anita thought about the finger emerging as Mrs. Eappen unfolded the handkerchief. She must be running out of time if the moneylender was not one to give warnings.

"But she is there, with Dipak, yes? He is holding her, yes?" Anita asked.

The man lowered his eyes in acknowledgment. "Do you come to rescue her?"

The minute he said the words, Anita could hear how ridiculous they sounded, even though there was no mockery in his voice. As she stood before this cagey man, she could see how she must look. She was no more than a young woman traveling with a servant and looking for an employee; she looked out of her element and unprepared for danger. But his words made her bristle. "I have something he wants."

The villager nodded, considering her reply. "You have brought about the death of Dipak's rival?" He waited. "Ah, I see by your expression you have not."

"I have something equally valuable to him because it will ensure his safety." Anita watched, wondering just how much she dare tell this man. "Do you know where his house is?"

"I do." He studied her. His eyes flickered, and she could see his mind moving from one idea to the next.

"Well?" She was growing impatient. "If you help, I am grateful, but otherwise I must be on my way."

That made him smile, and he said, "I will take you some of the way and you will find it easily after that." He took a few steps along the road toward her car. "I walk, you drive. Not far." He turned around once more. "He is a wily man, this moneylender. But smart also. Do not underestimate him." He folded up his lungi again.

She climbed into the car, thinking she had come this far and would not be deterred. Only as she started the engine did she realize that Brij had disappeared. She called out the window for him but he seemed to have vanished into the jungle. On the lane ahead the villager was taking a turn around the bend. Anita slapped the steering wheel, angry with Brij for going off on his own. But she couldn't wait for him. She put the car in gear and drove after the villager. She'd have to come back for Brij later.

Anita followed several feet behind the man, swinging the steering wheel to avoid ruts, feeling the wheel bounce back and forth in her hands. When he came to a fork in the road, he stepped to the left and waved to Anita, pointing to the other road. She drew up beside him.

"That road is going there. Driving half a kilometer and you are almost there. You must park and then you are walking another ten meters or so. You will not be lost. Going." He turned and walked on down the lane, not waiting to see if Anita had any questions. He seemed uncurious, which surprised her because she expected the opposite. Perhaps his attitude was the result of living in an area with someone like Dipak. Perhaps villagers just learned to keep their curiosity to themselves, learning what they needed to know in discreet ways. Anita drove on and parked when the lane narrowed to a small track unfit for cars.

A pye-dog came onto the road from a narrow wooded path up ahead, stopped to gaze at her, then continued on across the road. Its teats hung low and full to the ground, its tail angled oddly as though broken, an ear torn away, its eyes assessing her and finding nothing promising. The dog picked up its pace and dove into the bushes on the other side, rummaging among piles of trash. She must be nearing the house.

The dog picked up its head. Anita stopped. Was the dog going to turn on her, attack her? She watched. The dog swung its head about but looked in the opposite direction, lifted one leg and kept peering deeper into the forest. Apparently satisfied, it relaxed and went on rummaging while Anita passed by.

She walked on, and came to a bend in the lane. As the trees and shrubs receded, she saw a small house perched on a low rise. The road continued on, making a turn around the house and winding down the hill. In a nearby ditch were a few cigarette butts, the ends of beedis, a few plastic bags caught among brush.

A cascade of pebbles tumbled down the slope to her left, but when she glanced up she saw no one—no dog, no human, no cow or goat meandering or grazing. *Someone is there,* she thought, *hidden but there, watching me.* She felt the sweat trickling down her back.

The house appeared to be empty, silent and perhaps abandoned. An old gateway, about ready to tumble to the ground in a strong wind, stood in stately isolation at the edge of the property. In the yard, to the right, was a small hut with a few plates and pots stored along an outer wall. Three chairs lined the front veranda, but the front door was closed and padlocked. Above the door, in the place of honor, hung the framed photographic portrait of an austere-looking man in a suit, the homeowner's father or grandfather, Anita guessed. She looked for the framed images of Shiva or Vishnu spreading out along the wall beneath the eaves, but there were none. *Odd,* she thought. Even in the most modern homes the deities were never missing.

At the sound of rustling, Anita took a quick step back and scanned the property once again. A man emerged from the side of the house.

"*Namaskaram.*" Anita greeted him. "I'm looking for someone. I sought information from a villager and he sent me here."

"Who sent you here?" The man lifted his eyebrow.

"I don't know the man's name. I am not of this place."

"Whoever you are looking for, they will not be here." He paused. "Go on. Go." He jerked his head to the side, sending her away. She was cemented to the spot, like a house post waiting for the monsoon wind. His rudeness was unusual in a village greeting, but she ignored it.

"It is Nisha I want." In that moment she felt the weight of her undertaking. She had no weapons, no men to threaten or fight on her behalf. She must have been insane to come here, but she didn't feel insane. When she looked at this house in front of her, she saw only Hotel Delite and Nisha's little bungalow. She had no room for second thoughts, only alertness. She pushed aside fear. Everything she said or did had to be delicately calibrated. She'd put her own life into the balance.

"Wait." The man walked around to the back and Anita waited. In a few minutes he returned. He waved to her to go around the other side. She took a path running between the house and a little hut, pausing for a moment as she passed, caught by a smell, or was it a sound? She hesitated for half a step, but the man noticed and snapped at her. She walked on.

The back yard was like any other in a village home—the broad veranda filled with the pots and pans of kitchen work, large colored plastic buckets filled with clothes or dishes to be washed, bags of vegetables or herbs hanging from the rafters, gardening tools leaning up against the back wall. But here there was only one chair, and only one man sitting. Two men leaned against the veranda posts as they watched her approach; they were joined by the man who had met her at the front.

A man well into middle age rolled a cigarette along his fingers till it reached his knuckles, when he let it roll down his loosely held fingers and caught it. He twirled it among his fingers, back and forth. He was entranced by this for several minutes, until all at once he put the cigarette to his lips and looked down at her standing there.

"I don't have visitors coming to this house. It is a retreat for me. No visitors." He offered her a thin smile, as if to apologize for his rudeness.

"You are Dipak, a businessman of this place?" Anita asked.

He nodded.

"I am looking for a woman named Nisha. That is why I have come here." Anita paused. "She works for me and she has gone missing. I think she is here and I want to take her home."

The man blinked twice. His head jerked as though he had a spasm and he leaned forward. She took note of his reactions, filing them away. She needed to understand everything about him—every twitch, every blink, every smile or sneer. He paused to study his stubby fingers.

"Why would she be here?" Dipak asked. "I have a cook, a maidservant, anyone I want to care for my household. Why would I want another?"

"She is Panju's wife," Anita said.

His eyebrows went up in a semblance of surprise and confusion. "Panju?" He looked to his minions. "Do I know a Panju?" The men began to babble but he shut them up with a flick of his fingers. "Ah, that Panju."

She kept her eyes on him, unimpressed with his little mime.

"And what is he to me?"

"He owes you money," Anita said. "His father took out a large loan."

"Ah." Dipak nodded. "Yes, of course. Girjan's younger brother. I am remembering him." He lowered his chin and glowered at her with a smirk spreading across his face. "I do believe the debt is unpaid."

"It is not her debt," Anita said. "She and Panju were not married when the father took the loan from you."

"Is that so?" Dipak's eyebrows went up once again and he shifted in his chair to better see his minions. "Did you know that?" Once again the men began to babble and once again Dipak silenced them with a wave of his hand. "And you think this Nisha is here, to pay the debt?"

"I do."

"And you want me to give her to you?" This time only one eyebrow went up, thick and black.

"I do."

"And why should anyone give her to you?"

"She is not useful to anyone else."

"Perhaps she is useful to me."

Anita smiled. "If she were useful to you, the deed would

already be done. The debt would be repaid and you would have no further interest in her." For a second she thought she saw a flash of something—what? anger? surprise at her temerity?—in his eyes before he looked down, reached into his pocket and drew out a matchbox.

"Do you smoke cigarettes? Surely not beedis."

"I am not a smoker of anything."

"No, of course not." He struck the match and watched the flame shoot upward, then shrink. He lit the cigarette and tossed the match to the floor. An old woman leaned out the back door and swept it up in her hand. "Do you think I cannot persuade others to do my bidding?"

"Some, yes. Not everyone."

"Not everyone?" He drew on his cigarette and exhaled, watching the smoke travel across the veranda and sink in the heavy air. The wind had turned and felt ready, ready to bring the monsoon, ready to carry the heat away, ready to draw in rain to kiss and soothe the parched, starving ground. "Do you not think people should pay their debts?"

"What is her debt? She is a widow. She knew nothing about her husband's family's debt. Why should she pay it?"

"Not a family debt?"

"Not worth her life."

"Hmm."

"Think of her life as her *stridhana,* her woman's wealth taken with her into marriage. Her life will always be her own," Anita said.

He smiled at that. "Hmm, very fanciful, using the old customs in that way, but I enjoy a little joke. And you think I hold her here for this debt?"

"I have heard many rumors."

"Ah, rumors." He smiled, his expression growing thoughtful. "Did rumors tell you I cared about you and your opinion?"

She saw his eyes flicker, the ear twitch, and calculated her first lie. "Your interest in a camera told me that."

"Ah, yes. The camera. Yours?"

Anita glanced at the men inching closer to her on either side. Dipak had taken the bait, but he could still catch her out. Her lies were getting complicated. What would give her away? Did her ear twitch? Did she blush uncontrollably when she lied? "How much money is it? How much is Nisha's husband's family's debt?"

"I do not want money. I have plenty of money." He dropped the cigarette to the floor and crushed it with his foot. The man standing nearest winced, glancing quickly up at him. A hand reached out and swept it up, including the little shreds of tobacco.

"What is it you do want?" Anita pretended to struggle with his chameleon-like changes in mood.

"What does anyone want? What do you want?"

"I am certain we are not wanting the same thing," Anita said.

"Many people try to divine what I want and offer me many things," Dipak said. "Panju offered me a mobile." He smiled. "Did you know that?"

"My offer is better," Anita said.

"Can you be so sure?"

"The phone number of a debtor is nothing special, but the place where that debt resides is." Anita adjusted her dupatta, as though there was nothing more important at that moment than her wardrobe. He watched her, and when she glanced up she had the sense she was meeting a sulky child, a little boy who had been told he couldn't have whatever he wanted just because it was his birthday.

"You come here thinking we are different. I know your type. You are a person of standing. You are thinking we do not think alike. But yet you know why I was interested in you and your camera. You come with an offer." A man standing just behind her shifted enough for her to hear the movement of his sandal on the ground, a scuffing too soft to hear in normal circumstances but at this moment it seemed loud. "We are alike, isn't it?" He lurched forward. "Detestable, isn't it? To think you are like me." The spittle gathered in the corners of his mouth, his eyes glistened. Anita stiffened and tried to hide her contempt.

He was right, of course, in part. She could be business-like and hard-nosed when necessary, but she had something he would never have—the unshakable self-confidence that came from being born into a certain class. It was like an accent. You could hide it, but it never went away. He knew that, and groped for a way to bring her down, pulling on her offer to negotiate someone's life. But even he knew that in the end what she had he could never have, no matter how much money he made. She lowered her eyes and smiled, ready to continue.

Dipak leaned back and began to laugh, a little chuckle at first, then a deeper belly laugh, until he was laughing so hard that he had trouble catching his breath. He gasped and waved away his minions, until gradually his heaving and hooting subsided. "No, you don't want what I want." He wiped the tears from his eyes and blew his nose on the end of his red plaid lungi. "The only people who say they don't want power are those who already have it. Or think they do," he added as if to himself. His eyes clouded and he leaned forward in his chair. "I know this. I can see it in you. What other sort would come here so bold? You think I can't do any harm to you because you are known in Trivandrum as a good honest citizen? I wouldn't dare harm you for fear of what it might bring down upon me. Isn't it?" He paused, smiling.

"Perhaps," Anita said. "You may be right. I've never been truly afraid. I don't know what it's like. I've never known real danger." She waited while he enjoyed a moment of satisfaction.

"But you too like to feel safe. Perhaps that's as important as the debt."

He leaned back in his chair, a thoughtfulness creeping over a scowl, like a cloud moving over the shade of a tree and passing on. "For the sake of discussion, perhaps."

"Girjan borrowed money from someone who was new to this area," Anita said, "New competition for you." Anita paused, warning herself not to grow overconfident. His shoulders stiffened as he listened to her, but he didn't lift a hand to silence her. "But that man was only an agent. It wasn't his money that flowed into your valley."

All three minions stirred. Dipak lifted his hand to forewarn them, then suddenly, in a whisper, gave an order to the nearest one.

Chapter 24

A burly man gripped Nisha's upper arm and dragged her along the dirt. She flopped and twisted as she tried to get a purchase on the rough ground. He pulled her to the veranda and shoved her the last few feet. She lay in a torn and dirty heap, her face bruised and encrusted with dirt. He gave her a gratuitous kick as he stepped away. Anita rushed to her and knelt down to help. She wrapped her arms around Nisha, pulling the other woman to a kneeling position. Instinctively Anita looked up at Dipak and saw only a look of amusement in his eyes.

"She insulted me." He gazed out over the yard, apparently bored with the two women before him.

Anita offered comforting words as she smoothed Nisha's matted hair, touched her grimy fingers, testing for broken bones, wiped dirt from the other's face with her dupatta. Nisha's eyes were dark and bloodshot but her gaze from her one unswollen eye was steady. She seemed to offer a warning, but also reassurance and encouragement for Anita to go on with her plan. Anita blinked slowly to show she had understood. The man was dangerous. She didn't need to be reminded of that.

"So, why should I let you have her?" Dipak said.

Anita stood. She wouldn't talk to him on her knees. "She is no good to you, but what I have is. You want to be secure in your business here. And right now you have a formidable competitor, someone who is really, in this business, an enemy. And you don't know who he is."

Dipak's glance flickered to the men standing behind her. He leaned back in his chair and took another cigarette from his pack, tumbling it over his knuckles, watching it dance in the heat-crackling air.

Anita watched him amuse himself with his cigarette. Behind him loomed the back door, opening onto the dark inner rooms. Every now and then she caught a glimpse of the near invisible old woman whose hand removed matches from the veranda floor, or set out a glass of sweetened water, or simply waited to be of use. Anita wondered if she were a relative perhaps, an old woman who had no one else to care for her, or just the old woman who had once lived here and was grateful for some income, any income, for serving the man and his minions. Out of the corner of her eye, Anita caught a flash of color, light on a steel bowl, perhaps, or embroidery in the old woman's pallu. She felt Nisha's steady pressure against her leg, and turned again to Dipak.

"This is your only idea? To offer me a few photographs?" The moneylender rearranged himself in the chair and waved to his men to take a look at this pathetic creature, this woman come to save her friend. He laughed and the men roared along with him. "Could I not as easily take it from you?"

"I am not bringing it with me," Anita said when they had quieted down.

"Could I not force you to tell me where it is?"

"If I tell you, it would still not be available to you."

"Ah, this is cryptic. You are trying to be clever." He tipped his head back and closed his eyes.

"You want to remove your competition, but you don't know who he is. You know there is an agent, but you do not know there is a man behind him." Anita stood with her hand resting on the side of Nisha's head. She had him now, though he would be loath to admit it.

"Do you find it tiring to stand in the sun?" He leaned forward. "Hmm? I see the sweat. And her." He stuck out a foot and nudged her shoulder. "I could tie you in the sun for hours and days. You would die."

"And with me or Nisha would go the information that identifies your biggest threat."

His eyes flashed with anger. He didn't even try to conceal his feelings. He shifted in his chair. "All this talk of heat makes me thirsty." He paused. "Thirsty!" He shouted. The men started to speak but Dipak silenced them with a wave of his hand.

"How do I know you have this information as you say?" He swung one leg over the arm of his chair, swinging his foot. "How do I know?"

"Look at this." Anita pulled a fragment of a small photograph from her cloth bag and held it out to him. "You can see the agent you are so concerned about."

He nodded to the man standing closest to her, and he took the photo, studied it. She saw his shadow move and knew he had nodded to Dipak. Whatever question the moneylender had asked his minion by his look had been answered. He leaned back in his seat and crossed one leg over the other. As he did so an arm shot out and left a glass of cooling spiced water on the floor by his chair.

"I like you," Dipak said. "You are bold. You are showing courage in coming here. And you are not pleading and begging." He rolled his eyes and looked away. "Ah, you cannot know. So many of those who owe me they come and they beg and they whine. They can't pay this, they can't pay that. One has a broken leg, another has a sick mother, someone else has a drought. I listen. I soothe. But inside I am thinking, they are so pathetic. They are not even on the level with the animals. What animals beg? What animals make excuses, twisting themselves into knots to appeal?

"But you. You come with a proposition. You are a businessperson like me." He looked down at Nisha. "You offer me photographs from your camera for this one. Yes?"

"Yes." Anita's answer was firm, her hand still resting on Nisha's head. So far Nisha had only softly patted Anita's leg, as if in approval. She knew what the photographs were.

"You come with an offer. I like that. I like that." Dipak glared at the still form at Anita's feet. "She defied me. She was rude to me. I did not like that. What would happen if others did something like that? How am I to feel?"

"She is nothing to you, just an instrument," Anita said. "I offer you more than anyone in Girjan's family could bring you even if they followed all your instructions. I bring you knowledge." Anita had him and they both knew it. But Dipak had a game to play, and she would play it with him. The end was determined already; she'd let him have his fun.

"Yes, this is what you tell me. And you have shown me this." He nodded to the photograph still in the hands of one of his minions.

It was just a matter of time, Anita thought. He wanted to play with them, she understood that, and she would let him. They were almost home, she thought, almost home.

He stretched out in his chair. "You are showing courage. This should be rewarded. It is just a photograph from a camera. But I will take it."

Anita nodded as though sealing the deal. "And I will take Nisha."

He looked around him, as though hoping this annoying woman would just go away, but she was still there when he looked back. "Yes, you will take her. She is nothing but a nuisance for me. I am tired of her. She eats too much." He snapped his mouth shut and pouted. "My man will follow you to the city and you will give him the photographs." He leaned forward. "But if you try to trick me—"

"No trickery," Anita said. She spoke without fear, and she knew he understood that. This was a business deal, and he could trust her. "It is a fair trade, and when it is done you will never hear from me again, and I will never hear from you."

At the end of her little speech Anita hoped she hadn't gone too far. But once again, he smiled. He burst out laughing, pointing to her and Nisha and laughing. His minions laughed too before he silenced them. "I believe you. You are not complicated enough to cheat me. You are still naive." His face relaxed, and at that moment he looked like any other person she might meet on the street, pass a few words with in a shop, an unassuming man going about his business with no ugly secrets. "I believe you will keep your word." He stared at her another moment, as if imprinting his agreement on her body. "It is done." He nodded to the men behind her to confirm the order.

Anita reached down to gather up Nisha. The young woman got to her feet. She leaned heavily on Anita as they stepped away from the veranda, but Anita sensed her effort to walk on her own. They began the long and painful walk to the front of the house and to Anita's car.

Dipak seemed to take pleasure in watching them struggle, and settled back in his chair to enjoy the scene, but he quickly grew bored, even when Nisha stumbled. As Anita steadied her, she glanced back, barely turning her head, worried the man would change his mind, but he was no longer interested in them it seemed. He looked down at the glass of cool water as though just remembering he had asked for it. He swept it up in his hand. He held the glass up and tipped it, to let the liquid pour into his mouth. Abruptly the glass spilled its liquid on his shirt and he spewed out what was in his mouth. The liquid spattered his clothes and bare arms. He threw the glass to the veranda where it shattered, shards and liquid splashing on him, on the veranda, on Anita and Nisha.

Dipak spun out of his chair with a roar and charged into the kitchen shouting barely coherent curses. Startled, his minions looked at each other for a long moment, listening to the roaring, before starting for the steps. As they did so a burst of flame filled the doorway. The men jumped back.

Dipak fell through the opening onto the stone veranda. He struggled to his feet, almost lifted by the rising fire. Flames shot up from his clothes, his hair, his feet. The men tried to get near. One picked up handfuls of dirt and threw it on the flaming body but the dirt had little effect—if the fire was suffocated on one limb, it burst out on another. The men fell back and a moment later they melted into the jungle, disappearing among the trees.

The flames shot higher, into the roof. The woven palm leaves crackled and smoked, like mist rising from a lake in winter. In a moment the dry leaves exploded into flame. In the thundering, roaring noise Anita thought she heard the screams of the old woman. By the side of the house a figure fell out a window, then straightened up and skittered into the jungle. Right behind her came a figure in a pale yellow lungi. Tajji. Brij crashed out of the jungle, running straight at Anita and Nisha.

Dipak stumbled around the veranda, a column wrapped in a sheet of fire. Anita thought she heard him shouting but no, it was the flames. She reached out for him—her hands not her own, acting on an impulse from deep inside her—but the heat was too intense. Like a sudden gust of wind, the heat knocked her back. Flames roared through the roof above, the leaves crackling and shriveling almost instantly. Large fiery fragments flew into the air and floated away on the breeze.

The column of fire folded and twisted. Dipak stumbled from the veranda, collapsed onto the ground, and crawled a few inches. Could she hear him calling? The flames burned on and gradually abated as he rolled in the dirt. His men were gone, and Anita's pitiful handfuls of earth did no good. Her dupatta shriveled as she patted it over him. The flames died down. In the waning fire he began shaking, trembling, and shivering, twitching so hard his legs banged against the veranda steps; one twisted back on itself as though he had broken it. He choked and sputtered but didn't wail. He seemed to open his mouth, his teeth still white, and she peered into the red flesh of his throat. His fingers were blackened stubs; his face was a mask of cinders with two little white dots that saw nothing.

"Is he dead?" Tajji came up behind her and looked down at the dying man. Startled, Anita jumped away, then turned to look at him. He ignored her and stared down at the blackened form. Occasionally a groan emerged from the jerking body. The boy's voice was quiet, matter of fact.

"I . . . I don't . . . He must be—almost. Perhaps his heart is still beating." Anita crouched down, helpless to save him but listening for some sign. She wondered if the body was now twitching of its own accord, the soul that had once animated it gone, returned to the Atman.

"Is he dead?" Tajji asked again.

"Almost." Anita repeated. She looked up at the boy. "He had just agreed to let Nisha go in exchange for information. He was letting the debt go."

"I heard that," Tajji said without looking at her.

"You heard?" Anita struggled to understand what the boy said.

The boy stared at the charred body, his face hard and set, his head occasionally nodding in satisfaction. "It is done."

"What happened? It was something in the glass, wasn't it?"

Anita stared at the boy, who seemed not to understand what he had done. Or did he? "What was in the glass?"

"Kerosene." Tajji spoke without taking his eyes off the man dying. "He spit enough on himself to be his own match." He paused. "But I added more. He came into the kitchen to beat the old woman, as I knew he would. I threw a bucket of kerosene on him—and a match."

The fire crackled in the silence. Remnants of the roof and rafters shifted and collapsed into the now empty rooms. Sparks and cinders flew up. Whatever was inside would be burned to black ash.

"What about the old woman?" Anita said, looking in the direction in which the wizened creature had fled. "It is a miracle she didn't give you away."

With that Tajji turned to her, a look of wonder on his face. "Did you think she was loyal to him? She was as much a captive as Nisha. The old woman despised him."

"Oh, Tajji!" Nisha said, falling to her knees. She spoke so softly that Anita wasn't sure she'd heard her.

"The police will come," Anita said as she helped up Nisha. "The word is spreading even now. Villagers can see the house burning. People will be coming with water and sand."

Tajji gave no sign he heard her. He stared at the moneylender. He spat on the body.

Anita pulled Nisha farther away from the burning house. In the stillness of the day the fire undulated upward, straighter and straighter as though pulled by an unseen hand, shaped and reformed to reach high above, as though Agni, God of Fire, carried their prayers to the greatest heights. At the edge of the jungle the old woman knelt and stared at the house, then inched her way into the jungle again. Anita watched her go.

"We must leave here, Tajji," Anita said. "I must get help for Nisha."

Instead of following Anita, Tajji knelt down at the dying man's head. Smoke rose from the burning house, its few furnishings smoldering; occasionally something made of paper or dried reeds flared up, but most of the house had been reduced to pockets of flame slowly burning out. The house was gradually turning into a giant cinder. Anita looked back at Tajji one last time. Squatting barely three feet from the body of Dipak, oblivious to the flashes of heat still exploding from the house, Tajji watched the moneylender. He stared hard at the cindered body, waiting, waiting to be sure Dipak was dead. He watched every twitch and followed every robotic eye movement without a single flicker of feeling in his own eyes.

CHAPTER 25

Anita watched the two sleeping forms, Nisha and Theti, sprawled over the mattress, their arms and legs intertwined, feet dangling over the edge. The quiet breathing from the two was as peaceful as the color of peaches sitting in a bowl on the kitchen counter. Anita closed the door as quietly as she could and finished dressing in the sitting room. She had left her room to Nisha and the child, to give them at least a few hours of privacy and peace.

"It's not over," Nisha said when Anita ushered them into her bedroom.

"The police are not interested in us, Nisha." Anita offered an encouraging smile.

There was little to be done for a house in the countryside that bursts into flame. Nevertheless, Brij had run to the village for help, and the police had arrived at the burning house by the time Anita and Nisha reached the car. A truck carrying buckets of sand followed soon after. The constable inspected the house and the corpse in the back before returning to the two women.

"Cooking fires are very common," he said, looking back at the house. "No cook here?"

Anita shook her head. "She fled."

"What is happening?"

"Something upset him and he went inside. And the next thing we saw, he came to the door aflame." Anita shivered at the recollection. The body on the ground hardly seemed human

229

anymore, but she would never forget the vision of Dipak in the doorway.

"And you are alone?"

Anita nodded. "There were others, but they ran off."

"Ah!" The constable did not seem to find this surprising.

"And this one?" The constable nodded to Brij, who had hurried to help with the buckets of sand. All the while the constable watched him, his lips pursed, his eyes narrowing.

"He works for me. He wandered off into the jungle—he is not used to this area." Anita gave Brij a comforting nod. "He came running when he saw the flames."

The constable scowled, pulled his shoulders back, and took another turn around the house. The little hut that had been Nisha's prison had caught fire soon after the main house, and was now a little pile of cinders, along with disintegrated clay pots and melted plastic buckets.

"And how did it start?" the constable asked.

"I don't know." Anita lost count of the number of times she said this. The constable pretended to be confused, uncertain, but she wasn't deceived. He poked and prodded and nudged and scowled and frowned, and every time Anita said, "I don't know."

"Yes, kitchen fires are very great danger." He sighed heavily. "You are leaving your house address." Anita did so, and with a wave of his hand, they were dismissed.

"It's not over," Nisha said as she slid down in the front passenger seat. "He knows things and is not asking. But he will in the end."

"If you mean Tajji," Anita said. "I suppose the police will search him out and interrogate him. Some of Dipak's people might come forward. The word will spread. But there is nothing we can do for him now. He has made a desperate choice."

"That's not what I meant," Nisha said, laying her head back

and closing her eyes.

She must be exhausted, Anita thought. *She'll make more sense after she's rested.* She slammed the car door and started the engine. She was relieved to drive away from this nightmare and refused to look in the rearview mirror at the villagers scrambling around the burned-out house or the constable standing in the middle of the road watching the car disappear.

Early the following morning Anita took a quick peek at Nisha and Theti sleeping, then closed the door to her bedroom. She felt an enormous rush of relief. Only now could she admit to her deep inchoate fear that Nisha would not come out of her ordeal alive. But she had. And now she was reunited with her daughter. Anita rested her head against the door and allowed herself a moment of satisfaction and gratitude. Outside she could hear water pouring into a plastic bucket, the initial roar softening to the sound of a small waterfall. She heard a hose being dragged along the concrete as someone began the early-morning chore of watering the dozens of potted plants that would otherwise die in the tropical sun.

Anita finished dressing and made herself a cup of coffee. She found the newspaper at the front door and took it along with her coffee to the balcony. It wasn't yet six o'clock, the sky was only beginning to lighten, and the breeze floating in from the terrace carried the scent of jasmine. Someone had come to work with flowers in her hair. Anita smiled.

"Nisha!" Anita turned in surprise at the sound of bare feet on the concrete floor. "You should still be asleep."

"I wish I could, but I fear I have very little time."

Anita put down her coffee and motioned for Nisha to sit. "What do you mean?"

Nisha sank down on a chair and closed her eyes. "I must tell you what has happened." She took a deep breath and opened

231

her eyes. "The police will come soon to arrest me."

"Then you will tell them the truth," Anita said. Startled by Nisha's expression, she said, "Perhaps you should tell me what happened. You will have to tell the police."

Nisha smiled without warmth. "You don't understand. I can't tell them the truth."

Anita studied her. "It wasn't Dipak or Riyas who was responsible for your husband's death? I thought you hid Theti here because of threats against you and your family. No?"

Nisha shook her head. "No, it wasn't either of them. Dipak did threaten us, but he wasn't behind Panju's death."

Anita put down her coffee. In the back of her mind she had first assumed that Panju's death would be laid at the feet of Dipak. Later she concluded Riyas Patel was the murderer. But Nisha was telling her she was wrong. "You had better tell me, Nisha. Who was it? Who did kill Panju?" Anita winced at the pain in Nisha's eyes. "You must tell me. Only then can I know how to help."

"You cannot help, not this time."

"A man came to your home that night, the night Panju died." Anita waited. "I know there was a man who came. Who killed Panju?"

"I did." Nisha looked her straight in the eye, calm, soft-spoken, and repeated her words. "I did it. It was me."

"You're lying." Anita was too stunned to say anything else except what she believed. "There was someone else in the house that night, wasn't there?"

"Yes, that is true."

"Who was it?"

Nisha took a deep breath, ran her hands over her face, and closed her eyes. "It was the other moneylender's agent."

"Tell me the rest, Nisha."

"Panju found the agent's mobile. Well, Tajji found it and gave it to Panju. It was an accident. Panju arranged for the man to come to the house. He was setting a trap for him, gaining his trust, he told me." Nisha's face began to shine with sweat and Anita touched her hand, which was clammy, to calm her.

"Keep going," Anita said.

"The man came but he fell—tripped—in the dark and lost his mobile. He must not have realized it right away. But Tajji found it and gave it to Panju. An unexpected stroke of luck, Panju told me. He could use it."

"How was he going to use it?"

"He wasn't sure at first." Nisha began to shift in her seat, moving forward to the edge of the cushion, rubbing the palms of her hands together. "He had been tracking the new money-lender's agent to learn who he worked for."

"He took photos," Anita said. "I found the card. It was in my camera."

Nisha nodded. "I knew you would know something was wrong when you found it. Perhaps I shouldn't have done that, but I had nowhere else to turn. Panju told me Meena Amma had gone to the same lender because of him. I knew it would be trouble for her." She took a ragged breath. "He showed me the card and when he wasn't looking, I took it and left it with Nirmala. I told her to hide it if she couldn't get it to you. I told her Panju was in trouble."

"She put it in my camera." Anita turned toward the open balcony. Beyond was the Arabian Sea lightening to a rich blue beneath the last few ships of the fishing fleet on their way to port. "What did he mean to do with the mobile?"

"He told Dipak about it. It had phone numbers on it, Panju told him. It excited Dipak. He thought he was getting information on the new moneylender." Nisha stared at her hands.

"That's why Dipak told me about it when I offered the camera," Anita said.

Nisha nodded. "He was going to trick them both, Panju said, both moneylenders. His anger was white hot—I could not make sense with him. He was terrifying—he was a stranger to me."

"So the man came back the next night, and killed him for it?"

"No, no! Panju never told him he had the mobile." Nisha looked shocked. "He was going to use it as bait, but I took it and hid it. Panju was furious. But I would not tell him where it was. I thought if I could stop him from acting on these insane plans, take away these things he thought would help him, he would stop and think and see what a foolish idea it was. I took the card and then later I took the mobile. I hid it well."

"I know."

"Do you have it? Where is it?"

"Hidden." Anita could see the doubt in Nisha's eyes. "Who is this man who came to your house?"

"I never knew his name—only that he was the other money-lender's agent. He was the one Girjan and Panju were supposed to kill, to pay off their debt." Nisha shook her head, drawing in her arms.

"The agent was there when Panju died, yes?"

"Yes."

"Why do you say he didn't kill Panju?"

"He didn't do it. I killed my husband."

"You're lying. I know you are. I don't believe you."

"The police will believe me." Nisha wouldn't look at Anita after that, not even when the police came and took her away in the early morning, arresting her for the murder of her husband, Panju Eappen.

In answer to Anita's many questions they only answered one. "Poojapura," the oldest police man said when she asked where they were taking Nisha. The Central Jail in Poojapura, on the southeast side of Trivandrum.

"I'm sorry," Brij said to Anita as he lifted his hands in a sign of resignation. "She got away from me."

In a corner of the parking area, Theti sat curled into a little ball crying uncontrollably. Brij reached down and picked her up as though she were a bundle of laundry and headed for the stairs to Anita's suite. Anita ran ahead up the stairs and opened the door, directing Brij to the bedroom. He laid the child down on the bed.

"I'll call Mrs. Eappen," Anita said.

Brij left and Anita stood by the bed for a moment, uncertain what to do. As much as she liked children, she wasn't used to them, and a child who has just seen her mother taken away by the police must be even more challenging. She couldn't think what to say that would soothe the little girl. She sat down on the edge of the bed and rested her hand on Theti's back.

"I'll take you to see your amma as soon as they let me," Anita said, thinking the offer was little better than nothing at all.

"When will that be?" Theti sat up and lifted the skirt of her dress to wipe her eyes and runny nose. Anita handed her a box of tissues.

"I don't know."

"Why did they take her? Because of that bad man who burned up?"

For a moment Anita was surprised that Theti knew about this, but she guessed that Brij had told her in order to explain how her mother ended up so dirty and tired, with bruises and cuts all over her, not to mention her missing finger.

"No, it's not about that man."

Theti stared at her, and Anita could feel the child willing her to speak.

235

"It's about the other man, the one who came to your house in the night a few days ago." Anita paused to take a breath, but before she could say anything more, Theti looked down and started to shake her head.

"We're not supposed to talk about that," the child said.

"The police don't know about the bad man who came to your house," Anita said. "They think only your amma was there when your acchan died."

"Amma didn't hurt Acchan," Theti said.

Anita felt a surge of relief. She wanted to wrap her arms around Theti and hug her in gratitude. "That's what I said. I don't think she did that either." After Tajji insisted he hadn't seen anything because he had been outside, she had assumed that only Nisha knew what happened, other than the real murderer, which Anita thought had to be Riyas Patel. Anita hadn't considered that little Theti would know, but then she had known about the purple mobile and where it was hidden, and she had heard the arguments between her parents. Little Theti knew everything that was going on.

"I know she didn't hurt Acchan."

"Can you tell me exactly what happened?" Anita asked.

Theti took a deep breath and exhaled, the dramatic sigh of importance. "That man came and he talked to Acchan about money, and Acchan said yes, he would do what he wanted. So he went to get something. Then, something happened. Acchan was quick. He turned and there was the knife. Amma said no. She put her hand out. I put my hand out." Theti looked up at her with large questioning eyes, the pain as sharp as the knife that had killed Panju. Anita knew what the question was.

"You didn't hurt your acchan, Theti." Anita reached for her little hands. "Your hand isn't strong enough to move the knife, Theti. It was the bad man who did that."

"I did not do this?"

"Did you think you had?" Anita asked.

Theti nodded. "Yes. I didn't mean to. But I could feel the knife. It was sharp." The words came out in such a soft whisper that Anita wasn't even sure she had heard them. She stared at the child, tried to make sense of what she'd said, to understand that night from the child's point of view. Theti looked up at her, waiting for a reaction.

"You did not do this," Anita said. "You did not hurt your ac-chan."

Theti nodded. "That's what Amma said. She made me promise I would never say such a thing again." The child leaned forward and whispered. "Is it a secret?"

"No. There is no secret here. That man who came did this," Anita said. "Not you, and not your amma."

CHAPTER 26

Mist still shrouded the sun as morning light seeped onto the parking area. Workers on their way to hotel restaurants who had stopped in the lane to watch the police arrest Nisha continued on their way. The early-morning vegetable vendors in small open-backed trucks swerved around them. Anita swung the hotel door shut and turned back to the desk.

"We have little time before the guests want breakfast." Anita looked at the large clock over the desk. It read six thirty-five. The cook passed by the open window, glanced in, smiled, and walked on. "Ravi will be here soon, to take the desk."

"What is happening?" Auntie Meena looked stricken. The sight of Nisha being carted off had brought home as nothing else could just how dangerous their current situation was. Anita had extricated Nisha from one nightmare only to see her enveloped by another. And Anita still had one more threat to face.

"How do you contact your moneylender?" Anita asked.

"I do not do that. Never." Auntie Meena shook her head vigorously.

"But you know how to reach Riyas Patel, the agent, yes?" Anita leaned across the desk. "Tell me the telephone number."

"Oooh! Child, you must not call him. This is making such a one very angry." Meena cringed.

Anita thought of the moneylender's purple mobile she'd ordered buried in the back compound. "Let me see your purple

238

mobile, the one the moneylender's agent gave you."

"Why are you wanting this?" Meena pressed her hands together in front of her face.

"Riyas Patel gave me his business card at the accident," Anita said. "If the phone number on the card is not the same as the one in the mobile, I will have an advantage, and he will understand that."

"You mustn't tempt him to anger," Meena said.

"There is no time to waste," Anita said. "Right now we have the advantage. No one knows what happened in Panju's village exactly. They only know Dipak is dead and that Nisha and I were there. We can use that. Right now the grapevine works for us, but that won't last." Anita hurried around the desk and into the office. She found her aunt's purse and dumped its contents onto the table.

"Ayoo!" Auntie Meena rushed in behind her. "You are not to be doing this."

Anita grabbed the purple mobile from the pile and turned to her aunt. "You have mortgaged Hotel Delite, my home and yours, for your daughter, whom you love—yes, I know this—but we must save the hotel. There is only one way."

"There is no way but money, and I am truly working as hard as I can. Have I not cut back on all frivolous purchases? Have I not sent away—"

"There is no way we can pay back that total sum, Auntie. The amount is huge. The hotel is all but lost unless I can force him to give it up."

"Why would he do that?" Auntie Meena fell into a chair.

Anita punched buttons on the purple mobile. After a moment, the screen produced a number for the last incoming call.

"What are you doing?" Meena shifted closer to Anita. "I promised no one is seeing this. No one is knowing. Do not look at me like that, Anita. I am trying my best."

"Now I must do for us what I did for Nisha."

Meena stared at her. "You mean to burn his house down?"

Anita would have laughed if she hadn't felt so desperate. "Is that what Brij told you?" She swore softly, and then pulled out her own mobile. She punched in the number of the last incoming call from Auntie Meena's purple mobile and sent a text message. She had no doubt Riyas would understand.

Over the years Anita had watched the city change, with little guesthouses torn down to make way for air-conditioned glass towers of hotel rooms. She supposed other people noticed the new traffic lights, or perhaps reconfigurations of city streets, or new housing developments. When Riyas invited Anita to meet him at the new hotel just behind the old college, she knew exactly where he meant. She'd visited the hotel once before, a year ago, to see what the new business offered. It was good to keep up with the competition, she thought, even though Hotel Delite would never rank in the same tier. And this morning, her visit reminded her once again just how powerful and rich was the new crop of businesspeople in Trivandrum, including the new moneylenders.

The hotel was glass, marble, and gold leaf, and furnished with antiques that guests were expected to appreciate. The coffee shop, one of the few in the city, looked as though it had been lifted from a Mughal garden by way of New York, bright paisley tablecloths set within an exotic garden. The atrium could be cooled or opened to the sun as desired. Today it was darkened, as the sun rose to its zenith. Hotel guests and others dawdled over breakfast and studied maps and brochures, planning their day. Riyas was waiting for her, in a booth at the opposite side of the room.

"Is this your usual morning place?" she asked as she sat down. She had decided to be cordial, since she needed something from him—cooperation—and she was more likely to get it that way than if she waved a threat in his face. Riyas nodded to the waiter, who had hurried forward, and he reappeared in seconds with another coffee cup and filled it.

"Can I order something for you?" Riyas offered. Anita shook her head and rested her hand on the table beside the cup steaming in front of her. Riyas leaned back and twisted the handle of his cup back and forth, back and forth. "I am always delighted to see you, Anita. But I think you are not so pleased yourself to see me."

The quiet of the room seemed to be the quiet of the world, with only Anita and her conscience still engaged, thinking of life beyond this serene and false interior. In her heart she listened, she argued, she debated, and then she did what she always did.

"Do you work for Mr. Varjen?" Her voice was soft, casual, and without a hint of accusation. "It is in front of his mansion where you do business, isn't it?"

Riyas pushed away his coffee cup but kept his eye on the swirl of cream.

"I searched some records. The mansion looks abandoned, but I know it isn't and I know beneath all the layers it is Mr. K.K. Varjen who owns it."

Now that she had begun staking out her position, she felt steadier. She took a careful look at him, watching for his reaction. He didn't look the same this morning. She studied each feature of his face, looking for the barely visible change that made him seem a different person. Once his mask was gone, she knew, his expression would have to change, reveal how he truly felt, but the mask seemed to be still in place.

"Your competition is dead now. Dipak burned to death."

"Yes, I know." His smile faded, and he looked like any man who might take coffee in an expensive hotel.

"Did you arrange that car accident when we first met?"

"Had I known you were so charming I would have done it years ago."

Sure, she thought. *Years ago.* "Dipak is dead. You look like you do not fully believe the rumors."

"He really did burn to death?" Riyas seemed caught by the manner of death, wanting to dwell on it.

His words brought back the image of the moneylender falling through the doorway with flames shooting from his body, the whites of his eyes showing only terror and shock before they disengaged from the immediate, his body falling and shivering and trembling. She wondered if she'd ever forget it, if her mind would ever be clear of the horror. "He did."

"It's hard to believe he let anyone get that close to him," Riyas said.

"He didn't 'let' him," she said. "And we're all vulnerable sometimes."

"The son?" he queried. Anita nodded. "Where is he now?"

"Tajji went back to the family farm. For the time being anyway. It is hard to know what the police will uncover in an investigation into the fire and Dipak's death. Tajji could still be arrested. What is your interest in him?"

"No interest. He is of no interest to me. And what of the woman Nisha?"

"Nisha?" Anita frowned. "You know about her?"

"Everyone in this—business—knows about her." Riyas sipped his coffee, moving a little in his seat, but otherwise looking as comfortable as any man who has pulled off something special and was trying not to look smug. Anita wondered, what if it was a pose?

"Interesting," she said. "I suppose it's naive of me to say that I find it disturbing no one tried to rescue her."

"It is, but you did it."

"I had to find her first."

"Ah. You wanted pointers."

No, thought Anita. *I wanted someone to send in the police. But perhaps they already knew.* She pushed that thought aside.

"She has been arrested for her husband's murder, yes?" Riyas asked.

"She has. She confessed and the police took her."

"Confessed? How brave of her," he said.

Anita pushed away the breakfast pastries provided by the waiter and watched him refill the coffee cups. He disappeared again as unobtrusively as he'd appeared.

"So, she truly confessed?" Riyas folded his hands in his lap, the coffee forgotten. "Do you believe her?"

"She seemed quite insistent. But no, I don't believe her. She has worked for me long enough for me to think I know her, and I don't think she would kill someone."

"No other reason?"

She started to shake her head.

"You are a good friend. Are you choosing friendship over truth?"

"I have no reason to believe she would murder her husband," Anita said. "But I wasn't there, was I?" She leaned forward. "When I told you she confessed, you hesitated, Riyas. Only a second, but you hesitated. You were surprised because you were there."

"You make too much of nothing," Riyas said.

"Do I? Tajji saw you. He found your purple mobile, the one you have been searching for. The one you searched Hotel Delite for—and didn't find." Anita felt the weight in the room shift. What had been pressing down on her suddenly lifted and floated away. She turned her head a little to the left and saw the last of the late breakfasters leaving the room. In a moment, she and Riyas were alone.

"Yes, the mobile," he said.

"You know the truth," Anita said.

"The truth. I can't see it would do Panju and Tajji any good," Riyas said, lifting his right hand to the table and once again twirling the coffee cup.

The truth, Anita thought. The truth was never as simple as people wanted it to be. "Panju was going to give the mobile to Dipak," she said. "Use it as a way to discharge his debt."

Riyas shifted, crossing his legs. "I hardly think there was enough in the mobile to warrant that. It wasn't worth such a large debt." He looked confident again, and Anita had to admit that with his charisma and confidence he would go far. His life would not be ordinary. He could shrink into a charming, bumbling pal, expand into a deadly crime leader, and inhabit any number of personalities between the two. It gave her chills to think how many people Riyas would destroy in his lifetime. He was a young man. He had years ahead of him to ruin lives.

"The phone had value, and Panju meant to use it against both you and Dipak," Anita said.

Riyas chuckled. "Oh, my, such a devious fellow, our Panju. If Dipak had known Panju meant to betray him, he would not have kept Nisha alive. He would have tortured and killed her."

"If Dipak hadn't died, he would have killed her. Yes, you're right about that." Anita understood the minute she started talking with the village moneylender that he had come to a dead end with Nisha. He wanted to be rid of her. It wasn't Anita's brilliance that won him over in negotiations; it was his desire to be extricated from the entire situation without facing a murder charge.

"And why didn't he do it anyway?"

"I offered him something valuable," she said.

"You offered him the mobile?" He lifted his eyebrow in query, and Anita caught a glimmer of uncertainty before he blinked it away and looked down his nose at his coffee.

"I offered him proof of the identity of his competition."

Riyas's eyes sharpened as he looked at her, and she felt like she'd been stabbed. He lifted his coffee cup and offered her a smile. "I doubt you have such a thing."

"But I do. At first I was going to offer Dipak the purple mobile," she said, watching for his reaction. "Only it had so little information on it, just phone numbers of those in debt to his competition, just those people one agent was handling. You. Not so much in value. So I looked for something else, something someone would want but only I would have. That's when I thought about the photographs from a camera card. They would be much more valuable."

"You have this device still?" Riyas stiffened. "And the phone?" The change in him was palpable. She could see a tiny scar along the ridge of his cheekbone, which she hadn't noticed before, and yet it seemed so obvious now.

"If I do, why would I tell you?" *You can't negotiate for anything unless you put something on the table,* Anita thought. *And once it's out there, you can't take it back without undermining your own credibility. I have just told him,* she realized, *what I have.*

His eyes studied her and she knew he was sizing her up. He had searched the Hotel Delite compound and buildings, and not found either item, but then he wasn't searching for the camera card. He only wanted the phone. She idly wondered if the moneylender K.K. Varjen, for whom Riyas was merely the agent, would change his practices, or if he even knew about the use of little mobiles. Riyas gave a choking laugh. "An interesting game you have started. All right, Miss Anita. What do you want for them?"

"You were there, weren't you? The night Panju died. You came to meet Panju."

"Does it matter?"

"Of course it does. You came the night before and lost your mobile, and you came the next night. You agreed to meet Panju twice at his house. The second night he died." She leaned forward. "This was part of Panju's plan, to bring you to the house and kill you, and then go after Dipak. Panju asked you to come, to lend him money. But it was a ruse. You saw through it. You killed him."

The minute the words were out of her mouth she felt a reckless fool. Here she was in an empty restaurant and she was accusing a man of violence, of the most serious crime. She looked into his face. Instead of anger, though, she saw amusement.

"You think this is funny?"

"No, not at all. I find it amusing that you would think that I would bother carrying out such a crime." Riyas moved to the edge of the banquette. "I would never work that hard."

"So someone was with you."

"Ah, no. You were correct up till the end. And then you jumped to a conclusion. If I was there, I had to be the killer. After all, I am a moneylender, or the agent of one—of one, I should point out, who is the most powerful man in the city. I must be a villain. But no, you are wrong. I did not kill him. I was there, I saw through the ruse, and I watched him die. But I did not kill him."

"I don't believe you," Anita said.

"Why? Because you don't want to? You have no reason to doubt me except you dislike me and think me a criminal."

"You are a criminal," she said. "Why would I believe you?"

"Even criminals can tell the truth," he said.

"Convince me," she said.

Riyas smiled. "I knew Panju meant to kill me when I walked into the house," he said, pausing. For a second Anita wondered how it must feel to go through life knowing people hated you enough to want to kill you. "We were face to face in the sitting room, almost directly under the fan. Panju waved the knife at me. But he seemed to change his mind. Suddenly, he was weak, surprisingly weak. Physically, I mean. It was easy to push him aside." He paused. "Panju lost his will. But I cannot be accused of killing him."

"Tajji could testify against you," Anita said.

"He cannot. He was outside," Riyas said. "And even if he tried, he wouldn't live long enough to enter the courtroom."

Anita cringed at the casualness of the threat. "All right. If you didn't, then who did kill Panju? You just said he had the knife and you pushed it away."

"You have the mobile?"

"I do. How did you figure that out? Or were you merely searching every home of every person Nisha was associated with?"

"I am much more careful than that," he said with obvious contempt. "If you had the child, there was a good chance you also had the mobile. Nisha must have taken it when she fled with the child." He paused.

"How did you know we had the child?"

Riyas laughed. "Kovalam is a village. Anything different speeds through the workers. Suddenly a child is hiding in Hotel Delite." He shook his head and laughed, looking down at his coffee.

"So you guessed we had the mobile too," Anita said.

"The police searched Nisha's house and did not find it. They even went back a second time," he said. "Twice they searched but did not find it."

"Perhaps they missed it."

He stiffened. He didn't like thinking his associates, even those in the police force, could miss something like that. It was a serious failing. "I want the mobile."

"I want to know who killed Panju."

"Give me the mobile and the card and I will tell you what happened." He paused to lean back against the leather seat. *He must be feeling clammy,* Anita thought, watching the way his shirt sleeve clung to his arm. *He's not as confident as he seems,* she thought. "The mobile," he repeated. "My men searched everywhere for it. Where is it?"

"Hidden."

"I know."

"Your men drugged my dog."

Riyas shrugged and looked annoyed. He turned around as though to call a waiter, saw no one, and turned back to face her. "Where is it hidden?"

"You will tell me who killed Panju if I tell you where it is?"

"I will tell you." The strain in his eyes startled her.

"In the midden, beneath the dog poop." Anita smiled. "I knew no one would look there. I can tell by your expression I was right."

Riyas stared at her, his mouth opening just enough to show his white teeth and pink tongue. Then he began to laugh. He threw his head back, spread his arms across the back of the banquette, and roared. The tears streamed down his face, his chest heaved and shook. A waiter came out to see what the commotion was about. After several minutes, Riyas grew calmer and smiled again at Anita. "You do know what Dipak's community is?"

"Yes. His people collected night soil. He despised his caste."

"If you had told him where you'd hidden the mobile and the card, he might have killed you on the spot." He began to laugh again, more quietly this time but with deep satisfaction.

"But I didn't hide the card with it." Anita smiled. "You promised to tell me. You won't get the card till you do."

"So I did." He slid out of the banquette, stood up, and reached into his pocket. He dropped four hundred rupees on the table. "Panju brought out the knife and charged at me. His wife and daughter were there. Perhaps he was so mad he didn't notice, perhaps he didn't care. I don't know. But he charged. Nisha tried to stop him and his little girl also stepped in. She may have thought he was charging at her mother, I don't know. But he saw them, saw how close they were. They reached out to stop the knife. I think they tried to take it from him. It is fatal to hesitate, as you are quick to notice. They saved me my work. It was easy for me to push his hand away. I told you. He lost his will when he saw what was happening. Nisha's hand was on the knife that killed Panju. So was Theti's. I had no trouble guiding it into Panju."

Anita listened to this explanation and felt a shock spread through her body.

"It's the truth." He ran his hand down the placket of his shirt. "But don't bother asking me to tell the police anything."

She saw his hand twitch and rise. She wondered, if they were alone, what he might have done. "Will you send your men to dig up the mobile?"

"I will dig it up myself. I dare not trust anyone else with this. My life could depend on it." There was no laughter now. "I want the card too."

"I want the original of my aunt's secret loan document returned, marked paid in full," Anita said. "No document, no card."

CHAPTER 27

The ashy light of early morning crept onto the balcony. Anita had fallen asleep on the settee and her leg felt numb where it had been wedged against the carved frame. She sat up and looked around the sitting room. She was hungry, hungry to the point of pain. *Stress,* she thought. *It must be stress.*

"Are you there?" Auntie Meena banged on the door.

"Coming, coming." Anita pulled open the door. Auntie Meena clutched a robe around her, her hair flying out in all directions like Kali set on revenge.

"You must see." Meena turned to go back down the stairs. "This trouble will never end, will it? We are condemned to this misery forever." Auntie Meena didn't wait to explain. She led the way down the stairs and Anita followed.

At the top of the steps to the lower compound, Anita stopped. She looked down at the grass and rock outcroppings, the cement enclosures for the dhobi, the clothes lines strung along one side for when the wind was too strong to dry clothes on the beach rocks. In the far corner, where the hotel staff burned trash, beneath the copper pod tree where the hotel midden was barely concealed, lay a pile of dirt and trash. This was where Anita had hidden the purple mobile. The ground had been dug up, the detritus tossed back in little piles.

"So, he has come already," Anita said.

"Who? Who has come?" Meena had gone on ahead, and now stopped halfway down the stairs. She swung around to face

Anita. "What are you talking about, Anita?" Auntie Meena was distraught, and Anita wondered if she should have warned the older woman about what might happen. Well, it was too late now.

"I told Riyas he could have something he lost if he told me about Panju's death," Anita explained. "I didn't think he would come so soon."

Auntie Meena turned back to stare at the midden. "He did this? A man so fastidious?"

"He must have been desperate." Anita recalled his last words about collecting the mobile, that he would do it himself, as though his life depended on it. She had thought them mere hyperbole at the time. She shivered and pulled her bathrobe tighter.

Just before seven o'clock Anita again made her way to the dining room, ready for breakfast, though not as hungry as she had been. She nodded to the woman sweeping the front steps and walkway. Anita noted the little pile of leaves, scraps of paper, and other debris being pushed along the ground.

"That seems like a lot of trash for this early hour," Anita said.

The sweeper straightened up and waggled her head in agreement, smiled, and bent over again. Before she could swing her broom down to the ground, Anita called her to stop, and with the backs of her fingers Anita brushed away leaves and bits of plastic. She plucked from the pile a square envelope of good-quality paper. She turned it over. Her name was written on the outside in small letters by a hand that pressed the nib deep into the paper. "I'll take this," she said, standing up.

Anita slapped the envelope against her thigh to knock off the dust and dirt and stepped into the hotel lobby. Beyond the office she could hear the cook telling his assistant to bring more eggs from the storeroom, and a metal tray clanged beneath the clatter of cutlery. The day was beginning, as if nothing were wrong anywhere in the world.

"What have you there?" Auntie Meena leaned toward Anita from a chair at the office table.

"I found this in the trash being swept up outside." Anita pulled open the flap. "I don't recall it being out there when we went down to look at the midden."

"Some fool throwing trash over the wall." Auntie Meena could not, would not, accept the degree of trash strewn about her beloved state. She was shocked and disheartened by the carelessness of her fellows.

"I don't think so, Auntie." Anita pulled out the sheet of paper from the envelope, unfolded it, and read it.

"Really, Anita. It is filthy. Put it here." Auntie Meena held up a trash basket and waved it at Anita. But Anita ignored her aunt and sat down at the table, still holding the sheet of paper in front of her.

"I think you will want to keep this." Anita handed the sheet, with its crabbed handwriting, florid signatures, and revenue stamps, to her aunt.

"Must I touch it?" Auntie Meena wrinkled her nose and pulled her mouth down.

"You already have, once." Anita dropped the paper onto the table.

Meena reached for it. She read it through without touching it. Then she picked it up and read it through again, this time very slowly. Then she burst into tears.

"I thought the revenue stamp was a nice touch," Anita said, leaning back in her chair, "especially for a document that is illegal in every way."

The Hotel Delite dining room began to fill up at seven-thirty, when the Danish tour arrived to take one of the long family-style tables for themselves, leaving the smaller tables for the remaining guests. A few guests were known not to arrive until a few minutes before ten o'clock, dragging themselves downstairs as though forced at gunpoint. Sometimes Anita was annoyed with them for keeping the kitchen open past the time when the chef should have been on his way to the market, and sometimes she felt bad for them because they didn't seem to know how to behave. Today she didn't care. They could show up at eleven o'clock demanding breakfast and she'd welcome them with a smile. She had never been happier to be her aunt's mainstay and assistant, her backup and helpmate, her whipping girl and girl Friday.

Anita chose a table by the window, one of her favorites, and checked to make sure all was as it should be. The tablecloth was bleached clean and well pressed, the salt shaker was recently filled, so no clumping yet. The pepper shaker was just right. The glass and cutlery sparkled, and the single flower in the little vase was fresh.

"Coffee, Amma?" Moonu arrived with a tray of coffee pot, sugar and creamer, and cup and saucer. "Newspaper?" He deposited every item properly on the table and Anita felt a little light headed with all this well-being. Everywhere she looked, life seemed to say, yes, all is resolved, all is settled, all is back to normal. Life is good. She ordered idlis for breakfast.

In the back of Anita's head was the nagging thought that the phone was gone but not the card. It made her uneasy, as though the whole affair was unfinished. She had learned about Panju's last moments, even though she doubted Riyas's story. She had traded him the mobile, his purple mobile, for the truth, and she had listened to his story. She had offered the card with its damning photographs in exchange for Auntie Meena's loan document. And now she had the document, stating the loan was fully discharged. But she still had the card. It unsettled her. She had entered into an agreement and she would have to deliver on her end. These men were not the forgiving sort. She wondered when he'd contact her, and how.

Anita poured herself a cup of strong black coffee and opened the newspaper. She loved the feel of the world sitting on her lap, the paper crinkling in the morning quiet, the urgency of stories she could ignore simply by turning the page or reading another column. She scanned the national news, and then glanced at the local news. Festival season would begin soon, and arts programs would fill the pages. She enjoyed those stories, all those young people with so much talent performing as brilliantly as seasoned professionals. It was inspiring. She glanced down at a shorter item with a headline in bold.

"Amma! Amma! Your coffee!" A waiter hurried to Anita's table and began mopping up the coffee pouring out of her cup now resting on its side, the black liquid streaming across the table and down the wooden leg, to puddle on the floor. But Anita didn't hear him, didn't see him. She was reading a headline at the top of the column.

"Petty Criminal Found Dead in Canal. Foul Play Suspected."

Anita reread the first sentence. "Thirty-seven-year-old Riyas Patel was found drowned in the Chakka canal with an old-fashioned landline telephone cord tied around his neck."

Anita stood up, crushing the newspaper to her, and ran into the office. She pushed away the plate in front of Auntie Meena and put the newspaper in its place.

"What is this, Anita?"

"Read it. Riyas Patel is dead, murdered last night." Anita fell into a chair.

"Oooh!" Meena read the story through and looked up at her niece for an explanation. She wiped the perspiration from her face. "Truly! He is dead! It is shameful for me to say this, but I am not sorry to read this. Not at all, no, not at all. Am I awful, Anita?"

"No, no, of course not," Anita said automatically, but her thoughts were elsewhere.

"He is dead, Anita. He can do us no more harm. I will not fear meeting him unexpectedly in the market or at the taxi stand." Auntie Meena began to smile timidly, the corners of her mouth and her forehead twitching. "Are you not relieved?"

Was she relieved? Anita tried to think. She and Auntie Meena had gone to bed at their usual time. This morning, inspecting the mess that had once been a tidy midden, she had assumed that Riyas had come late in the night, or early in the morning. He had assured her he would dig up the phone himself. This wasn't something he could trust to anyone else—it meant his life, he said. She had thought he was exaggerating, for effect. But if his death could be reported in the morning newspaper, he had to be already dead by the time someone sneaked into the compound and searched the trash heap. At least this time the dog was not poisoned, just sedated through food.

And the phone cord.

"It's a warning, Auntie. The phone cord is a warning."

"What sort of warning? We are safe now, isn't it?" Meena began blinking and her breathing grew short and fast.

Anita rested her hand on the older woman's arm and tried to soothe her before explaining. "It is a warning. But perhaps not to us."

"But to who then?"

"I'm not sure. The purple phone, like the one you have, is a link to an illegal activity."

"Oh."

"I am thinking I should give it to the police. You still have it, yes?"

"I have not thrown it, Anita."

"See if it is in your hiding place, Auntie."

"Of course it is in, well, that place." Auntie Meena turned around and began rummaging in a drawer. When her efforts were unrewarded, she grew frantic, shoving papers around and pulling the drawer almost out of its cradle. "It is gone, Anita. Gone!"

"Of course it is gone," Anita said. She leaned back in her chair, her arms gripping the sides.

"But why? Why are they doing this?" Auntie Meena looked at the drawer and then at the office door. "How did Riyas get in here?"

"He did not do this, Auntie. Someone else did."

"The one who signed the document, yes?"

"Yes, but not him personally. Someone who works for him."

Auntie Meena once again looked confused. "But it is given, yes? I have the document now."

"Yes, it is given. With a warning. But not to us, I am thinking." Anita leaned forward, resting her clasped hands on the table.

"I don't understand."

"Riyas was careless, Auntie, so his employer, K.K. Varjen if that is the one, could not trust him, so he killed him. Someone else came to get the phone from the trash heap." Anita paused. "Riyas was killed as a warning to others." Anita didn't add that in fact the warning could include her and Auntie Meena.

Anita thought about the card still hidden in her flat. She had promised it to Riyas for the document. She had received the document, though she almost missed it. It could have been swept up and burned and she would never have known the loan had been released. The deed would have been lost, and the uncertainty would have haunted her and Auntie Meena for the rest of their lives. The manner in which the deed was returned was a cruel game, and Anita and Meena had been lucky, nothing more.

But even more confounding, there had been no effort to take the card. She wondered if Riyas had failed to tell his boss about it. Had he planned on keeping it for himself, as his own insurance? Did anyone other than Riyas know about the card? If she sent it back, K.K. Varjen might consider it a threat. If she kept it, he might still come after it—if he knew about it.

"So I am safe?" Meena started to perk up.

Anita smiled and patted her aunt's hand. "Forgive me for saying this. Yes, you are safe—except for one thing."

"What is that?" Meena's expression of hope sagged.

"Except for the influence Padma has on you," Anita said. She didn't like reminding her aunt of what had gotten her into trouble in the first place, and the expression on Meena's face broke her heart. But Padma was a problem that would have to be addressed, even if not at this moment.

"You are being unkind, Anita." Meena pouted. "I am relieved of a great burden and a great fear, and you chide me." Her mouth trembled into a smile. "But truly, I am safe?"

"Yes, Auntie, I think you are safe." Anita leaned back in her chair again. She could still hear Riyas's voice describing the night Panju died in such matter-of-fact terms, like a story he had read in the newspaper. But she especially remembered the way he had told the tale, as though his fingers had merely skimmed the knife rather than seizing the opportunity to thrust it into Panju. Yes, Nisha's hand was on the knife, and so was little Theti's. That's all Nisha saw, all that Panju saw. But there Riyas saw his chance, a ruthless man who would let a mother and daughter pay for his violence.

If Anita came out with Riyas's story, she would sound ridiculous. She had no way to prove he was there. She couldn't rely on Tajji, a minor, who hadn't witnessed the murder, and certainly not Theti. Nisha wouldn't help either. Anita had already tried to persuade her. No, Nisha had taken the terror of that night, seen only her presence, and expanded that into guilt. Yes, her hand was on the knife, but only Riyas had the strength to direct it. With no witness except little Theti, Nisha had little chance in a court of law.

The digital record of the photos was another opportunity for Riyas. Anita could see that now. No one but Nisha had known about the card until she gave it to Nirmala. But neither woman knew what was on it. Riyas didn't know about the card until Anita told him, but it must have terrified him. He had extracted the loan document from his employer, but Anita had no way of knowing how. Had he promised the mobile alone? Had he hinted at some additional evidence, then said he found nothing during a search? Did Varjen give up the document, or did Riyas steal it?

The whole situation was diabolical, she thought. Riyas had probably meant to keep the card in reserve, until he needed some leverage over his employer. He knew Anita had it, and assumed he could get it any time he wanted. She knew what sort of man he was, and he knew she knew. But now he was gone, and with him the threat. The printed photo she had shown Dipak was also gone, turned to ashes, but the card remained just where she had hidden it, in plain sight. Unless she destroyed it, she'd be looking at it for the rest of her life, every time she sat down at her desk and looked up at the collage about photography, with its fragments of photos, batteries, and now a card.

CHAPTER 28

Anita placed each of the three photos on the table, aligning the corners and watching the light shift and settle on the shiny surfaces. Each was a version of the sun rising through the mist as the sun rose above the horizon. Rahul leaned over to study each one. These shots were good, special. She could feel it.

"I think we should include at least one of these," Anita said. She felt the heat rising to her cheeks. She was used to being calm and nonchalant about her work, even cavalier, but she couldn't hide her feelings now. This exhibit had come to matter to her. It had been Anand's idea, and she'd been flattered, but hadn't really taken it seriously. But the idea had got under her skin. Now it did matter. It mattered a lot, more than she dared admit to herself. She waited for Rahul to comment.

"Yes," he said after almost half an hour. "I think so too. This one definitely, and perhaps the other two." Without looking at her, he gathered up the photos. He called a name and an older man came out of the back room and shuffled over to them. Rahul gave him instructions as he rested the photos on the man's uplifted palms. The old man shuffled out again. "He does superb work, but he's going deaf, unfortunately."

"Ah." Anita grinned happily. *I must look stupid,* she thought, *but I don't care.* She followed the old man's progress across the room.

"Anand will be here soon," Rahul said, giving her a brilliant smile as he turned to his desk. "I'm hoping he'll give me some help with all this." He waved at the papers cluttering the surface.

"I'm sure he will," Anita said.

"He tells me you knew that man found dead in the canal. Is that true?" He rested his hands on his hips and peered at her. She hadn't noticed before the fine lines near his ears and how heavy his beard was. He was older than she had originally thought, but his physical bearing was that of a younger man.

"Someone who worked for us was put in serious danger because of him, and, well, I helped her." Anita felt reluctant to say anything more about what had happened.

"That's not what Anand told me."

"Really? I think you've seen more of him than I have of late," Anita said, watching him walk to the other side of the desk. Rahul looked up at the sound of the door opening. "And here he is now."

Anand crossed the polished stone floor and reached Anita first. He leaned down and air-kissed her on the cheek, to her surprise. They had never been demonstrative, a natural reticence considering their culture and families. She blushed as he pulled away.

"Rahul," Anand said by way of greeting.

"We were just talking about you," Rahul said. "Weren't we, Anita?"

"In a manner of speaking," she said. But neither man was listening to her.

Rahul launched into a discussion of arrangements for the exhibit. Anand frowned, nodded, made suggestions, glanced at Anita in case she had any objections, and offered a few comments about subcontractors for the opening. Anita leaned against a crate of artwork and listened as the two men grew more involved and animated. For a moment she felt the same fey relief she'd felt when she sat down to breakfast and knew Auntie Meena was no longer in danger, just before she read the morning newspaper.

She would have lingered there in that moment if not for the shock of discovery and understanding. She watched the two men handling the stash of papers, joke about Rahul's work habits and Anand's pared-down lifestyle, and allude in coy snatches to a trip that seemed to be on the horizon. As she watched she recalled Anand first telling her about the offer from Rahul's gallery, when she didn't even know who Rahul was, and she remembered the first time she had come to the gallery and found them both here and marveled at their easy camaraderie. She closed her eyes and felt a sharp pang, and then her heart sank. She turned away to stare out the window, blinked rapidly to clear her eyes. Now, as she watched them plan her exhibit, she knew it was a parting gift from Anand to her, and a gift of another meaning from Rahul to Anand.

She should have known there was a reason her relationship with Anand never grew beyond friendship, an intimacy of equals but not of lovers. She wondered when he was going to tell her. She hoped it wouldn't be for a while. She hated the idea of telling Auntie Meena that she was right. Anand wasn't suitable for her after all. Anita tried to get used to the dull throbbing in her chest, telling herself it wouldn't last, the pain of disappointment would fade, there would be other men, and Auntie Meena would be gleeful at the prospect of playing matchmaker again.

"What?" Anita heard her name called and turned back to the two men.

"Haven't you been listening?" Rahul said.

"I've been listening very carefully," she said.

Anand lifted an eyebrow in query, then his eyes narrowed. "And that means?"

Anita studied his still face and smiled. "It means Auntie Meena is no longer in danger," she said. She'd never told Anand everything that had happened, or could happen. "Nisha is in prison on remand but with a very good vakeel to plead her case, and her daughter, Theti, is now living with her great aunt. Tajji has not been arrested yet and may never be—I don't know. But the danger to life and limb is past." She smiled. "And now I feel like the world makes sense."

The two men smiled at her, as though she were a particularly clever younger sister.

"I'm glad to leave the details to you," she said to Rahul.

The two men looked at each other and laughed, and then returned to planning the exhibit that would be one of the great events of the year in Trivandrum.

CHAPTER 29

Late in the afternoon a matron dressed in a starched sari led the way through a large room appointed with a row of bed frames. She pointed to a sleeping mat rolled up and standing in the corner. Nearby was a red plastic bucket. "For washing," the matron said. Nisha leaned forward to see a bar of soap sitting on the bottom inside. She pressed a towel and a change of clothes to her chest as she listened to the matron's instructions.

Nisha had heard the murmurs as she passed the other women prisoners on her way to the dormitory. They had already heard about her, the story her advocate had told in court, the story the judge had listened to, frowning and occasionally tugging on his thick white eyebrows, his sharp chin jerking forward if he thought he'd missed something. By now, she knew, everyone had heard. Nisha had insisted on her plea, and the wheels of justice had started their noisy, creaky turning on a bumpy road. It would be ten years of lying, lies so persuasive that by the end of her sentence even she would believe them. But it would be worth it. Her daughter would never see the inside of a courtroom, and no one would ever know how far Panju had fallen. He died an accidental death in a fit of anger, but nothing more. There would be no talk of murder plots.

She balanced her pile of clothing and towels on top of the sleeping mat and looked around the room. A shelf at eye level over her bed frame was wide enough for her meager possessions.

"You are here on remand," the matron said, "but we do not have facilities to separate such individuals so you are with the general population."

Nisha nodded and followed the woman to the doorway.

"Your arrival coincides with tea. First meal 6:30 a.m., lunch at noon, tea at 4:15, and supper at 5:30. Menu is set and everyone is knowing it." The matron recited the information without looking at Nisha, scanned the room once more, and turned to leave. "Tea is outside," the matron said as she stepped out into the sunshine.

Through the open doorway Nisha could see one of the gardens the inmates tended. She had heard about the various projects in the prison—making chapattis and chicken curries to sell to the community outside, the fish pond, all the weaving and other crafts projects. But right now she was grateful for the sight of the gardens. They might look a bit arid and limp in the heat, but the sight of them refreshed her. Nisha heard a voice and looked down.

"Tonight is vegetable kurma and green gram curry." A woman sitting on the ground seemed to be talking to her foot, which she had propped up on her knee while she inspected her toenails. "There's never enough. Keep us weak so we can't make trouble."

Nisha looked down on the woman's black hair tied into a knot at the nape of her neck. She didn't know what to say.

"I am requesting leave, to see my son get married." The woman tipped her head back and smiled, as she imagined the wedding of her son and his bride. "Five days I am getting." She nodded and turned her attention back to her foot. "And then six more months and I am gone."

Something had caught the attention of the other women and they gathered near a gate. Not knowing what else to do, accepting that her life was no longer her own, Nisha took a place at the edge of the group and moved along as it reshaped itself into the semblance of a line. In a few minutes someone handed her a small metal cup of sweet milky tea.

"This is the only way it comes." The speaker was a wiry old woman with most of her teeth missing and the remaining ones yellow from smoking beedis. Nisha had been told no beedis or other smoking materials were allowed, but the staining of beedis was usually permanent.

"It is not so bad, Amma." The minute Nisha said it, she froze. No, she thought, I cannot be myself here. She hoped the old woman had not heard her, the tone of respect in her voice and address. But she had.

"You think so now." The old woman studied her. "Ten years is a long time to protect someone."

Nisha felt herself swaying unsteadily on her feet—it wasn't possible for anyone to know. Not possible. The old woman poked Nisha in the stomach, ran a bony finger along her arm, then turned over her own wrist and arm so Nisha could see the long, deep gash running the full length of her arm down into her palm.

"I should have done what you did. Instead, I got a knife and stabbed him while he slept. It is one thing to beat me—I am his wife—but to go to the child." She clucked and shook her head. "I know what comes after that. So I killed him while he slept."

"How long have you been here, Amma?"

"This is not important. I am not leaving, so how long I am here is not worth knowing." She finished her tea in one gulp. "But I was young. And pretty."

Nisha was on the verge of offering sympathy when she thought better of it.

"We are like a family here—only thirty of us. It is crowded, yes, but we are comfortable with each other. We bicker like family, push each other around like family, and then we forgive."

The old woman gazed around at the women in their light blue prison saris as though she were the teacher looking over her students, admiring some and disapproving of others. "Later I will tell you who is who. They already know who you are—the smart one—and you should know who they are. But now, it is evening and time for us to rest and perhaps do some laundry and think our own thoughts."

Nisha returned her cup to the cart and walked back to the dormitory. She could hear voices in the distance and turned in their direction. Two women walked among the rows of vegetables. A heavy raindrop fell on the ground in front of one woman, and she looked up. The second woman followed suit. Nisha too looked up at the sky. The northeast monsoon, *thulavarsham*, was late this year, so late the farmers had wondered if it would come at all. But here it was. The heavy dark cloud dropped low and began to shed its burden. It looked so low Nisha thought she could reach up and squeeze it. The women came out of the dormitory to stand beneath the cloud, their hands held out to catch the cool, clean rain and feel it pour over their bodies. Outside, in other parts of the prison and beyond the walls, Nisha heard a few shouts and cheering. But here, as the first moments of the monsoon took hold, the women were quiet, looking up, as though the clouds had brought them messages from another world.

ABOUT THE AUTHOR

Susan Oleksiw writes the Anita Ray series featuring an Indian American photographer living at her aunt's tourist hotel in South India; *When Krishna Calls* is the fourth in the series (the first is *Under the Eye of Kali*, 2010). She also writes the Mellingham series featuring Chief of Police Joe Silva (*Friends and Enemies*, 2001; *A Murderous Innocence*, 2006). Susan is well known for her articles on crime fiction; her first publication in this area was *A Reader's Guide to the Classic British Mystery*. She co-edited *The Oxford Companion to Crime and Mystery Writing* (1999). Her short stories have appeared in *Alfred Hitchcock Mystery Magazine* and numerous anthologies. Susan lives and writes outside Boston.